His Glowing Eyes, Light Streaming from Them, Paralyzed Me!

I was transfixed, and while fear climbed into my throat and choked off my breath, he smiled. It was a terrible, knowing smile, inhuman—alien! A shriek of terror died within me as he reached up with an enormous hand and removed *it* from his gaping mouth. As I cringed helplessly beneath him, the towering figure held the offering before me—the Communion offering of the mysterious Church of the Brotherhood—a pulsing, amorphous object of translucent white jelly. I trembled and gagged.

It Was Alive!
As I Stared in Horror, It Transformed
Itself into a Mouth—and Smiled!

By Furies Possessed

Ted White

PUBLISHED BY POCKET BOOKS NEW YORK

POCKET BOOKS, a Simon & Schuster division of
GULF & WESTERN CORPORATION
1230 Avenue of the Americas, New York, N.Y. 10020

ISBN: 0–671–83308–1

First Pocket Books printing November, 1980

10 9 8 7 6 5 4 3 2 1

POCKET and colophon are trademarks of Simon & Schuster.

Printed in the U.S.A.

To Roger Zelazny—
friend and patron

PART ONE

BY STRANGER TAKEN

Chapter One

It was a routine run. We made liftoff at 03:00 hours and were down on the Moon three meals and two naps later. I always slept well in freefall.

Simmons was waiting for me when we docked, and I sensed the annoyance of several of my fellow passengers when he ushered me through the VIP corridors and past Bio-Customs with a total lack of red tape. It pulled a small smile to the corners of my lips.

"Have they docked, yet?" I asked as soon as we had the corridor to ourselves.

"The *Longhaul II* should be down in, oh, thirty minutes," Simmons said, glancing at his wrist-chronometer. It is standard Bureau issue—I had one identical to Simmons' myself—with concentric faces for Greenwich Mean, local (adjustable), and local-A (which in this case was set for Luna Standard—I'd set mine on the ship). Simmons was one of those incredibly precise, fussy-clerk types who will refer to his watch for confirmation even if he last scanned it a minute earlier. He seemed to be one of those people who only know where they are in relationship to a fixed and immutable constant like Time. If the power-cell fell out of his unit, he'd probably have had heart failure the first time he noticed the sweep-second hand wasn't moving.

But Simmons' office was here, on the Moon. Simmons had been out to Mars once, and Ganymede once. (I know; I once looked up his file.) And my office remained on Earth. It stuck in the craw, sometimes—and sometimes when I found myself in the company of this prim-mouthed little man I really detested him.

We took a lift down to office-level, and a capsule over

to his quadrant; the *Longhaul II* might be coming in within the half hour, but interstellar ships are not docked as casually as an Earth-shuttle, and we had some time to kill. Simmons felt it would best be occupied by another briefing.

I always felt a certain measure of satisfaction when I was in Simmons' office. It measures exactly ten feet square and is seven feet high. I usually have to watch my step with the low ceilings because with Earth-normal muscles my walk is too bouncy; I don't have that slouchy walk you find in a Luney. Each time I've been in Simmons' office I've been able to endure it with equanimity for less than fifteen minutes. After that time, the confined space (every wall surface littered with the oddiments of Simmons' seven-plus years there) starts working on me. It starts at my temples with a kind of inward pressure that makes me want to jerk my head around. Then the air starts feeling close. I find myself breathing through my mouth in panting gasps. Finally, I have to stand up and start pacing.

As I say, I found a certain measure of satisfaction in that office—knowing that it was the price Simmons had paid for his deep-space clearance.

"I must say, Dameron," Simmons said, looking up from his microfilm viewer, "I questioned the advisability of your assignment to this particular project."

I said nothing. My first fifteen minutes were not yet up. I leaned back on the narrow couch and crossed my legs, only lightly brushing the edge of his desk with my toe.

"However," Simmons continued, perhaps annoyed with my lack of response, "I have been assured by Geneva that you are the best man for this task. Then too, you will be escorting your subject back to Earth, where I'm sure you are more at home."

I ran my fingers through my hair, brushing back my bangs and lightly massaging my right temple. *Score one for you, you bastard.*

"Perhaps I should go over the few facts we have with you," Simmons suggested.

"Why not?" I said, shrugging and nearly boosting myself

off the couch. "I can't have gone over the entire file more than a dozen times so far. I'm sure I can benefit from your superior judgment."

He looked up, a flash of annoyance crossing his petulant face. This game was supposed to be played by *his* rules. I was stepping over the line.

The *Longhaul II* was one of seven interstellar ships built in the last forty years, and the second to make use of the Feinberg Drive, which takes us as close to the speed of light as we're ever likely to get. The *Longhaul II* was coming back from Farhome, our first colony beyond the solar system, and, more important, was the first to make the round trip since a one-way long-sleep ship left our system with the original colonists early in the last century. According to the laser-beam message sent in by the *Longhaul II*, from somewhere then not much beyond Pluto's orbit, the ship was also returning with an emissary from Farhome, a man identified only as Bjonn. We didn't have much more than that to work with; The Bureau of Non-Terran Affairs has an impressive name, but ranks low on the worldwide pecking order. Most of the ship's message was concerned with scientific data, accumulated both from Farhome and from the trip itself. We've had the Feinberg Drive for forty years now, but the *Longhaul II* is only the third of seven ships to make its return (although *The Rolling Stone* has been back twice). My Bureau was interested in Mr. Bjonn— but most of the bureaus were more concerned with the physical details and data of a thirty-year round trip between the stars.

Simmons let this vast fund of information out to me with exquisitely deliberate slowness, rather like a cat playing with a catnip mouse. I think he enjoyed watching me squirm in that claustrophobic den of his. He referred often to his watch, but whether to check his schedule or to ascertain the speed with which I was reacting and exhibiting my now-classic symptoms of confinement, I couldn't say. Perhaps both.

In due time, he checked his left wrist again, sighed, and

rose to his feet. I remained seated, mostly in order to score points against him. I had manfully restrained myself from pacing, despite his obvious impatience for me to begin. If I leapt to my feet now, he might very well sit down again, his ploy a success.

Instead, he threw out a new gambit: "Well? Are you waiting for something more? We'll be late—" and turned on his heel (a remarkably casual gesture in the low gravity) for the door.

We went through corridors, a capsule, more corridors, and then a lift for the lunar surface; we more or less retraced our earlier route. Never having had to live on the Moon, I have never tried to figure out Lunaport's elaborate system of corridors, levels, and transit systems. Most pastel-hued concrete-walled corridors look the same to me. Each intersection is dubbed with enough letters and numbers, each in its own arcane sequence, for a city the size of Megayork—but I'm told the system was created for a much larger Lunaport than has yet been built. Rather like a twenty-square block village with 1021st Streets, and the like: hopelessly confusing to a non-native.

Eventually, we were standing in yet another room, this one perhaps twice the size of Simmons' office, but unfurnished and sterile in appearance. We waited among various functionaries and dignitaries while media-service men moved in and out around us with their recorders and cameras, and portable laser-scanners set up in each corner of the room for hologram recordings. It seemed to take Simmons down a peg or two, waiting here among men most of whom were more important than he; he was here as representative of a Bureau which did not rank in the upper third in clout or importance. For a few moments I actually found myself identifying and sympathizing with Simmons—but only for a few moments.

The doors in the opposite side of the room slid back, and four men, fresh from Bio-Customs, walked in.

I recognized Captain Lasher immediately—and at the same moment I felt a sort of freefall vertigo. *He looked hardly a day older than he had when he'd left, almost thirty years ago.* It's one thing to speak knowledgeably of the Einsteinian Contractions and all that, and quite another to confront in the flesh a man who bears such obvious witness to their truths. Lasher had left our system when I was three. I had seen his pictures and holograms in the textbooks, on 3–D specials, and I'd even done a tape-report on him and the *Longhaul II* when I was in Third Form and a teenager. Hell, I'd been so space-happy in those days I'd put pinups of Lasher and the others all over the walls of my sleep-cubicle, more than once provoking my den mothers to extreme annoyance.

And here he was, back again at last, the same reddish cowlick in his eyes, the same boyish freckled grin, *live and in solid color,* as the saying goes, not aged more than a few months in all these years. He was smaller; he'd always struck me as a big man, but that was my boyish hero worship. He was at least a head shorter than I, and tired looking, too. The same, and yet not the same. The more I watched him—the media-service men fighting the officials to cluster around him and his group—the more small changes in detail I catalogued. But these were the details of humanity, as viewed by older, more cynical eyes than those I'd once had.

"What do you think of him?" Simmons asked in a low voice, under my ear.

"Living proof that if you want immortality, just space out," I said, absently.

"No, no," Simmons spoke chidingly. "Not *him*—your charge, the colonist!"

I really hadn't noticed him. He stood between the other three ship's officers, and there was absolutely no reason why I shouldn't have noticed him first. He stood at least a foot taller than anyone else in that group, his hair (short, brushed back, looking a little like the style antiquarians affect) was only inches from the ceiling, and a startling white-blond color. His skin was dark, either deeply tanned or naturally pigmented a burnished walnut. His eyes, which seemed to be scanning the room with lighthearted thoroughness, were the palest blue. All in all, he was a very electrifying sight.

But I beg an excuse: Captain Lasher was a boyhood idol; Bjonn was just an alien.

I sensed it immediately, and it had nothing to do with his appearance. I've seen more outlandish-looking men in any Open City, and his clothes were so anonymous that I had to conclude (rightly, as it turned out) that they were standard ship's issue. Part of it was his eyes: not their color, but the way they moved, the way they seemed to see, digest, correlate, and pass on—in machine-like efficiency—at the same time that they seemed to twinkle with unguessable secrets. Call it a hunch, if you will—I think of it as an intuitive assessment, and it happens to be one of my more valuable talents—but I felt a tingle, a certain feeling that this man Bjonn, with no first name, no second name, just one, all-encompassing, all-purpose cognomen, was not human in the same fashion that I was human, or indeed as anyone else in that room was human.

Alien: I sensed it, and I knew it. In some subtle, indefinable way, this man was alien. And it was my job to find out just precisely how, and why, he was whatever he was.

He moved easily through the flanking media—sensors, cameras, and mikes all pressing against him and falling away again—and the congratulating functionaries, palms all outspread in that ageless gesture of pressing flesh which every politician learns at the cradle, and reached me with his own hand outstretched.

The contact was electrical; I felt as if I had been given a brief static charge, the hairs at the nape of my neck bristling for a short moment. I'd thrust out my own hand automatically, and been prepared for the brief, automatic squeeze.

Instead he took my hand, enveloped it in his own, held it, and locked his eyes on mine. I found myself looking *up* at him, and my heart did something too fast and too irregular.

"You are Mr. Dameron," he said, his voice seeming to confirm the truth of this statement. The pressure of his hand around mine was firm and unrelenting. His speech was flawless and without accent—but then he'd had some time aboard ship to lose it if he'd had one. "You will be showing me Earth. I'm pleased."

I felt flustered. He hadn't released my hand yet, and I wanted to extricate it without further embarrassment. I felt as though every eye in the room was on us (although a later check of the records showed they weren't)—and I could feel Simmons, virtually ignored thus far, bristling at my side like a hostile terrier.

"Tad Dameron," I acknowledged. I gestured with my free hand. "This is our local Bureau man, Phelps John Simmons."

Graciously, inevitably, as if he had planned it from the start, Bjonn released my sweating hand and reached for Simmons'. "I'm very grateful," he said, and he seemed to bow as he funneled his concentration into the short figure of my colleague. Simmons looked as though he wanted to jerk his hand away after a single touch, and I wondered if I'd shown that much anxiety myself. But Bjonn did not tarry over Simmons as he had over me, but straightened up and seemed to dismiss the man. I felt a sort of obscure triumph at that—as if Simmons and I had both been den-mates, competing for the attention of the local sports champion—and it wiped away for a moment my own anxiousness.

Then the media-service men were closing in on us again, and the air was thick and heavy with questions: "What are your plans?"—"Will you be spending much time on Earth?"—"What is your itinerary?"—"How do you like our system?"—"What are his plans?"—"Can you tell us about Farhome?"—"How long will he be here?"—the same questions were asked over and over, while sensor units were covertly pressed against us and passed over our bodies. I was grateful for the debug implanted in my chest. At least they wouldn't have all my chemical-emotional reactions down on tape, although from the perfunctory way they scanned me, I was certain they knew, or suspected, I was debugged.

Simmons had to be debugged too, but it was fascinating to watch the way the big blond colonist handled their insinuating mechanical caresses. Moving without seeming to move, he somehow kept the sensors from ever quite contacting his clothing or skin. I wondered if he knew what they were, or if he simply moved instinctively away from them. This triggered other questions I wanted to ask: What kind of a planet was Farhome? How comfortable in the confinement of Lunaport could Bjonn be? How would he react to Earth, when he got there?

"That's enough, gentlemen," Simmons said, after consulting his watch. "Mr. Bjonn will be available for depth-interviews later, on Earth. Just now he is encountering us for the first time, and he must be overwhelmed"—he didn't *look* overwhelmed; he looked calm and confident—"by your attentions. I must ask you to let us pass." And, reluctantly, they did.

Simmons apparently had no plan to subject Bjonn to the tortures of his tiny office. Instead he led us into a quiet lounge, adjacent to the Earth-shuttle docking facilities. I recognized it by reputation as a V-VIP lounge into which I had never before gained admission. It was, by Lunaport standards, a vast room, and its floor was thickly carpeted and broken up into several levels offset by one or two steps. It must have been my imagination, but even the air seemed cleaner, fresher.

"Mr. Dameron will be your guide and companion during your stay on Earth," he assured our guest. "The Bureau will act as your host. You may make any request." He smiled a brief and wintry smile. "We may or may not be able to fulfill all requests, but you should feel free to ask." I realized that Simmons had told what was for him a joke. I felt a sense of wonder at the good fortune involved in my presence upon such an august occasion.

"I certainly hope you will enjoy your visit with us," Simmons continued, "and I hope you'll find our Mr. Dameron an adequate guide through our no-doubt complex and mystifying civilization." (I wanted to snort when he said that.)

Simmons mouthed a few more platitudes, and then consulted the time again before announcing, "I believe you may now enter the shuttle for the final leg of your epic journey. May I wish you all luck and success." It was Simmons at his floweriest.

They gave me a better berth going back with a definitely superior menu. After checking out both berth and menu (the latter with much private pleasure), I rejoined Bjonn in the common lounge, where I instructed him on the use of his berth.

There is no privacy in a shuttle lounge, and there were many questions I wanted to ask the man but avoided, simply because of that fact. Still, we talked a bit while we awaited liftoff.

I felt ill at ease. Bjonn had a disconcerting directness to him. I had the feeling that he was totally unpracticed in the art of small talk. I was unwilling to pass beyond vague generalities here in public, and yet he seemed determined to stare directly into my eyes and ask me the most direct questions. I answered them as best I could, but I was quite relieved when the announcement came and we had to return to our berths for liftoff.

Chapter Two

A lunar liftoff is a gentle thing, compared to the raw and jolting waste of power one experiences on leaving Earth. There was really no reason for retiring to our berths except that of tradition. Berths are for liftsoff and eating. We liftoff from the Moon; therefore, we retire to our berths for lunar liftsoff. *Quod erat demonstrandum*. On this particular occasion, however, I welcomed this mindless example of bureaucratic tradition. I stepped into the berth, closed the folding door, inflated the supportive restraint cushions, and relaxed. It sometimes struck me as peculiar that I could relax as easily in a tiny closet, the dimensions of which only slightly exceeded those of my body, when a relatively much larger space like Simmons' office hit me with such a strong wave of claustrophobia. Perhaps it was simply the difference reflected in my attitudes: Simmons' office was intended to be moved about in, but offered little opportunity. A shuttle berth is intended for use as a sort of womb-like bed, and as such is excellent.

After the warning bell I felt the gravitational shift which signaled that the shuttle rocket was being raised into vertical launching position. Soon I was lying flat on my back, when moments before I had been standing upright. We waited, and with my arms laid flat I couldn't check my chronometer, but I knew from experience that this wait would seem the longest and be the shortest. Finally a faint vibration penetrated the inflated cushions that enveloped me. Right. Engines firing: testing. We would either abort, or lift; these were the crucial moments. I've never been on a shuttle that aborted, but I know it has sometimes happened. Only important people go to the Moon—and beyond—people with whose safety no one takes chances.

The vibration ceased—or seemed to. Then I felt a gentle push against my back—still less than one G—and I knew we were lifting off. I felt a strain in my chest, found I'd been holding my breath, and released it gustily.

After indulging in my first meal—I'm afraid I sucked the tube more greedily than usual; but then, eating *is* one of the greatest personal, private, and sensual delights—I deflated the restraining cushions and opened my berth.

Bjonn was waiting for me outside.

He seemed used to moving in freefall; his movements had a catlike grace and I was reminded again of the way he had moved through the crowd of media-men back on the Moon. There was something more there than simple suppleness; he had a body-awareness, a total knowledge of where every part of his body was in relation to his immediate environment. I could never imagine him being clumsy, or bumping into or against anything. Following him into the lounge again I felt stiff and awkward, and very adolescent.

Perhaps you are beginning to understand that which I did not yet comprehend about myself: that I was coming to dislike Bjonn. It was a deep-level reaction, the reaction of the pimply adolescent as he follows his heroes around: he envies, but he also hates, because every moment he spends in the company of those who are better, more skilled than he, he is reminded of his own inferiority. But, as I say, I was not yet aware of my reaction. It was to gnaw and nibble at me for a long time before surfacing.

The shutters were open and the lounge viewport offered a beautiful sight of Earth, rising over the Moon. Technically, we were still in lunar orbit, but for me this was a senses-shattering sight, and one I treasured every trip. The Earth was jewel-brilliant in its three-quarter face sun-washed brightness, all pinks and sapphire blues and snow-bright whiteness.

"This is Earth," Bjonn said to me as we hung from handholds a little behind the main cluster of passengers. His voice was breathy, and it seemed to me to be tinged with a strong emotion.

I agreed, not really wanting to talk.

"'Land of our fathers,'" he quoted. "Most beautiful."

"What does Farhome look like?" I asked.

He chuckled. "I really do not know. There was no opportunity to view it when I boarded the *Longhaul*, and none afterward. I've been shown recordings, of course, but they are never the same, are they?" He paused, then added, "We have less water; from space the world looks browner, I think. The cloud-layer is heavier—most of our days are overcast. Whites and browns, a little blue."

"How do you feel, leaving Farhome and coming here?" I asked. "You know, when you go back your friends, family—they'll all be thirty years older."

He sighed, a curiously human sound which I hadn't expected. "True. And yet, I am the Emissary. I could not have stopped myself from coming here, even had I wished."

I wondered, even then, what he meant by that.

* * *

Mostly a shuttle trip is routine, even a little dull, but for all that it represented the sum total of my travels in space. Familiarity dulls even the finest sensations. The menu must vary. This time, however, I found myself looking at the trip through Bjonn's eyes, trying to anticipate his reactions, sensing all over again the newness, the *differences* he must be finding all around him.

All too soon, however, we were back in our berths, restraints inflated, and dropping down through Earth's atmospheric window to Hawawii-port. I found myself supping abstractedly from the meal tube, my mind still turning over and analyzing the things Bjonn had said and done in the lounge.

"Ours is a sparsely settled world, you know," he'd said. "We erected a vast landing port with radio-beacons against the day your ships would come, because we knew you'd never find us otherwise." And on another occasion, "Farhome has much larger land-masses, of course. We've settled only one southern continent, and we haven't even mapped much of the planet by air. The oxygen content of our air is about the same, but the humidity much higher. It's a corrosive atmosphere, and things don't last as long as they should."

And always those very pale blue eyes staring, unwinking, into mine until my eyes would water and I'd blink and find an excuse to look away. Disconcertingly direct, and somehow everything he said carried the import of deep personal meaning. I found myself wondering what I'd do with him in the weeks to come.

The sub-orbital express took us to Eastern Long Island, of the Megayork complex, where a Bureau pod was waiting for us. We had booked Bjonn a suite above the fiftieth floor in a modest hotel in southern Brooklyn for the duration of his stay in eastern North Am. The swift changes in transportation and scene left him quiet but unruffled. As always, his eyes seemed to be tracking methodically, noting everything with computer-like accuracy, while a quiet smile lurked behind them. I showed him his facilities, pointed out the infomat, the information-console, and demonstrated a few of its uses. I felt like a bellhop.

"Enough, please—enough," he said, waving his hand at me and chuckling. "I shall have enough to do just in exploring this amazing suite of rooms to occupy me for the next few weeks. Let us relax for a few moments, and enjoy the quiet amenities. Have a seat. I know you are dying to ask me many questions that the presence of others has inhibited. I will summon some food, and we can talk and eat together."

I'm afraid my reaction was entirely too obvious. I felt the blood leave my face, and my limbs went watery. I all but collapsed into a handy chair. Well, yes, bad taste to be so demonstrative, but after all, the *shock*—

"Ah—perhaps, perhaps," I stammered, "you are, umm, not acquainted with our, umm, ways."

He had already taken the chair facing mine, and now he was leaning forward, an expression of concern tugging at his face. "Have I said something wrong?" he asked. His voice was gentle, but I could not forgive him as easily as that.

"One of man's most private—most personal—moments," I said, forcing the words out past stiff lips. "Most *private*—do you understand?" I found my breath becoming more regular again.

"I'm afraid I don't," he said.

"A decent man—a person of sensibility," I said, trying again, "does not offer to intrude upon the privacy of so personal an act."

"Please forgive me if I have offended you, Tad," he said, "but I remain unaware of the nature of my offense. I understand that its nature makes it difficult for you to speak of it, but surely you must understand that I come from another culture and that my education in your ways is far from complete." He was leaning on the edge of his chair, his voice low, intense, striving to communicate something to me—something more than appeared on the surface of his words. "How have I violated your privacy?" he asked.

I felt my stomach clench as I pushed the words out: "Food," I said. "You offered to eat with me."

A wave of sadness seemed to move over his face, and then was gone again. "The people in your society do not share food together?" Disappointment tinged his voice.

"Never," I said. "The act of food-partaking, like its twin and consequent act, is man's most jealously guarded privacy. It is an unbroachable intimacy. I shall say no more. It is not a subject I can or care to discuss."

"I see. . . ." he said. His eyes had dropped. He was staring at the floor.

I stood. "I think it is best that I leave you to your own devices for now," I said. "You may reach me any time you need me via infomat—" I gestured at the console. "It is a part of the entire vast worldwide Telex System communications network, as well as a computer-outlet for North Am IBM. I'm sure you will find much to amuse you, and that you'll want to rest after your journey. . . ." I was babbling, and the sound of my words embarrassed me. I said goodbye, and left.

In the pod on the way to my office, I wondered at the extremity of my reaction. Very well, eating *is* a private, personal thing—but a proposition to share a meal is not beyond the bounds of comprehension. Why had I felt so deeply shocked? Was it because of Bjonn's own intensity? Or was it because I sensed something that underlay his apparently innocent suggestion? Why had he seemed so disappointed in my refusal? Not surprised—not contrite for unknowingly violating the mores or custom—but disappointed in me. In *me*. Why?

And later, in the lift, I wondered how he could have escaped knowledge of so basic a custom while aboard the *Longhaul II*. But that sparked other thoughts, other questions, the answers to which—if I had them at all—were still locked in my unconscious, awaiting their release in a "hunch."

"Tad! What are you doing here?"

A scent of gardenia: I knew it was Dian before I turned.

She was just closing the door of her office-cubical. I paused, with my hand on my own door.

Dian Knight has been working out of our office for three years now; previously she put in five years advancement in the Bureau's Tokyo office (I checked her file). In the three years I'd known her, I had invited her to social gatherings on four occasions. She refused the first three—all in that first year—and accepted the fourth, two months ago. But it had not been an unqualified success.

Dian was now about five years my junior—a comfortable age gap, I think—and, to me at least, a very attractive woman. She wore her hair conservatively, and rarely revealed more than her breasts. She had a good sense of humor—a nice balance against my own lack—and a generally sunny disposition. To the best of my knowledge (and that of the Bureau), she had never had a marriage contract.

"Come on inside," I said, gesturing at my office. "Let me tell you about our man from Farhome."

We settled down in comfortable chairs, and while I stared abstractedly out my window at the gray waters of the Sound, I sketched in the details of my initial encounter with Bjonn.

"He bothers you," she said, when I had concluded.

I steepled my hands and rested my chin against them. "Yes. It's not a simple cultural difference. God knows, I've encountered that before. It's something more subtle. It's—it's like those Religious Archivists. You remember them?"

A man named Schobell had been digging around in the literary debris of earlier centuries, and had uncovered several works of fiction which he released—suitably edited, of course—to the world as the bible of a new, but authentically ancient, of course, religion. It had to do with pre-space-age visitations by alien creatures in arcane vehicles, reincarnation, "engrams," and a civilization which lived, or still lives perhaps, in caves beneath the earth's surface. He hit the media during a lull, a dull period; and provoked a wave of summer madness (in the northern hemisphere—below the equator it was winter madness; ah, well) that swept the public. Overnight his churches had sprung up everywhere, he was "auditing" people by the millions, and was boasting he'd licked "the deros" for the first time in five hundred—or was it a thousand?—years. Like all fads that gain momentum so quickly, it had played out equally quickly and lapsed into obscurity within its second year. I understand Schobell retired on the fortune he made, but a few dedicated cells of his followers still persist.

One such man was at the party I'd taken Dian to, and she recalled him without further prompting. "Oh, you mean that strange, intense way of speaking he had? So sincere, and always looking you in the eyes, and like that? Don't tell me it's spread to Farhome!"

"Not likely," I said. "And Bjonn hasn't the, oh, call it the studied artificiality, of an Archivist. He's, well, *genuine*. It's not something he's learned—it's something he *is*." And as I spoke the words, I felt a nagging idea in the back of my mind. But I couldn't reach it.

Dian let my silence lengthen and then said, "How strange. But perhaps they have some similar religion on Farhome. After all, things were very different here before they left."

"No," I said, shaking my head, but replying more to myself than Dian, "that's not it. It's in there, worrying its way around the back of my brain, but I can't touch it yet."

"It will come to you," she said confidently. "When it's ready."

I glanced at her in surprise; it was an unusually perceptive remark. "There's something else," I said. "Something I didn't tell you yet."

"What?"

"He asked me to eat with him." I felt an icy fist clamp over my intestines as I said it, and I rose and went to the window to stare out of it.

She said nothing for a moment. I watched the safety-pane vibrate from the winds outside. Far below the incongruously white sails of a racing yacht darted over the water. Then:

"He must be ignorant of civilized customs."

"I thought so at first, myself. But then, after I left, I

started to wonder. What about the time he spent aboard the *Longhaul II?*"

"Fifteen years . . ." she breathed.

"More like five months, for him," I said, "but still time enough. No, I think he knew our customs well enough. I think he faked ignorance in order to gain an acceptable excuse for his blunder."

"But—why? If he knew—?"

I turned around. Dian dropped her eyes momentarily to her lap, then looked up again, her eyes meeting mine. It was disconcerting. Her face seemed a little flushed.

"I don't know," I said. "That's what I can't figure out. He really *wanted* me to—to eat with him." This time we both blushed.

Properly speaking, I should not have been in my office. I should have been with Bjonn, filling his head with wondrous tales of our marvelous land and civilization, all the while covertly noting and filing his behavior and reactions. But I had a relatively free rein with the assignment. If I chose to leave him on his own, it was my own decision to make. After all, we controlled his suite; he could do little there which was not monitored, and if he left he would be discreetly watched.

Nonetheless, when the buzzer sounded on my infomat I was not surprised. Dian stood up quickly and said, "I'll check with you later," and then was gone. I gave her a goodbye nod and punched for audio-visual.

It was Tucker. He's my boss. His office is in Old Town Chicago, in Great Lakes City, but scuttlebutt travels fast, and by now he'd probably heard from a half dozen sources that I was in my office.

Tucker is the Old Man to me. He can't be much more than twenty years older than I am, but he has one of those midwestern faces that's etched with weathered lines: laugh lines, worry lines, and all the rest. His face is a contour map. And since he is a practicing antiquarian, he affects steel-rimmed glasses. Naturally, he has a drawl.

"Okay, son. Want to tell me about it?" were his first words of greeting.

"Not particularly," I said. "Since when do you need progress reports?"

"Something has your wind up," he said. As I said, he cultivates Quaint Sayings.

"Ayup," I said, giving him one of his own. "But I'll handle it."

"I hope so," he said. "I suppose you know your boy is out on the streets?"

"No," I said, feeling a shock of alarm. "I thought he'd stay put. After all, he just came down from the Moon."

"Better think it through again, son."

"Is he in any kind of trouble?"

"Nope. Just rubbernecking, I gather."

"And you think I ought to be with him."

"Well, that's your job, isn't it?"

"He's a big boy. You should've seen him handling the media."

"I did."

"Oh. Yeah."

"Do as you think best, son."

"I'll get down there," I promised.

The screen blanked out. For some reason I always feel chastened after one of Old Man Tucker's little spiels.

Chapter Three

I punched our Restricted Code into the infomat, and asked for Monitor Central.

When Bjonn went through Bio-Customs on the Moon, he received the full treatment—although of course his five months or so on the *Longhaul II* served as a sort of quarantine. Once checked out, he had been given a small pellet of an extremely weak radioactive isotope. It had been surgically inserted under his skin in his back, just below his right shoulder blade. He probably didn't know it was there; they'd have been sticking things in him for half an hour or more by then. The pellet was a tattletail—it would activate automatic monitors wherever Bjonn went.

It could be argued that this was a fundamental invasion of the man's privacy. But I think I could make an equally valid case for the notion that it preserved his real privacy. As long as machines can watch, human beings will not. Monitoring a man's movements can be the dullest job in the world, and I think if I was faced with the choice, I'd rather the eyes which surveyed me in my public and private actions were mechanical, and not human and knowing. More important, Bjonn *required* watching, as much for his own protection as for anything. As the first representative of man's first interstellar colony, he was an enormously important and valuable person. He required protection. In an earlier age, when fewer people clogged the cities, he would have required a phalanx of bodyguards, and his fame would have guaranteed him a mobbing every time he ventured out into public. He could hardly have enjoyed himself; his "freedom" would have been minimal indeed.

But this is the modern age, the Age of Anonymity. His image had been broadcast over the entire world; and was on recall for printout at any infomat. Ergo, no one really needed to "see" him in the flesh, and few indeed would even recognize him, so accustomed are we all to the anonymity of the teeming masses we move about in. Over one billion people live in Greater Megayork these days: compute the odds, if you will, of *your* likelihood of bumping into Bjonn.

Thus, the Monitor System: a way of keeping easy, automatic, unrestrictive tabs on the man. A way of letting him enjoy his freedom without danger. And a way for me to find him, now.

Shortly I had his present coordinates, a graph of past movements, and a projection based thereon. I keyed in a printout, tore off the sheet of plastic, and all but bolted from my office.

Dian poked her head out of her office as I rushed past. "Trouble?"

"Come along, why don't you?" I suggested. "Unless you're busy?"

In the downlift she asked, "Why the rush?"

"Our man is out on the town," I replied.

"Aha! Is that bad?"

"Yes and no. Not really—I can't imagine him unable to handle himself." I pointed at the printout still in my fist. "He's just ambling along, looking to see what there is to see."

"Around the Stiles Arms?" Dian laughed. "Not much!"

"Not if you're used to hundred-story buildings, podlines, park strips, and all the rest, no," I agreed. "But he isn't."

"But you don't think he's in any sort of trouble, do you?"

"No, but I can see where I might be, if something *did* happen. Ergo, I'm in a rush."

I put her into a Bureau pod, slid in beside her, and punched out the coordinates of the point Bjonn had last been near.

"You haven't told me why you want me along," Dian said. The pod zipped out of the holding lane, and into the traffic stream. We were less than fifteen miles away; we'd be there in minutes.

"I'd like a woman's opinion," I said, hesitating a little.

"A woman's opinion? Of Mr. Bjonn, you mean?"

"Yes," I said, more or less thinking out loud. "We'll say you're my secretary—and, uhh, you wanted to meet him. First man back from Farhome, all that. You've seen a recording of him?"

"On the morning show," she said. "Live and direct—solid color, you know?" Again, the bubbly laughter in her voice that had always warmed me to her.

"Think you'll have any trouble playing the awestruck female bit?" I asked.

She gave me a lingering smile. "Now, how'd you guess?"

* * *

We found Bjonn sitting on a bench on the park strip only five blocks from his hotel. An old man wrapped in a trundle-suit sat at the other end of the bench, feeding pigeons from a large bag. The messy birds were fluttering all around the man and the bench, and went swirling into the air when we walked up.

"Don't you know that's illegal?" I said, flashing my badge—impressive, so long as you didn't read what it said—at the old man. "Pigeons breed disease, and they create filth."

The old man looked up at me. "How's that, now?" he said. His hand dipped into the bag and he scattered bits of dried algae or something on my legs and feet. I kicked a pigeon away from my ankle.

"Leave him be, Tad," Dian said, laying a hand on my arm. "He's wired for sound. Can't you see?" And then I noticed the flesh-colored bits of plastic in his ears that were feeding him a constant diet of pop sounds in mind-numbing aural stereo. He couldn't hear a word I said.

Bjonn had been watching us in silence. Now I turned to him to introduce Dian, and he said, "Am I violating my parole?"

Dian laughed, and I put a brief smile on my lips for him. "You're not under guard," I said. "But you are unused to a city this size, I imagine."

"It stretches for miles in every direction, I'm told."

I nodded, and slipped in an introduction for Dian, "my secretary," who had been dying to meet him. He gave her a smile that lit his face like the sun.

"I've just been sitting out here, trying to encompass it all," Bjonn told us. We began strolling down the strip, away from the old man and his pigeons. "These monstrous buildings. . . ." He gestured with his arm at the buildings which lined each side of the strip and then pointed at the narrow band of yellowish sky overhead. "And the sky so far above. I feel that at any moment they will all topple down upon me; I feel their enormous weight."

It was warm, out here in the open, and I wasn't dressed for it. I didn't have nose filters either, and the smell was vaguely annoying. I didn't normally spend much time out here. "I had expected you would be tired, after your long day," I said, "or I would have offered to show you around the town a bit."

"I slept on the shuttle," Bjonn said, "when we were, ah, berthed. Very pleasant." We had spent almost all our free time in the lounge—but I didn't bring that up.

"Well, *I'm* tired. My day started with the shuttle flight *up*," I said. "Perhaps you'd enjoy seeing some of our nighttime entertainments with Dian?"

He glanced from me to Dian, his smile deepening. "If the young lady has no objections?"

"Oh, none at all," she said. "I'd love it." Either she was a fine actress or she was giving him a better reaction than she ever had me. "I wish you'd tell me about your home— Farhome, I mean. . . ."

I left them there, happy—I thought—to get back down to traffic level and a pod. Dian was a Level Seven Investigator—my own rank. Bjonn would be in capable hands. So—why was I annoyed?

I took a high-speed tube to Vermont. I lived in Rutland, which is still a small city by modern definitions, but has a direct tube into Megayork. My aptrooms were located on the top floor of a ten-story coop, and not only is the sun closer and the air cleaner, but I can see green mountains from my bedroom window—if it isn't polarized (which it usually is).

I stripped, took a mist in the 'fresher, and slipped into my meal chamber for the total pleasure of a complete dinner and evacuation. Then, cleansed, drained and refilled, finally at some sort of peace with the world, I went to bed. The events of the day slipped off me like an easily shed skin, and I forgot the whole troubling mess.

It was with me again when I awoke, though.

My alarm clock, having sensed that the sun would strike me full-face and that the day was clear and not overcast, had depolarized my window. I turned my back, but the back of my neck and my shoulders grew uncomfortably warm. I had my usual pre-waking dream of being trapped in a burning room.

Finally I turned over, stared at my light-washed window, squeezed my eyes shut again, red and green afterimages still dancing under my lids, and groped my way from the bed to the door, where the clock and window control are. The light died to a blessed underwater greenish murk, and I peeped my eyes open.

Standard ritual.

When are they going to invent a clock that will wake a man up painlessly?

After my morning meal and ablutions, I dressed and punched the recall button on my infomat. No messages. A nice day, according to Eastern Seaboard Weather Central: average temperature-humidity only comfort-plus-five-degrees, smog index of .25, prevailing winds from the northeast at five miles an hour with gusts to fifteen. No messages; that meant Dian had encountered no problems the night before. Well, that was good, anyway. No news is good news. Yeah.

I stared at the console for about five minutes, and then got up and went over to my storage room.

I went into my storage room about three times a year, on the average, although it had probably been six months since I had last used it.

Actually, it was intended as a second bedroom for the apt, but I had converted it into a virtual replica of the den in which I'd spent my teens. The dimensions weren't exactly the same—the storage room was larger—but I hadn't been after a faithful copy, right down to the last nick in the wallplastic. And, since a great deal of my time during the years of my boyhood had been spent in both that original den and many others before it, in a sense the storage room was a four-dimensional replica spanning the years of my growth from age six—when I'd left my parents—through mid-adolescence.

The walls were papered with posters and pinups. Astronomical charts and photos covered one entire wall. A replica model of the *Star Voyager* hung from the ceiling, turning slowly in the vagrant air currents. Captain Lasher beamed a merry salute to me from the niche opposite the door.

They weren't all originals—I'd lost many of those. But those I no longer had I could still easily buy, most of them on the open market and a few from antiquarian collectors, although most of my boyhood junk was of too recent vintage to interest a collector.

I walked into the room, let the door slide shut, and I was standing again in my own past. The room was bigger—the ceiling was higher—and the scale nearly matched that of my den when I had myself seen the world as a much larger place. Entering that room was like entering my younger self. I didn't do it often.

I went over to my bunk and sat down on it. The foam was old and no longer very resilient; its lumps corresponded to my younger body, and the place where I sat now had been hollowed out long ago. I stared moodily up at the *Star Voyager*.

Her sister ship, the *Deep Space*, had set out at the same time she had, bound for the planet we even then were calling, hopefully, *Farhome*. An earlier series of unmanned probes had penetrated Farhome's system, orbited Farhome and sent back their data. They said man had a chance on that planet. The *Deep Space*, loaded with one thousand people and all the implements of necessary technology, had set out soon after the probe returned. They made it. The *Star Voyager* did not. There was, and is, no record of what happened to it. The *Eternal Hope* is *still* embarked on its journey, and we will not know its fate within my lifetime.

What kind of people must have volunteered for those long and dangerous journeys, so long ago? How must they have felt, entrusting themselves to a primitive cold-sleep and the protection of untested machines? Those hardy few were our last pioneers. They were selected for genetic soundness, for survival talents, put through mazes of tests in order to prove themselves, five hundred men and five hundred women, all young, fit, virile, ready and willing to make and populate a new home on a new world.

They didn't all survive the trip; we knew that now. (Cold-sleep has been discredited by modern science. How did those star-voyagers beat the average failure rate of 42 percent?) But most of them did; enough of them did. Four of them were Bjonn's grandparents.

I looked at that great and monstrous fat globe of a starship hanging in the center of my den, felt all my old awe and wonder and worship for the men and women who had made a journey in a ship so much like it—and knew a violent, twisting pain in my gut at the thought of Bjonn, the offspring of those people.

They were the impossible ideals, suffering birth, life, and death before my time. Bjonn was reality; the reality I had been denied.

It was at that moment that I first learned of my hatred for the man.

Perhaps I should have had myself disqualified from the project then. But, as I turned it over in my mind and viewed it from as many angles as I could then comprehend, it did not seem to me that my personal reaction to Bjonn should enter into my professional relationship with him. What was wanted was my professional opinion—not my personal like or dislike. There were two separate and distinct factors here. The first was that I was bitterly and hatefully jealous of the man—for all the things he was and could be that were forever lost to me. The second was the alien quality I had sensed in him—a quality I recognized with certain awareness long before I had learned to dislike the man. It was that quality I was probing for. It made no difference whether I liked the man or hated him. And as for the way I felt about him—I was self-aware. I knew my own limitations, I'd seen my own file, my own personality profiles. No one had ever hidden my disqualifications from me. I knew my reaction for what it was, and I could handle it. I hoped.

When I sat down at my office desk, I found a message in my infomat; Dian wanted to see me. I wondered why she didn't just pop in, as she so often had, but I rose and went down the hall to her office, knocked, and entered.

Tucker was sitting behind her desk. Dian was at the window, her back to me.

"Good morning," I said. "You both look serious. What's happened?"

"You tell him," she said, without turning.

Tucker looked up at me, and then gestured to the spare chair. "We're dealing with an unusual man," he said, all traces of his drawl gone. "I went through your prelim notes on him. You're on to something, all right. Last night he propositioned Dian."

I glanced at her. The back of her neck was red, and her shoulders were flushed.

"Not for bedtime fun?" I asked. I had wondered if that might happen. Dian had repulsed me quietly, nicely, very firmly, the one time I had suggested it to her.

"No. For a meal." Tucker had not smiled.

I said something profane and emphatic, then apologized to Dian. It had been unthinkingly appropriate. Then I added, "But he knew damned well—!"

"Of course he did. We know that," Tucker said. "But he went right ahead."

"What did he say, Dian?" I asked. "I mean, did he pretend ignorance again, or—?"

"No," she said. Her voice was low and muffled. "No, he was perfectly honest about it. He told me that you—that you told him—"

"I don't get it," I said, shaking my head. "It makes no sense."

"He—he said it was a customary ritual on Farhome. He wanted to share it with me. . . ."

"A 'customary ritual,' you say?"

"That's what he said." She sounded on the verge of tears.

"I think our problem is one of communication," Tucker said. "It's pretty obvious that not only are meals handled differently on Farhome—it's a primitive planet, after all—but that they mean something very different there as well."

"Like what?" I asked.

"Well, son," he said, the corners of his mouth twisting

down with his familiar drawl, "that's a question I'm sure we'd all like answered."

Tucker stood up. "It's your baby," he said to me. "You've rung Dian in on it, and I'm not complaining, but just you remember where the responsibility lies."

"Thanks a lot," I mumbled, shortly after he'd closed the door.

I looked back at Dian. "Why don't you come over here and sit down," I suggested, an idea starting to take shape as I said it. "It's okay—we've both gone through it now, that's all." I tried a small chuckle on for size; it was meant to sound comforting.

She turned and I saw that her eyes were glistening. She nodded and sat down in her chair at the desk.

"I'm sorry," I said. "I didn't think anything like this would come up, you know, or I'd. . . ."

"I know," she said. "It's not your fault. It's not his fault, either."

" 'His'? You mean Bjonn?"

"He wants something, Tad; I wish I knew what it was. The look he gave me just pinned me to the floor and made me want to bawl like a baby. He was so—so *disappointed*."

"Yeah," I said. "It was that way with me, too. Well, maybe not that extreme, but. . . . Uh, otherwise, how'd you hit it off?"

A little of the old sparkle came back to her eyes then. "Oh, we had a marvelous time! A concert at the Consenses, a live show in Old Manhattan! Everything was just grand, until we'd come back to his suite and he, he wanted to— you know. It was so much fun, being with him. He's like a newborn baby when it comes to all those dull old things we take for granted. And yet, he's so much a *man*. . . ."

"Do you want to see him again?" I asked.

"I—don't know," she said. "I told him I would, but. . . ."

"Listen," I said. "There's something about the man that is definitely number five, you know what I mean? Offkey. This whole emphasis on meals, on—sharing food. He knows it isn't done. He has no excuses left. And yet he's still pressing the point."

"What are you getting at?" she said. She knew what I was getting at; she just wanted me to be the first to put it into words.

"It's something we have to know," I said. "It's something we must find out. Somebody is going to have to share a meal with him."

Chapter Four

In the back of my mind an insane little line kept repeating itself like an endless tape loop: *Who should it be? Me? Who should it be? Me? Who—?*

"I don't think you have the right to ask that of me," Dian said.

I sighed. "No, you're right. I don't." I stood up. "I'm sorry to have involved you in this, Dian." I slid back the door.

"Wait," she said, her voice very low. "Just a minute."

I closed the door and turned back to face her. Her head was bowed and I couldn't see her expression. I waited.

"I—I guess the man has gotten to me," she said. Well, that made two of us—each in his own way, of course. "But . . . I just don't know if I could go through with something like that. I just don't know. . . ."

"I have a suggestion," I said. "Why don't you take him out sightseeing today? You know—the hovercraft cruise, the moldly old landmarks, all the tourist stuff. All public, all in the bright light of day. Take your time, see if he brings it up again. Maybe he won't. But don't make up your mind in advance; see how you feel when he makes the proposition—if he does. How does that strike you?"

"I—don't know," she said, but she looked up at me with a small smile. "I guess that might be an idea."

I leaned over her and lightly kneaded her bare shoulders. "Remember," I said, "it's all for the good of the Bureau."

She straightened up, shrugging off my hand. "Oh, you—!"she said, but the look she gave me was that of the old, mischievous Dian.

The next several hours were spent at routine work. I called Bjonn and told him Dian would be taking him sightseeing, and then I plowed into the exhausting details we'd been furnished by Data Central on Farhome, following the debriefing of the *Longhaul II* crew and staff. It was, for the most part, dry and boring: a welter of facts and figures, tables and tabulations which constituted the scientific code for the substance of what Farhome really was.

The thing is, the *Longhaul II*, an interstellar ship designed for use only in orbit or weak gravitational fields, could land only a shuttle craft (a so-called lifeboat, but no one has yet tested their potential for deep-space survival)— and the amount of gear that could be carried in such a small craft was minimal. So what I had to work with was largely useless: spectrographic readings of Farhome's atmosphere (no significant improvement on those brought back by the original probe), and a lot of other data on the atmospheric content, trace elements in commonly grown food sources, general makeup of the planet's crust, salt content of Farhome's oceans, and so on. It was broadrange stuff, no doubt of immense value in determining the nature and variety of goods to be shipped out next trip, but having little of value to me. Only one section stood out amid all this weights-and-measures data: the observations of the ship's resident shrink on the colonial society. I had that put on printout, and sat back to absorb it more fully.

The average family on Farhome had at least six children. Of the 873 original survivors of the cold-sleep, 460 were women, outnumbering the men by forty-seven. Apparently accommodations were reached in what remained an essentially monogamous society so that every woman became a mother. (None of the colonists had been contracted in marriage to any other colonist at the time they were selected.) The goal was six children, spaced over twelve years, during which the women joined the men in setting up their first townsite and developing nearby farms. (The *Deep Space,* designed with lifting surfaces for its oneway trip, had been glided in, and furnished food from its stores and prefab hydroponic units for the early months. It stayed in production on a supplementary basis, I learned, more than twenty years thereafter.) There were nearly three thousand in the second generation, fairly equally divided in sex. Current projections had Farhome's total human population at over eleven thousand. Of these offspring, a significant number, perhaps one in six, were the products of the ship's supplementary sperm bank, which was intended to combat genetic drift in such a small, relatively closed community. There was talk of supplying a fresh addition to that sperm bank on the *Longhaul II*'s next trip.

But obviously, from what I'd noted, genetic drift or no genetic drift, there had already been changes worked in Farhome's colonists.

The shrink noticed them too, if less perceptively.

"It has been noted," he noted, "that the social structure of the colonists is far more fluid than might have been expected. Despite the strong need for survival skills and specialization, and for the resultant differential in status, class, etc., between agricultural workers and industrial technicians, no actual class structure has been observed.

"Particularly noticeable is the colonists' unusual willingness to communicate at length with this observer, despite the interruption thus imposed upon their tasks. One meets unfailing courtesy, unruffled tempers, and a welcome reception anywhere one goes. Fights, disputes, altercations are apparently so rare as to be remarkable. Although the colonists have evolved a political structure commensurate with their needs in such an open and unpopulated land, they have made no provision for policing their society. They have provided no courts, or other means of dealing with disputes. Crime seems unknown to them. When queried, they remark that they have little time for the trappings of an idle society. This observer found their sincerity unmistakable, but nonetheless naïve, and predicts that within the next generation—observable on the next journey to Farhome—population density will require the adoption of these institutions."

He'd given the colonists a battery of tests, and found that to the man they ranked within the top percentiles of intelligence and personality adjustment—although he questioned the validity of the latter tests, and remarked in passing that inasmuch as a proper curve had not yet been established for the colonists as a whole, his findings were relevant only to Earth norms.

I suppose if you're used to measuring everything around you, the only way you can relate to something new is to say, "I found different measurements." He surely didn't know what he had.

The environment of Farhome was not particularly hostile—at least within the area settled. A few native plants had been cautiously tested and found edible. A number of native animals were domesticable. A small town—it simply can't be described as a city; it has less than a hundred dwellings, all individual and set on their own acreage—constituted the main concentration of the colonists, but outlying farms were being established, and mechanized industries had been located near deposits of petroleum and ores. A typical scene, on the tapes, showed a low, sprawling dwelling in the foreground with plantings of varying hues of green surrounding it. To one side would be a garden, and beyond a backdrop of rolling hills that were purple in the distance. The sky was usually heavy with the puffy undersides of gray-gold clouds, which helped to filter out much of the local solar radiation. The whole picture looked very much like an idealization of our own less populated past, and a bit like a put-up job. Staring at it I couldn't help wondering if a man wouldn't feel a bit lost and alone in such an empty place.

We used to think the discovery of a world like Farhome was the answer to our own overpopulation problems. We were wrong. A man named Leiberson did a study and a breakdown for us. At the present, the population is more or less stable at twenty-seven billion. If an interstellar ship were filled to its capacity (for life support) with new colonists, it could not hold more than a few thousand—and it would be forced to dump them out on their new world without any luggage, any cherished possessions from their past.

Say three thousand colonists a ship; round-trip time to Farhome is roughly thirty years. Seven ships, if all were diverted to the task—which is impossible right now. Twenty-one thousand people every thirty years. Sure.

There's been some loose talk about building a vast fleet—mostly from a few demagogues after they'd heard from the *Longhaul II* that the colony on Farhome was thriving. But it costs billions to build an interstellar ship, and at the present state of the art it takes about ten years to do it. Supplies have to be ferried into orbit, an enormous expense in itself. They're building refractories on the Moon, but that's a separate project and one not expected to pay dividends for the next fifty years.

The way Leiberson figured it, it would cost the present population of Earth the entire lifetime earnings of every living man, woman and child to export one hundredth of their number to Farhome within this century.

Besides, how many of us would really want to settle a desolate planet with fewer than a million neighbors stretched out over a landmass almost double that of Earth's? The solutions—if they are ever to be found—will have to be home-grown.

I had a buzz from Dian late in the afternoon, just as I was getting ready to go home. Her picture was blurry, but she looked radiant. "Tad? Will you meet us at Bjonn's hotel? I really want to see you."

I told her I'd meet them there, and cleared the board. I'd finished taping my prelims, and I was exhausted. I joined the changing of the shift (thank God I don't get on the swing shifts any more; rank hath its privileges) at the lifts, and used my priorities for a pod, picking up a few grim looks in the process. I'm inured.

Minutes later, I was pushing my way into the lobby of the Stiles Arms, and taking an uncrowded lift up to Bjonn's floor. I shook out my clothing and popped a pill for sweat odor, wishing at about that moment that I could be in my own 'fresher in my own apt.

Dian opened the door at my first knock, and at first I didn't notice the difference in her. She invited me in, her eyes sparkling, but I was too tired. I just didn't notice.

Then Bjonn said, "We're glad to see you again," and I looked up. There was a note of something—almost gleeful?—in his voice, and the "we" was subtly underscored.

Dian had moved to his side, looking pert and diminutive against his tall figure, and suddenly I understood. The "we" was no figure of speech.

Something had happened.

Dian was changed.

"It's so marvelous, Tad—so wonderful!" she said. "We want to share it with you." Her eyes were focused directly on mine—why had I never before noticed the color of her eyes?—and the accents of sincerity changed her entire speech pattern.

I saw that, and in that moment I realized in an intuitive flash that the bubbly, happy Dian I'd always known was a facade, a defense that held me—all of the world—at arm's length. And now it was gone, and here before me stood a different Dian. She stood straighter, taller. The funny little quirky smile she used to wear, a lopsided way of smiling as she cocked her head the other way, was gone. Her face looked relaxed and open, in a way I'd never seen it.

And I knew, in the instant I saw and recognized these things, a fierce and violently passionate stab of jealousy. *He'd reached her*. In some strange fashion he had seduced her—seduced her mind.

She was alien now, too.

"Sit down, Tad," Bjonn said. "You look troubled. Is something disturbing you?"

Yes, I wanted to scream at him—*You are, you smug bastard!*

But I just shook my head. "I'm tired," I said. "I've spent a long day at the office."

Dian laughed a slow, warm laugh. It was very musical, very relaxed, the sound of a woman satisfied.

"Poor Tad," she said. "Poor Tad." She seemed almost intoxicated.

Bjonn flashed her some sort of look and then she was contrite. "I'm sorry," she said. "I didn't mean to sound patronizing. But *you'll* understand."

"Easy, now," Bjonn said to her. He seemed to be cautioning her. "Not all at once."

"I guess I haven't had time to become used to it," she said. "Oh, Tad, I'm *free!*"

I shook my head again. "Must be a loose connection," I said. "I hear sound, but it doesn't match with the picture."

"Tad, I want you to relax, to put your day's worries from your mind. It is all so unnecessary, you know," Bjonn said. He moved to the window control, dimmed them, and left the room deep in shadow. Then he led Dian to a low couch opposite the chair I'd found to sink into. His face was highlighted by the remaining glow, his features half lost and etched in appearance. Dian snuggled up against him like a kitten. "Dian has told me about your assignment," he added.

That, too! "Thanks," I told her, the sarcasm rolling in heavy droplets from my voice. "I hope you didn't forget anything or leave anything out."

"You mustn't feel she has betrayed you, Tad," Bjonn said. His voice was somehow disembodied, but very close, almost overpoweringly intimate. "It was in your own best interests."

"You just twisted her around your little finger, and she told you all," I suggested. "'It's in Tad's own best interests,' you told her, and she just couldn't resist telling you."

"It's not that way at all, Tad," Dian said in a dreamy tone. "Not that way at all."

"What I'm about to offer you will make your assignment superfluous," Bjonn said. "She knew that."

"Forgive me if I doubt that like hell," I said.

"Why are you so tense, Tad?" Dian said. "No one is threatening you."

"No?"

"No," Bjonn said. "You are among friends, here, Tad. The closest friends you have. Can you believe that?"

"Can you prove it?"

"Yes," he said.

"Then tell me just what the hell is going on here," I demanded. "Why the dim lights, all this, uh, seductiveness? Just what is it you two are pulling?"

"Tad, you are being so hostile," Bjonn said. His voice was very gentle. "It is difficult to offer you a token of love when you are trying so strongly to repulse us."

"Let it all *go*, Tad," Dian broke in. "Let yourself go free! You don't *have* to fight all the time. Look at me, I thought I did, but now—"

"Okay, okay, enough," I said, waving my arms. "Just tell me what you want of me. Just lay it on the line, huh?"

"We'd like to share a meal with you, Tad Dameron," Bjonn said.

"Please, Tad?" Dian added.

I got to my feet, groped for the door, and ran down the hall. In the lift I threw up, soiling my moccasins.

Chapter Five

The buzz of my home infomat woke me a half hour earlier than usual. I ignored it for the customary three bursts, turned over and was half asleep when it started up again. Which meant it was urgent, because someone had keyed in an override in the courtesy-disconnect, and wasn't content to leave a message.

I stumbled out of my bednook and thumbed the audio; I had no desire to face someone just yet. "Yeah," I muttered. "Okay, okay."

"Tad—" it was Tucker's voice, hard as grit. "I want a visual contact."

Reluctantly, I thumbed visual. "Christ, boss, I was asleep—"

"That's all right. You're awake now." He looked grim—more grim than I'd ever seen him.

I tried to shake the cobwebs out of my brain. My eyes kept sliding out of focus, and either the vertical hold was slipping on the infomat screen, or I was. It was probably me. "Look, I'm really not functioning yet," I said, a little crankily. "It takes me time to wake up in the morning."

"Tough," he said. "I want to talk to you, and I want to talk to you *now*."

You'd think they owned a man, just because he worked for them. "Okay," I said. "You're talking."

"What happened last night?" Tucker said—less a query than a command.

"Last night?" I said, trying to arrange my thoughts in some sort of orderly sequence. "Last night. . . ."

"Come on—snap up!" Tucker said. "Something happened last night and I want the straight story—*now!*"

"Last night. . . ." I repeated. "It seems to me that I was sick last night. Took some pills. . . ." To judge by the racket going on in my head not all of them had worn off yet. "It's still very fuzzy. Look, boss, can't it wait a little?"

"Dameron, you're on the spot," he said. "And I want answers from you—straight answers. No more evasions. Straighten out your head, and tell me this: *What happened to Dian last night?*"

"Dian. . . ." I said. "She—she went over."

"She *what?*"

"Joined Bjonn. Sold out to him."

"Suppose you spell it out for me."

"Called me up, told me to meet her at his hotel. When I got there—really just early evening, you know . . . I was working at the office. I was doing my prelims—"

"I *know*," he said, interrupting me in a savage voice. "I've scanned the whole lot of your prelims. Get back to the point, you poor overworked, underpaid, civil servant!"

"Uh, yeah. Well, she was like him."

"Like who? Bjonn? How do you mean that?"

"Same thing—all the little things about him, you know? Hell, I don't know what it is; I just know when it's there and I can spot it. You know."

"Meaning, she also seemed 'alien' to you."

"Yeah, that's right."

"And you've got no idea how it happened."

"No, I didn't say that. I know how it happened."

"Would it be too much," Tucker asked in a buttery tone, "to share your knowledge of this subject with the man who is your superior?"

"She shared a meal with him," I said.

Silence. Tucker stared at me for a moment, his face totally devoid of expression. He looked like solid granite.

"She . . . shared . . . a . . . meal . . . with . . . him," he repeated, very slowly, very distinctly, as if I was a very stupid or very young person—or maybe both. "And just how did this come to happen? As I recall, I spoke with her only twenty-two hours ago, and she was so shocked by the idea that she couldn't even face me and talk about it. As I recall, she told me—on that very same occasion—that she never planned to see the man again. In fact, she told me flat out that even if it came as an order, she wouldn't do it. And now you are telling me she not only saw this Bjonn—she *shared a meal* with him?"

"Uhm, that's right, sir," I said, swallowing something bitter that had risen into my throat.

"At whose suggestion?"

"Mine, sir," I said.

"You suggested it."

"Yes sir."

"A fellow investigator—equal to your rank. Not even assigned to the case. But you suggested it to her. *And she went along with it?* Are you trying to tell me that?"

"Yes sir."

"You're a liar."

"No sir, I'm not."

"You're a liar, Dameron. And I'm going to pry the truth

out of you if we have to pull each cell out of your brain by hand."

"Sir, you're being very unreasonable—"

"Shut up. Dameron, let me tell you something. You may have been her equal in rank, but that's as far as it goes. You weren't half the person she was. Do you know that?"

"I—"

"You're a failure, Dameron. A straight-out, pretested failure. It's on your charts. Do you know that?"

"I—"

"That girl had a brilliant career ahead of her. She was just starting. Just starting, Dameron, and she held your rank. You've been a Level Seven for how many years?"

"Ten—"

"For ten years, Dameron. And you're never going to go any higher. You were *never* going to go any higher. You are bottom-of-the-heap, Dameron. Strictly Earthbound. Expendable. If you washed out of your job tomorrow, you wouldn't be missed. Almost anyone in the Bureau could do your job. Do you understand that, Dameron? *Expendable*. And you put that girl out on the limb, and sawed it off! You walked her right out of the fifty-story window. What did you do to her, Dameron? *How did you get her to do a filthy thing like that?* Dameron?"

"Look—why don't you ask *her?* Why're you throwing all this at *me*, fergawd's sake? If you don't believe me, why don't you check it out with her?"

"Believe me, Dameron, it would be a distinct pleasure to be able to do that one little thing. It really would. But—" Tucker leaned so close to his pickup that his features filled my screen and blurred. "She's gone, Dameron. She's not available."

"Gone?" I echoed.

"G-O-N-E: *gone*. Disappeared. With that Bjonn. Into thin air."

I shook my head. "Sorry. No, that won't wash at all, sir. Bjonn had a tattletail in him. He is definitely not gone into thin air."

Tucker let out a gusty sigh. "Ah, but for the sheer om-

niscient wisdom of our juniors where would we old fools
be today? His tattletail was precisely monitored by Monitor
Central, and I have the chart here before me." He flashed
an indecipherable chart at the screen for a moment. "It was
followed from the evacuation-disposal unit in the refreshment chamber, down sixty-three stories of sewage pipe to
the waste-disposal network under Fourth Avenue, thence
to the Owl's Head Processing Plant, and there reclaimed.
I have it here now." A huge thumb and forefinger filled the
screen; they held a tiny pellet and then disappeared again.
"It's completely sanitized, of course. Had it not been sensed
and removed, it would even now be in an algae vat somewhere on Staten Island.

"Have you any further comments?"

"No," I said. "I don't. What do you want me to do?"

He considered me for a moment. "Well, what I want is
not important right now. Report to your office. Your story
will have to be checked out by truth technicians." The
screen went blank.

I spent half a day wired to machines of various persua-
sions, and by the time it was over my arms ached from
injections, and my mind was numb. Everything I'd said
had been checked out, and it was all verified. I saw Tucker
in the spare office he used in Megayork, when they were
finished with me. He had my graphs spread out over his
entire desk and half the infomat console. He ignored me
for several minutes.

Finally he looked up. "Okay, Dameron, you get to keep
your job this time."

"Thanks," I said. I guess some of the bitterness I was
feeling leaked out.

"Don't get tight with me, fellow," Tucker said. He was
treating me as if he'd never met me before, as if no bond
had ever existed between us. "If you lucked out this time,
it doesn't change a thing. You had a responsibility—a moral
responsibility if nothing else—and you failed it. You failed
it one hundred percent."

"Maybe I'd just better hand in my resignation," I said.

"Why?"

"You've made it pretty plain to me, sir. I have no future here. I'm at a dead end, and you've thrown that in my face."

"Dameron, you've been in the Bureau since when? Graduation?"

"Just about."

"This is the only job you've ever held."

"That's right."

"What do you think the odds are on finding another government job?"

"If I walk out on this one? Pretty poor, I'd imagine."

"You'd be right. So what does that leave? The so-called 'private sector?' Have you any idea how tight jobs are there? You have to be *born* to them to get in the door—that, or be so goddamned *right* for the job that they can't afford to ignore you. If you walk out of here, you'll be on Public Care tomorrow morning, and you'll remain on Public Care the rest of your life. Do you know that?"

"I guess so." I hadn't thought about it, but he was right. A private job is a joke, there are so few left—and when you turn your back on civil service, that's it.

"So—on top of everything else, you're a quitter," Tucker said. His voice lashed me with scorn.

"If you say so, sir."

He nodded, as if in confirmation of some private thought. "I see. . . . You have just sold Dian down the river to that . . . colonist, and now you want to walk out, turn your back on the whole thing, pretend it never happened."

"What are you getting at, sir?"

"Just this: Dian is *still* your responsibility. So, for that matter, is Bjonn. Just because they've worked some sort of disappearing act doesn't let you off the hook. You're weak, Dameron. You disgust me. One setback, and you're ready and willing to call it quits!"

"I was under the impression that I was no longer wanted here, sir," I said, stiffly.

"Nobody is talking about whether you're *wanted*, Dameron. Who said you were *ever* wanted? The first time I saw your personality profile, I wanted to see you transferred to somewhere far, far away—like the Sahara reclamation project. You think I want some space-happy nut in my department? How many times have you put in for space duty? How many times have you requested transfer to Lunaport? And just why do you think I've been forced to deny those requests?"

"I've seen my file, sir." Yes, and the big, rubber-stamped, *"Refused—Unstable"* on every transfer form I filed. I've read the expert opinion, neatly entered into the appropriate spaces by some anonymous secretary, from a shrink's offhand remark: *Borderline paranoia—childhood fixation upon space travel, space career, tending toward adult instability. Acceptable for Earth-assignment only; clearance for Moon-shuttle solely in line of above assignment.* I had daily bouts of nausea for more than a week after I read that.

"However, you have your talents. Your major talent is your ability to organize data systematically, in such a way that a previously hidden fact becomes apparent. Which is to say, you make an adequate field investigator. Or so I thought, until *this* situation developed. Well, *what are you going to do about it?*"

"You're asking me to investigate their disappearance, then?"

"Hell, man," he roared, "I'm not *asking* you a thing! It's your *job!*"

"Yes sir," I said, and walked out.

It's funny how you can deceive yourself. I mean, without half trying. Take me: I wanted to believe I was liked. For some dumb reason, I wanted to think that Tucker was my Old Man—like a foster father to me. It had made me feel the job I was doing was more valuable, somehow—because I had a specific person to please in my execution of it.

Well, strike one illusion.

Then, as I sat brooding at my desk, I began thinking about another false illusion: Dian. Why *had* she gone so willingly with Bjonn? I hadn't known the degree to which his proposition had bothered her—but it had taken relatively little on my part to persuade her to see him again. Why?

I'd assumed it was because of what he was—and I wasn't. I had come to think of the man as an irresistibly romantic figure in her eyes. I had even thoought (hell, I took it for granted) she would go to bed with him, even though she had refused to do so with me (and, for that matter, with anyone else that I knew of).

Backtrack a bit. When she agreed so readily to go along with me, to be my "secretary" for that first meeting, I'd put it down to eagerness on her part to meet a fascinating man. It hadn't occurred to me that she had wanted to do something with *me*, to join in *my* enterprise. And for that matter, hadn't Dian always been more friendly with me than almost anyone else in the office? How many other guys had she gone out with? (Well, maybe a few, that first year, but not many since—I would have known.)

Rethink it: Could it be that Dian had steeled herself to take Bjonn sightseeing, had forced herself to join him in a meal, *solely because she knew how important it was to me?*

That was hard to accept. Probably the truth lay between the two extremes. She wanted to help me, but Bjonn didn't make it difficult. . . .

The way she'd changed . . . what had she said? That at last she was "free"? Free, how? In what sort of way? What had I thought when I'd seen her standing here? That she had shed her old facade—her old defenses? Could that be what she'd meant?

Had she been walking through life as thoroughly fright-ened of it as I was?

Put that on hold. Let's try another tack.

Bjonn had flushed his tattletail. Either he'd known himself it was there, or Dian had told him. Would she have known? I couldn't be sure. I hadn't specifically told her, but she might have checked the records on him, she might just have made an educated guess—or Bjonn himself might have worked it out. That would have to be checked later.

How else could they be trailed?

Credit.

You can't use a pod, you can't board a tube, take a plane or rocket—you simply can't travel at all except by shank's mare—without your molecularly-keyed credit card.

Bjonn had no card. Or did he? Check that out.

I consulted the infomat.

Okay. The Bureau had issued him a card as a courtesy, because he was an Emissary. But he hadn't used it. Obviously, he hadn't needed to.

Ergo, Dian. They'd used hers.

I used the infomat again, requesting and receiving Credit Clearance on Dian Knight, employment No. QW8490358–HG–465397A–F.

Nothing.

Oh, sure, bills for clothing, charges for transportation within the city, and so on, the most recent a hovercraft pleasure cruise around the islands, yesterday afternoon. Nothing since, not even a local pod. Nothing.

I was staring at the printout, trying to read something clever and nefarious between the lines, when Tucker stuck his head in the door.

"I'm glad to see you working," he said. "But you're still trailing the hounds. We've found nothing on their credit after a most thorough search." The door snicked shut behind him and I regarded its blank surface for several moments. His drawl was back. Just what did *that* mean?

Chapter Six

Dian shared an apt with another girl in Old Manhattan. It was in an old building in the seedy East Seventies, just off the park. Once a rich and fashionable area, it had resisted change longer than most of the core city, and when the rest of the original New York City was rezoned and rebuilt, the Upper East Side had become an island of blight, a "historical landmark," duly enshrined and preserved in all its amber glory. The pod-lines ran underground here, in old subway tunnels, and I had to walk the three blocks west on the surface of the old, original streets. Someone had put potted shrubs in the onetime traffic lanes, but refuse and debris cluttered the pedestrianways and when I kicked one pile of litter that barred my way, live rats scurried angrily out from under it. Sordid. I wondered why anyone as fresh and bright and attractive as Dian ever wanted to live here.

Of course these days the area is considered to be "quaint" and it draws its percentage of young rebels. At one intersection I saw a young man spraying brightly colored plastics from a hose attached to a portable machine. The plastics solidified on contact with the air, and he was "painting" an object of some sort—perhaps a sculpture—that took form directly in midair. Quaint. Sure, a return to antiquarian values and all that. Recreate the individual artwork: down with computers, all that sort of thing. He even had short hair.

I found Dian's building. Twelve stories and huddled against the ground. Stone facades showing the signs of many repairs, coated now with clear epoxies, a misguided attempt to Preserve The Past in a few of its glories. Six badly worn stone steps led up to an ancient door of wrought-iron filigree which swung inward after I'd leaned on it for several moments. There was an empty vestibule large enough for a one-room apt, and beyond it another set of doors, locked.

The light came from one dingy overhead fixture, an ancient tube-type light, and I had to get within a foot of the names over the bell pushes before I could read them clearly.

Knight—Carr 12F.

I pushed the button.

"Scrawkutt?"

I jumped, feeling guilty for no good reason. The sound had come from a tiny grill under the buttons.

"Hello?" it said again.

"Hello?" I replied, feeling foolish.

"Who is it, I said?"

"Miss Carr?" I returned. "I'm Tad Dameron. I work with

Miss Knight. I'd like to come up and see you a few minutes."

"Now?"

I sighed. "If I might." I had no intention of making another trip like this.

"Okay." And the inner door began an irregular buzzing sound.

I caught it before it stopped, and pushed it open. The lobby beyond was even larger than the vestibule, with stairs on each side. I had visions of climbing twelve flights of stairs until I noticed a red door with a round window in it and a button-push in the jamb at its side.

Another door that swung open, and the lift chugged and wheezed as it literally crawled up past each floor. Apparently there had once been an inner door, but it was long gone, and someone had rewired the shaft so that the elevator would work without it.

I found Miss Carr waiting for me at the end of the hall. She had a turban of some sort wrapped around her head, and a voluminous robe around her bulky figure. "Please come in," she said. "I don't want to stay out here in the hall." She sneezed. "I'm sick," she added.

I followed her into the apt. The ceilings were high, and it appeared to consist of at least three rooms, plus, of course, the eating cubicle. The room we'd entered was cluttered with objects I couldn't distinguish in the dim light. The air was oppressively hot and humid.

"Have you received medical treatment?" I asked, mostly to be polite.

"Ha!" she snorted. Her face was moonlike—round and bland; she'd apparently had all her facial hair removed, including eyebrows and lashes. "They *never* know!"

I removed several articles of clothing from a chair and sat down. "I believe the Bureau has been in touch with you," I began.

"Oh! Have they *ever!* Beginning in the middle of the night!" She slapped her hand against her forehead in apparent mock anguish; the effect was only partially successful since most of her forehead was under the turban.

"The middle of the night, you say?" That seemed strange.

"Well, no later than six, this morning," she conceded.

Not long before Tucker had called me.

"And you told them—?"

"What could I tell them? She wasn't home. Far as I know, she wasn't home all night. So? She's of age—*she* can stay out when she wants." This was offered up to me in the spirit of complaint.

"But she hasn't done so often?" I suggested.

"Well, no . . . not that I recall."

"How long have you been rooming together?"

"Oh, must be . . . let me see . . . almost three years, now."

"Have you employment, Miss Carr?"

She turned red. "Is that any business of yours?"

"You're on Public Care, then?"

"So what if I am?"

"I'm a little surprised to see you living in a building like this," I said. "It was my understanding that. . . ."

"Dian made up the difference," she said. "She understood how it was with me. I'm an *artist*. You can't be *creative* in one of those public hencoops. I told them that. I told them, just give me my allowance and let *me* worry about how far it will go, huh?" Her eyes narrowed. "Which agency did you say you were with, again?"

"I'm with the Bureau of Non-Terran Affairs, Miss Carr. I have absolutely no interest in how you choose to spend your allowance."

"Well, just why *are* you here, anyway?"

"I'm here because Dian Knight has disappeared," I said.

Her jaw dropped open, exposing neat, even rows of carnivorous teeth. "How do you mean disappeared?" she demanded.

"Disappeared," I repeated. "Without a trace. When is the last time you saw her?"

"I—yesterday. In the afternoon. I was just getting up."

"You were sick yesterday?"

"No, I—say, what is all this? I *normally* get up in the afternoon. And it's none of *your* business!"

"Okay, okay," I said. "Just tell me about Dian. Was she alone when you saw her?"

"No, of course not," she said. "She had that colonist fellow with her, that big, strange-looking man. You know, I bet *he* made me sick!"

"How's that again?" I said.

"He comes from some other planet, right? Who *knows* how many bugs he's carrying on him? He could be starting an *epidemic*, just wandering around this city!"

"You should only know," I muttered to myself.

"Hah?"

"It's not likely," I said. "He had to go through Bio-Customs. They don't even let stray spacefaring spores through."

"Yeah? Well, *something's* made me sick!"

"No doubt," I said. "Let's get back to Miss Knight. She had Bjonn with her, you say. Why did they come here?"

"I don't know," she said, a little reflectively. "Funny you should ask. She seemed, oh, I dunno . . . different."

"Different?" My ears were pricked up.

"Well, like, I don't really know . . . kinda glowy, you know, really happy, even."

"What did she do? What did she say? Did she pack any clothes or anything?"

"Ummm, yes, I guess she did. Not a lot, though. Nothing much more than you'd want for a night out." She smirked at that one. She'd figured it all out, she had. "Just a little bag."

"Were *you* out of the room at all during that time?"

"Me? No, I don't—oh, yes, I was for a minute. The fellow, Dian had told him I was an artist. He wanted to see my stuff. I have a studio—in there." She waved her arm vaguely at a closed door.

"This room in here is yours?" I asked.

"I use it, yes. It's really for both of us. But since my own room is just *filled up* with my equipment, I kinda use this room, too."

"I see. And while you were in the other room, with Bjonn, was the door opened or closed?"

She leaned closer to me, as though trying to make me out in the murk. I wondered if she'd thought of turning up the lights, and then dismissed the notion. She'd surely not want brighter lights in this slovenly room. "Just what is it you think you're pinning on me, mister?" she asked. She had the whole line down perfect, even the inflection was right off a nighttime melodrama on the 3–D.

"I'm asking if you could watch what Dian was doing out here, while you were in your, ah, studio with Bjonn," I said.

Her bristles withdrew. "Ummm, well, no, I guess I wasn't paying much attention. I, umm, probably closed the door—one of my best renderings is mounted on the back of the door, and. . . ."

"So Dian could have picked up something out here and you wouldn't have known," I finished it for her.

"Picked up *what?*" she said. "Just what are you talking about?"

I sighed. "Used your card today?" I asked.

"My card? My credit card? No. . . ."

"See if you can find it," I suggested.

She pushed herself to her feet and moved over to a piece of furniture half buried under a pile of something-or-other. She pawed through the pile for a bit, and then reached under it. Half the pile slid to the floor, where it was absorbed by a mound of clutter already there. She paid no attention to it. She rooted about in the chest of drawers, or whatever it was for a while, and then moved on to another high mound which turned out to be a chair, stacked with debris. Plastic infomat printouts went flying. An old and very musty towel landed at my feet. I leaned over to pick it up between thumb and forefinger, and an unpleasant odor assailed my nostrils. Given another week or two, and I think life might have been spontaneously generated in that towel, particularly in this hothouse environment.

By now she was beginning to look a little frantic. She stopped, fixed her gaze on me, and stated, "I can't find it. I know exactly where I keep it, and it is not there." She opened her mouth to continue, but I interrupted her.

"Did Dian know where you kept it?" I asked.

"She knew well enough that it was always in my sporan," she said, nodding emphatically. Her turban was starting to come loose.

"Where's your sporan?" I asked.

"That's it! I can't find my sporan," she said. Her chins quivered with indignation.

My eyes wandered aimlessly, then returned to the pile I'd moved from the chair I was in to the floor at my side. Amid the rumpled clothing was a shaggy tail of fur. I reached down and pulled it free: it was a side pouch of synthetic fur, ending in a floppy tail. "Is this—?"

"That's it," she cried, pouncing upon it and wresting it from my hand.

"Please check it out," I said, feeling a vague sense of anticlimax.

She dumped the entire contents out on top of what remained of the pile on the chest of drawers. Her fingers rifled through the new debris and emerged triumphantly. "Got it!" she said. Her tone was a crow of pleasure—as though she had somehow bested me in a covert contest.

"Let's see," I requested, holding out my hand. She surrendered the tab of homogeneous plastic to me with poor grace.

I turned it over and stared at its face.

Every credit card has its molecular key that identifies it to its owner's account. Every card is unique; no one has ever succeeded in counterfeiting a card. A card can be stolen, but once reported stolen it is valueless, and the rightful owner is issued a new card. A simple consultation with the infomat is all that is necessary. So cards are rarely stolen these days.

But one was. This card carried a name in simple block letters: *Dian Knight*. To its right was an embossed thumbprint.

Dian had switched cards. "This isn't your card," I said. "This is Dian's."

"What?" she screeched. "That's whose?"

"Where's your infomat?" I asked, wearily.

"In there," she said, pointing through a half-open door.

It was obviously Dian's room: the cheerful late-afternoon light that streamed in through the windows only pointed up the neatness of the room and its effects. I found the infomat next to a chair that folded out into a bed.

I punched in my code and got Credit Clearance. "What's your full name?" I called out.

"Terri Carr," she answered.

"No middle names, no marriage-contract names?"

"No, of course not," she said, her voice trailing off. I requested information on the recent uses of Miss Terri Carr's credit.

Paydirt, as the old saying goes: two continental hops to the west coast, to Southern Pacifica. Pod to downtown Santa Barbara in northern Southern Pacifica.

And then nothing. No further uses. Absolutely nothing.

"How much did you say your regular allowance was?" I called out.

She told me.

"Well, I think you'd better prepare to draw in your belt a little," I said.

"What do you mean?" She was filling the open doorway with her bulk. I was getting tired of her.

"It's been spent," I said.

I took the time to do a thorough search of Dian's room, although not with much hope of finding anything. Still, I hoped I might turn up something that would point in the direction she had fled. People rarely manage to just "disappear" on their own hook. It isn't that easy. When one thinks of escape, he usually thinks in terms of escape *to* some place—a place in some way familiar to him, or a place he's always wanted to see. More likely even, he thinks of escape to some place where he has friends, contacts: some place where he will not be alone.

Bjonn was an alien to this planet. He could hardly have contacts or friends anywhere. He would have no preferences for any one spot on the globe. And no real knowledge of any given area's advantages or disadvantages, either.

So that left Dian, and Dian had roots. She had grown up, left behind a family, friends, associates, playmates, roommates. She had lived in various cities during her life. Some she would not want to revisit; others might arouse nostalgia from her and a desire to return. I had to gamble on a clue in her past that would point out the direction she was taking—because unless we sighted her by chance, there was no other way.

This is, as I have said, the Age of Anonymity. This is an era when one can see, in the order of a day's business, several thousand faces. Commuting alone: I shared my daily trips on the tubes with tens of thousands, whose throngs I must push my way through. As a consequence, privacy is a very personal and closely guarded right. One does not stare at strangers. One *never* meets another's eyes when out in public. It isn't done. It strips your own defenses as readily as it does his; that shocking moment of *contact* can leave you shaking and nauseated.

Bjonn was a striking figure of a man—but how many of those he passed among would notice him, even to the extent of becoming aware of his striking qualities? We could blanket the 3–D with his hologram, and we would receive millions of false reports on his whereabouts, and—probably—none genuine. Talk about your haystacks and needles—!

I found nothing of value in Dian's room. She had a few private tapes, a thin sheaf of printouts, mostly fashion notes for women, and a privately made pornographic book, much thumbed through, its plastic binding in tatters. But there was no correspondence—if she received any, she did not keep printouts—and no personal effects from her childhood. I wondered if she had successfully boxed her past and put it behind her. Most people do; I wondered if I was the only exception.

"You've still got her card," Terri Carr said to me when I returned to the humid gloom of the other room.

"That's right," I said.

"Well?"

"Well, what?"

"Aren't you going to give it back?"

I stared at the gross creature with ill-concealed dislike. "Miss Carr, this is not your card. Your card was stolen, and you should report it and have another issued in your name. This card is evidence, and does not belong to you."

"But she *gave* it to me!" she yelped.

"She did not have the right to give it to you," I said. "If you used it you would be guilty of violating the law."

"But she used *mine!*"

"I'll see what I can do about having the amount she used refunded from her account to yours," I said. "You won't starve."

"She's not coming back, is she?"

"I doubt it."

"What am I going to do for *rent?*"

"I suggest you find another roommate," I said. "One who can be equally tolerant of your little foibles. It's a big city—you shouldn't have much trouble."

As the door to the apt slammed shut behind me, I heard her begin to wail with sobs of self-pity.

Chapter Seven

I had to put in for Bureau clearance for a hop to Southern Pacifica—that is, if I wanted to put the expenses on the Bureau account rather than my own. So I had to talk to Conners.

"Pacifica," he said. "Why do you need to go out there?" Conners is in Cost Accounting.

"Mainly because that's where our missing persons last were," I said, wishing I could thumb off the connection and terminate the whole inquisition.

"Is there some reason why one of our people in Pacifica could not handle it?" Conners asked politely. His detachment came to him easily; Conners' office is in our main

office in Geneva, and as far as I know he hasn't stirred
from that spot in twenty years.

"There are a number of reasons, but the main one is that
this investigation is *my* job—not that of some nit in Pacifica," I said, my temper fraying at the edges.

Conners tuttutted me, and then asked me to hold. The
screen flashed a couple of times, and lit up with "Please
Hold," while I sat in my office and twiddled my fingers.
I thought of waiting until he returned, then flashing him *my*
"Please Hold" signal for a moment or two. But I didn't. I
thought about things like that, but I rarely did them. A pity.

He was checking me out, of course, probably with
Tucker. I could imagine Tucker telling him in that lazy
drawl of his, "Oh, the boy is getting nervous; I lit a little
fire under him t'other day. Thinks he could ease his way
with a paid vacation on the coast and be out from under my
thumb." Or maybe, "You know how it is," a chuckle, "fellow takes his title seriously—'field investigator'—too seriously." Or most likely, "No need for him to go out; we've
got plenty of people out there can get the job done; fact is,
Dameron's under a bit of a cloud these days. . . ." It would
all come down to the same answer, I was sure. And the
thing was, I couldn't be sure it wasn't true—*was* I just
looking for a change of scenery, an out from the hot box?
Why *did* I have to go out there myself? Because I thought
I might just sniff out something a more dispassionate investigator would overlook? And just how likely was *that*,
anyway?

The screen flashed again and the speaker tweeted to let
me know Conners was back—just in case I might be preoc-
cupied with a finger count or something of the sort.

Conners looked up. Light glinted for a moment on his
bald head. "It's all been cleared," he said. "I hope you have
a productive trip." Then the screen cleared and went blank.

The HST took only a little over an hour; trips this short
usually take longer by air than those which allow a full
trajectory. Soon I was amid the sunwashed stucco cliffs of
Southern Pacifica, that vast man-made sprawl that covers

the entire southern half of the state of California and the western parts of Arizona and Nevada. Never my favorite part of the world, I found myself wondering what its attraction had been to Dian and Bjonn. Or was it just that she'd already discovered her roommate's credit went no further?

The terminal was built over a portion of what had once been the San Pedro Channel, only just east of Catalina Island. These days it was an island in name only, since the city of Southern Pacifica had been built on piers stretching out over the water for miles. I was standing in a passenger lounge, staring around me and trying to put myself into *their* shoes. What had Dian and Bjonn been thinking when they stood here? Had they been perplexed, or were they already certain of the next leg of their flight? Had Bjonn stared out the big polarized windows at the muted scene of bright sun and white concrete and the tall, rocket-like shapes of the HST planes, or had he followed Dian immediately across the lounge for the local tube terminal? I scanned slowly around the room. People, coming and going, few pausing to sit and rest. A big 3–D on one side of the room, a soap playing itself out on its scene-shifting stage. A screen, dominating the other interior wall, with arrivals and departures flickering across in bright-green block letters a foot high. A vending area, near the exit doors, headlines and come-on blurbs racing across the screen over its printout in mockery of the larger screen nearby. The few seats were hard and uncomfortable—no one lingered here long.

I joined the crowd getting off another plane and made for the exit. Every man, woman and child who had ever passed through this terminal had robbed it of a little of its life and individuality. It had long ceased to have any. It was just a place one went through to get from one place to another, not even a way station.

Several tubes terminated here. Dian and Bjonn had taken the through-express to Santa Barbara. I passed my card over the turnstile eye and went through to board a through-express.

The tube made the nearly one hundred twenty miles in

thirty minutes—slower than I'm used to, but then they take life at a more leisurely pace in Pacifica.

Santa Barbara is regarded by the locals as an island of culture and history amid the enormous population growth and mushrooming megacity of Pacifica, but to me it looked more like a slum. Narrow, twisting streets, ancient tumble-down architecture dating, it is said, from the time the Spanish first colonized the coast, and a jungle of untidy plant life that seemed to be winning an age-old battle with the artifacts of men. And no pods. The tube station had only lifts to the surface, and there I found no covered arcades, no climate control, nothing in fact but the bare face of the city. Appropriate as a shrine for visits, perhaps, but to live in? No thanks.

It was easy to see why no further record had been found. Dian and Bjonn could hardly have summoned up transportation with a credit card here even if they'd wished it. I stood blinking in the sun and wondered just what I'd do next.

"Hey, goodfella', you lost?"

It was a kid. I looked down at him and felt the shock of premonition. He didn't look over nine or ten, his grinning face was the color of teak, and his sun-bleached hair was golden white. His teeth flashed ivory in the sun, and his eyes were the palest blue. He could've been Bjonn's son or younger brother.

"You tell me," I said. "Am I lost?" I gestured around me at the white stucco, red-tile roofs so low that the whole street was awash in light, and the dark-green hues of the palms and ivy on the walls.

"Maybe you need a smart guide—show you around the town?" He winked. Clever little bastard; I wondered if his virgin sister—or maybe his virgin mother, they never do things by halves, do they?—was next on the ticket. I had the feeling I'd walked into a very bad old melodrama . . . *live and in solid color*. . . . I waited for the next cliché to drop.

"What you want," he continued, "is a cycle. The only way to get around." He gestured, and I saw a man down the street perched upon an ungainly device with two high, narrow wheels. As he pedaled toward us he took a wobbling route, and I wondered how much further he'd make it before falling off.

"One of those things?" I asked. "No thanks. It's too late in life to try that trick."

"They got them with three wheels, too—for the ladies and the old men," he said. I gave him a sharp look, but his face was bland.

"Tell me something," I suggested. "Is there a place around here that's cool and out of the sun, where a tired old man could sit down for a moment?"

"Sure. You want me to come along an' show you?"

"Why not?" I said.

It wasn't exactly what I had in mind—I could have used a place with eating cubicles for a fast bit of refreshment— but he led me into a little vest-pocket park just down the street. In the shade the dry air was much cooler, and the smooth plastic of a bench felt almost soft.

"Okay," I said. "Now tell me about cycles."

"It's the only way to get around, you know what I mean?" the kid grinned. "They pass a law—this town is a landmark. No cars. No pods. No nothing except cycles—the kind you work with your feet."

"You live here?" I asked. I didn't see any cycle around that belonged to him.

"Naw, I live down south," he said, waving his hand in the direction of most of Southern Pacifica. He shrugged. "But this is a nice place to visit."

"Everybody who comes in here—do they all get cycles?"

"Most people. Some walk."

"And if you wanted a cycle, how would you get one?"

"Oh, mebbe you buy one—or mostly you just hire one, by the day or the week, you know?"

"Most people who come here—they hire them?"

"Sure."

"How many shops hire cycles?"

"'Round here? Just one."

"I think I'd like to pay that shop a visit," I said, climbing back to my feet.

"Sure thing," he said. "'Bout time," he added with another grin.

The cycle shop was a pleasant little place just up the block in the opposite direction from that which we'd come. Old Spanish (or fake-Spanish) architecture provided a row of pillared arches, inside of which were grouped cycles in stands, and an old man in a relaxer. The old man wore a toga of loose-woven mesh, and not a lot else. The town fathers apparently held a casual attitude about such things. I stepped under another of the ubiquitous red-tile roofs, and he opened his eyes and looked up at me questioningly.

"Hey, Mr. Hoolihan, I bring you a customer," my guide sang out.

"Eh, Mitchell," the old man said. "Always in my siesta— you little smartass." He sat up. "What can I be doing for you, huh?" He cackled. "Would you like to hire a cycle, or perhaps do you want to hire a cycle?" He laughed at his joke.

"Neither," I said. Both gave me startled looks. What was this? A new joke?

"Yesterday," I said. "Last night. A man and woman came here to rent cycles from you."

"Ah, yes," old Hoolihan said. "Yes?"

"You remember them, do you?" I asked.

"I remember that men and women have come to me to hire cycles, yes," he said with evident pleasure. "All day long, and into the night. It is my business, and I have the monopoly here."

"A specific man and woman," I said with patient care. "A small woman, kind of bouncy"—but that wasn't true any more—"and uhm, very relaxed and certain in her manners. Short-cropped, green-frosted hair. . . . The man looks like the kid, here, grown up. Tall. Almost seven feet tall."

Almost reluctantly it seemed, the man nodded. A stray breeze poked its way into the open shop and stirred the fine white hair on his head at that same, precise moment. I felt a tingling.

"They were here," the old man said. "They were here. I remember them."

"They rented cycles?"

"One. A tandem." Seeing the question on my lips, he added, "Intended for two to ride—I only have two in the shop." He gestured and in the gloom I saw the second, two sets of handlebars, two seats, one behind the other, leaning against a rear wall, dusty and long unused. "Not many people want them. But those two—they saw them and they wanted one. Laughed a lot, they did."

"How long did they, uh, hire it for?"

"Told me a week. Lots of people do that, but stay longer, keep their cycles longer. No matter to me. I get paid. This is the only shop that hires cycles."

"A week. . . ." I reflected. They weren't just passing through, then. But where were they likely to have gone? Who did they know here? "Where's your infomat?" I asked.

"Infomat? I don't have no truck with those things," he said. "You want one, you try the tube station."

I guess I was staring at him a little strangely. He added, in a defensive tone, "This town is a landmark, mister. A place of the past. We don't go for all those modern gadgets. You won't likely find one anywhere else."

"You want I should show you?" the kid asked. He'd been standing to one side, acting like a natural part of the scenery until now.

"Sure," I said, although I really doubted I needed a local guide to find the tube station's infomats. But I wanted to talk to the kid some more. "I might be back for a cycle," I told the old man.

"Don't let go all your three-wheelers," the boy shouted back at him. He was laughing and grinning again.

I checked with the Bureau. A quick computer check hadn't turned up any known friends or relatives in Santa Barbara when I'd first discovered that had been the fugitives' destination. But such a search had been confined largely to names given on Bureau applications and questionnaires submitted by Dian each time she'd moved up a rank, and those forms had called simply for references and next of kin. Nobody had ever asked Dian to compile a list of her friends. And no one had checked to see if anyone she *had* listed had since moved to Santa Barbara. So the in-depth research took a little longer. It required some human programming and innovation. Setting these wheels in motion had been one of my jobs before I'd left.

I might as well not have bothered, for all the results I got. The Bureau had turned up absolutely no leads at all. "We're not a Missing Persons Bureau you know," was about the way it was put to me. For which, you may read: "Look, Mac, I don't know nothin' about this job—so whad'ya expect, anyway?"

In any case, I thumbed the disconnect with more force than was necessary, and ended up mouthing a small imprecation the effect of which was not lost on my erstwhile companion.

"No good, huh?" he said.

"Mitchell—is that your name, Mitchell?—let us find a place once more to sit and talk," I said.

Having nothing much else to do, and apparently fascinated by the oddity of my behavior, he assented cheerfully.

We ended up in the same little park, still deserted as before, and sat again on the same bench.

"You look to me as if you're the sort who gets around," I said for openers. "You see a lot."

He nodded, grinning.

"Did *you* see the man and woman I described?" I asked.

"Oh, sure," he said. "I saw them this morning. They was riding that cycle, you know, and wow! They sure was something!"

"How come you didn't tell me that before?" I asked.

"How come you don't ask me?" he replied, with flawless logic. It's little endearing traits like that which make me so fond of computers.

"Any idea where they're staying?" I asked. I knew already they weren't checked into any public hostelry.

"I don't know," he said, pulling at his lower lip with his fingers. "Maybe up in the hills. I saw them going that way. But maybe they just riding around, you know?"

"If you were me," I said, "and you wanted to find them, what would you do?"

"Oh, hell," he said. "That's easy. I'd just hang around for a while. They turn up. This is a small place, you know? Not like the city."

I rented a three-wheeler—a tricycle, it's called—and set out to see what I could of Santa Barbara.

It's not a big town—Mitchell was right. Many centuries old, it seemed currently in a state of genteel decay, aided and abetted by its curiously languid inhabitants. I rode down to the waterfront—still where the original waterfront was, and surrounded, in a great U, by the enveloping arms of Pacifica reaching out on piers over the water to both the north and the south. The water was brackish and oily, and slapped against the seawall under the docks with the same air of helpless lassitude that affected the rest of the city. "Used to be lots nicer," Mitchell, my guide, informed me, "before they built the city." He waved his arms to take in the white man-made cliffs of the city on each horizon. "No drilling, either." Squat black oil-drilling rigs worked thumpingly directly to the west, a few miles out. Well, a mechanized society runs on oil. It seemed curious and ironic that this town, huddled in the arms of the modern world, had turned its back on progress and a sense of tomorrow to dream of yesterday. Even the sun seemed faded and fraught with nostalgic haziness. But perhaps that was just atmospheric pollution.

We circled around the town. There was little traffic; either the locals preferred a cooler time of day, or there simply weren't that many people around. I favored the latter notion; it was easily accepted.

Time passed inexorably, and finally I'd had enough of aimless wandering and the pious guidebook inanities of my companion. And my legs ached. When I surrendered the tricycle to old Hollihan, my thighs and calves hurt in hundreds of novel places and I felt that the simple act of standing upright was a brand new accomplishment. Then Hoolihan told me, as he handed back my credit card after refunding the unused portion of my deposit, "Saw those people you were wanting."

Adrenalin surged through my system. I glanced back into the rear of the shop. *Where one dusty tandem cycle had stood there were now two.* The second sparkled with chromework and plastic highlights, and I wondered why I hadn't noticed it the instant I'd come in.

"Told them a fella' was looking for them," the old man added.

"What did they say?" I demanded, wanting to pound the facts out the stubborn old fool.

"They just laughed," he said, a twinkle in his eyes. "They just laughed to themselves."

I stared out into the long shadows of the afternoon street. "Where'd they go?" I asked.

"As to that, I wouldn't know," he said. "They took a tube, I'd guess." He paused and then dropped the bombshell he'd been saving. "All four of 'em," he added.

Chapter Eight

I got home late that night—and the time differential which had worked in my favor earlier was now against me. I skipped my final meal and went straight to bed.

. . . where I dreamed . . .

I was sitting in a dark room. Others were sitting in a large circle around the edges of the room, their faces in shadow. We were linked, our hands joined. I felt the terrible thrill of the forbidden. A light began to glow in the center of the room. It began searching our faces, passing quickly over faces I did not know and could not remember. Then it stopped, directly across the circle from me. The face was Bjonn's. His eyes were focused directly on me, even though I was certain I was not visible in the darkness, and I knew that the light must be blinding him. I stared into his eyes and knew that he could see me, was watching me. It frightened me, but it also held me transfixed. Then the light seemed to shift and I was aware that it was Bjonn's eyes which were emitting the light: twin beams that were held on me, pinpointing me, making me visible to everyone in the room.

I was naked.

Worse: I was sitting on, attached to, a food-evacuation unit.

Someone handed me a meal-tube.

That's when I woke up.

I was sweating profusely. I got up and looked at the time. Early morning, 04:12. I depolarized my windows and stared out. Moonlight and windows. Some were lit. Rutland is a bedroom community, but not everyone sleeps at night anymore. It's an old instinct, one of the oldest, but in a complex civilization you can't just shut down the machinery after the sun sets: After all, in other parts of the world it may be high noon. Life goes on, the world goes on, twenty-four hours out of twenty-four.

I used the 'fresher, and felt a little better. My stomach complained—I'd treated it to a pretty lopsided schedule—so I went into the meal-cubicle, attached myself, sat down and reached for the tube.

And stopped.

I was sweating again.

The dream: what did the dream *mean?* What was going on inside me? Something was messing me up. I pulled the tube to my lips, savoring the old familiar taste and feel, the plastic nozzle with its imbedded tooth marks, the big teat with its vari-flavored algae—and I had no appetite.

I sat there until my thighs went numb, and then decided in favor of expediency. I dropped a pill to start things moving, thumbed the evacuator to internal irrigation, flushed my system, and restocked myself. It was mechanical and joyless and I kept remembering my dream. Afterward, I had to stare at the menu on the wall to see what I'd had. My mouth just tasted sour.

I went back to my bed, lay in it for a while, and stared

at the aimlessly moving pictures on the backs of my eyelids. Finally I got up again. If I was going to keep running through the details of my work, I might as well do it in an organized fashion. I sat down at the infomat, punched the code for my office recordostat, and started dictating additional prelims.

Dian and Bjonn had flown to Pacifica, and gone up to Santa Barbara. They arrived late in the evening—they had left Megayork soon after I'd run out on them; I already knew that. Okay, they took out a cycle. (Why didn't we have a record of that before? Because Dian had simply left her roommate's card with the shop as deposit. But that implied—)

In a strange little town at night, with a cycle and no usable credit (they had Bjonn's card, maybe, if he hadn't already disposed of it—but they hadn't used it. Dian knew how instantly traceable credit use was. She was Level Seven, wasn't she?), it pointed to one obvious fact. They, meaning Dian, knew someone who lived there, knew someone well enough, or hoped she did, to drop in on him/her/them unexpectedly, without advance warning.

And the next day there were four of them. Four laughing, happy people, looking like people in love, radiant and joyful—*and somehow alien*.

He'd gotten to them, to Dian's friends. Bjonn had seduced them, as he had Dian. First just Bjonn. Then Bjonn and Dian. Now Bjonn, Dian, and two more. It was snowballing.

Bjonn was a point of contagion.

It was getting out of hand. It wasn't just a simple disappearance any more. It was something bigger, something strange with ominous overtones.

Something which wouldn't let me sleep.

I coded into Credit Clearance again, and had a search made. Object: Santa Barbara couple, four fares on the tube out of Santa Barbara, destination unknown, for a one-hour period in the late afternoon. It wasn't really a narrow enough criterion, but it might find me something.

It didn't. No one with an established residence in Santa Barbara had bought four tube trips out in the right time slot.

Where had I gone wrong?

Maybe the couple didn't have an established residence in Santa Barbara? Maybe they had a residence somewhere else, and were only extended visitors themselves?

Make it just four fares on one card, then, for the appropriate time slot.

Nothing.

I resisted the urge to do something destructive to the infomat, and told myself several times that it was simply a tool—a useful, if less than intuitively gifted, tool. It would tell me only the truth—and it would answer only the questions I asked.

Two cards, then. One his, one hers. Two cards, four fares. Narrow it down a little: two cards issued to a contracted couple. (Or was that cutting it too fine? What if they *weren't* contracted?) I pulled three replies on that. I had a fast biographical research made on each of the three couples.

I hadn't thought the traffic out of Santa Barbara had been that heavy. But then, I'd forgotten that the town was a tourist spot. I'd overlooked the obvious: a man and his wife and their two, state-approved, children. Or rather, to be more exact, three men, three wives, and three sets of two children.

So Dian's friends—relatives—weren't contracted to each other.

I thought about doing a make on each and every individual who had used his card for himself and someone else. I had the time slot right. There had to be a finite number, I knew that.

Two thousand, eight hundred thirty-six.

I had it verified, and there it was; 2,836 people had used that tube station at that hour for themselves and a guest. I shook my head in disgust. When I looked up I saw the sunlight streaming in through my bedroom windows. Still depolarized. I looked at the time: 05:18 hours. And the sun was already up.

Santa Barbara must be Southern Pacifica's very own

Central Park, for God's sake. I wondered where they'd kept themselves hidden all day, and then snorted in disgust. Every damned one of them would have to be verified. The data wouldn't take long; it was the idea of going over it all, trying to see where connections could be established, doing the *human* part of the job—

I set it up for printout in my office, and went back into the bedroom, pausing only to dim the windows and reset the alarm. Then I managed to go back to sleep. This time I slept soundly.

I spent the afternoon running cross-checks on my list of potentials. The idea was to eliminate as many as possible with the coarse comb before resorting to the fine one. The easiest method was an immediate check on their whereabouts. I had a strong suspicion that the two I was looking for would also have disappeared. Of course, a proportion of those who had been in Santa Barbara were vacationers, tourists, or otherwise not presently tied down to anything from which they'd be immediately missed. But I managed to account for 1,103 people that way. It was a definite step in the right direction.

By late that afternoon, I had my list narrowed down to thirteen.

Not one of them checked out on any list Dian had ever made, but I simply had to accept that. Three were from Tokyo, and that looked promising. Dian had lived in Tokyo. She must have known people there who didn't appear on her lists.

I decided to dwell on those three.

Two were young and in their twenties: Robert Linebarger and Karilin Mills. The third, one Arthur Ficarra, was in his eighties. I decided to eliminate Ficarra. He was on a retirement tour, anyway. He'd worked for the Bureau of Environmental Control—a garbageman.

Both Linebarger and Mills had taken the tubes north to San Luis Obispo, where Pacifica officially ends and the city tubes terminate. There Linebarger had hired a car. Mills hadn't used any credit there. Linebarger had taken a car with seats for four.

It was starting to add up.

He'd given his destination as San Francisco, in Bay Complex. He was taking the Coast Road. Just sightseeing.

I decided San Francisco could wait until the next day.

The okay for my second trip to the west coast came through without any questions asked. I decided my promptness in returning from the first one had been a mark in my favor, but I really didn't give a damn. Here I was, chasing down after-the-fact details, while something was going on out there, three thousand piddling miles away, and I couldn't figure what it was.

It was raining when we landed in Oakland, and the outside temperature was in the middle fifties. Fortunately, I was spared any direct contact with the weather. I tubed over to San Francisco, and took a pod to the main branch office of the car-rental company. They do a thriving business on the west coast with people who want to explore the mountains and the still undeveloped shore areas.

I was expected, and a lush young woman with dusky nipples ushered me into the branch veep's office.

"Your car hasn't checked in as yet," he told me after a handshake. Correy Burke was twenty years younger than I'd expected—a mere youth and not likely out of his mid-twenties. It made me bristle somewhere inside my Id: *clean young kid makes it into Private Enterprise*. He'd be retired and sitting on a handsome fortune before I was halfway to my pension. To give him his due, he seemed to sense the awkwardness of our relative ages and positions, and he was pretty nice to me. In itself that was a surprise.

"When do you expect them?" I asked.

"Them?" he repeated. "We have it down for a single— a Mr. Linebarger. . . ."

"I'm assuming he has three guests," I said.

"Oh, well . . . that would make a difference in our rate differential," he said, unobtrusively fingering a few buttons on his private console, and no doubt taking notes. Oh, he'd earned his position—that was obvious. He looked up again. "Sorry," he said. "About the projected hour of arrival—it depends a good deal on that particular run. It's the original Camino Real, you know—the Pacific Coast Road, we usually call it. Runs right along the coast. Historical—and unimproved. I've known folks to do it in a day—others have taken two, three days. Depends, also, on whether they stop often, or even lay over for a while." He smiled. "Our rates are based on both mileage and elapsed time. We encourage them to enjoy themselves, not to rush things. After all, with scenery like that, you want to let it really soak in, right?"

"So you really don't know when they'll get in, is that right?"

"That pretty well sums it up, yes."

"But you'll have a watch out—?"

"Oh, indeed. In fact, I'll have a special query on that car. We'll have it checked out for additional occupancy, you see." He consulted his infomat. "Yes, I see we have sufficient funds on deposit to cover it." He smiled up at me again. "We always encourage a heavy deposit on trips like these. Makes it more painless to spend it after you've transferred your credit on a provisional basis, anyway."

Yes sir, that boy was going right to the top of the heap.

He suggested I tube down to Monterey, where the car would actually be coming in. "We don't allow cars on city streets, you know," he told me, as if I was some hick who hadn't come from the first city to ban private vehicular traffic well over a century ago. So I went down to Monterey, and found the rental garage nicely located on the southern edge of the Greater Bay Complex, a convenient pod-lane stacked with waiting pods close by.

And then I waited.

And waited.

And waited.

After a while, I was bored out of my mind.

I was here because it was important to apprehend our two original runaways. I had no illusions about my abilities to do that; I had a court-issued restraining order ready to serve on Dian whenever I next saw her for desertion of a government job and betrayal of Bureau (ho, ho) secrets to a registered alien (small irony, that). I also had a Planetary Arrest to serve on Bjonn, since as an alien he had no citizenship and no rights here on Earth. It was a ticklish point, and one I was sure the legal department had agonized over, but it boiled down to the fact that Bjonn had been here on good behavior, and it was now felt he'd abused our hospitality. His dealings as an Emissary would necessarily be formally restricted from now on.

After we caught them, that is.

After *I* caught them.

If I did. Or, rather . . .

When I did.

Finally, a man at the garage suggested I get a room for the night. "We'll let you know when they pull in," he said. "You don't have to sit around here all night."

So I took a room in a nearby hotel, a nearly featureless cubicle with an eating nook off one side, a bed in the middle, and a 3–D facing the foot of the bed. Out of desperation, I turned on the 3–D.

An apparent hole opened up in the wall of the room behind the 3–D, and ghostly images moved about in it. The control was on the stand built into the bed's headboard, and I fiddled with it until the tuning was accurate and I had both sound and solid color. The 3–D stage was small—a cube no more than two feet on each side—but, after all, this was just a cheap hotel room. The set was probably twenty years old. The sound didn't synch perfectly to the figures—every time a player crossed the middle of the stage to the left side, his voice came from the far left—but that probably meant a couple of speaker-strips in the wallpaper were dead. So what else was new?

I had inadvertently tuned into one of the pirate channels—which probably explained the difficulty in properly tuning it. I'd heard rumors that you couldn't pick up a pirate channel on hotel sets or other "public" sets, that they had been fixed to reject pirate signals. But maybe the source of this signal was too close. Most of them broadcast from moving ships in the Pacific, beaming for one of the big overhead direct-relay satellites, and thus getting pretty close to worldwide coverage, but perhaps this one was broadcasting locally, on direct line-of-sight, ship to shore.

It was Shakespeare's *Midsummer Night's Dream,* so I watched it.

A good cast, I thought. Naturally, they played up the bawdy aspects of the play. Titania and Oberon were played nude, and Titania's lovemaking with Bottom, the weaver cursed with the head of an ass, was dwelt upon in lascivious detail. I found the pornography disturbing, but the play was, after all, Shakespeare, and vastly superior to the mind-rot to be found on the legal channels. Sometimes I wondered why the only interesting programming came from the pirate channels—but then I reminded myself that the vast majority of the populace, on Public Care and with little enough to abate their boredom, must prefer the lulling opiates of public 3–D. After all, anything too provocative might just provoke discontent.

I watched until the play concluded, and then switched off the set. I'd had my yearly dose of 3–D and could now return to the real world content. Soon after, I drifted into a hazy shade of sleep. . . .

. . . from which the infomat buzzer jerked me awake what seemed like only minutes later.

"Mr. Dameron?" It was somebody I hadn't seen before, but he wore the uniform of the rental garage, and I could see the word *"manager"* emblazoned on a small badge he was wearing.

I blinked a couple of times and assured both of us that I was indeed Mr. Dameron.

"The car you were interested in just came in," he said.

I glanced at the time: 01:10 hours. I sighed. "Are you holding them?" I asked.

"There's just one man—the driver. We've told him he has a refund due and that we're clearing it out. I don't know how long we can stall him. . . ."

"Are you checking out the car?" I asked.

"Sir?"

"There were four people in that car," I said, wondering if we had the wrong car, the wrong man, or what. "I understand you have ways of checking that out—and of adjusting the rates."

"Oh," he said. "I'll have them check that out. I just came on duty an hour ago, and I didn't find any memos on that. Thanks."

"Okay," I said, and thumbed off.

I dressed and went over to the garage. When I got there, the night manager and two men were standing in a semi-circle around the chair of a frightened-looking boy.

As soon as I approached the group, I knew something was wrong. I'd read Linebarger's biography, and he was a dark man in his late twenties. This kid could hardly be over graduation age, and he had red hair and very white skin, on which his freckles were pronounced blotches. He looked almost blue with fear, and he was hugging himself and shivering.

The three garagemen looked angry, but moved away in deference when I came up. The silence was hostile, and I guessed they'd found the evidence of additional passengers they'd been looking for.

"All right, son," I said, as I stood looking down at the boy. "What's your name?"

His eyes were wide, and his skin so pale I could see the veins under it. "Uh, Tanner, sir. Le-Leroy Tanner."

"How old are you, Leroy?"

"Nineteen, uh, sir."

"Nineteen," I repeated, for effect. "You didn't hire this car, did you?"

"No, sir. No, I didn't."

"You want to tell me about it?"

"Uh, will you tell me something, please? Am I in trouble? I mean—legal trouble?"

"You mean, do you need a lawyer? I don't think so. Not if we can get this straightened out." I saw the manager give me a nod. I didn't return it. "We're interested in the car."

"I met this man," he said. "He gave it to me. I mean, he told me I could have the use of it, if I turned it in up here. He said I might even get some credit transferred on it."

"You met a man," I said. "Tell me about that. Where did you meet him? And how?"

Chapter Nine

The next morning I took a rental car down the Coast Road, with young Leroy Tanner in the other seat beside me.

We were on automatic the first few miles, so I relaxed and turned to face him, picking up where we'd left off the night before. "You were hiking," I said. "Up from Pacifica? Isn't that quite a hike?"

He nodded, keeping his eyes on the road as though afraid to directly face me. "It seemed like a great way to do the summer," he said. "When I started, anyway. By the time I met Mr. Linebarger, I guess I'd had about enough."

"Tell me about it again. No pressure, just put it together the way you remember it."

He nodded again, and his Adam's apple throbbed convulsively, as if he was trying to swallow something too big for him. "Yeah," he said. "Well.

"By the time I got to Lucia, I'd really had it, you know? You get maybe three hours of sunshine a day, and the rest is fog and drizzle. It comes in off the ocean in the afternoon, fogs you in all night, and doesn't burn off until noon or later. I was damp all the time, and I had a cold—I *still* have a cold—and I still had a good way to go. So I thought, maybe I can get a lift, you know? Maybe somebody in a car will stop and pick me up. But they wouldn't. I'd stand on one of those horseshoe curves, and I'd wave, and they'd just crawl right by me. So slow I could see in and see their faces, and they always stared ahead, like I wasn't even there. I could've thrown myself right in front of them, and they'd just have run me over!" His voice cracked with emotion.

"It's a private world," I said. "People don't like to be intruded upon."

"I know," he said, snuffling a little. Maybe it was just his cold. "Well, anyway, I was up around Big Sur, and I was sitting in this fake lodge they have set up, you know, where they sell souvenirs and all that. I was just trying to get warm. And I saw this car pull in, and it had four seats, but just this man and woman in it. So I waited by the car until they came out, and I asked them, could I please have a ride. And the guy said—he was very nice about it—he said they'd like to, but they were on a short budget and couldn't afford it. So I asked what he meant, and he said if I rode in their car they'd get charged for another person for the whole trip, and they couldn't afford that. Well, I've got a card, of course, but not very much credit left for this month, and I was afraid it would run over what I had, because the rental on a car like this is pretty high from what I hear—"

"You hear right," I said.

"—so I just thanked them. Then while I was watching them drive away, this quiet-looking man comes up to me. He's tall, dark, and—oh, I dunno . . . he really seemed to understand about things and to, uh, to care.

"He said he'd heard me talking to the other man, and he thought maybe he had an answer for my problems. We walked over to this other car, and he said, how would I like to drive it up to Monterey. He said he'd rented it down south, put down a big deposit on it, and now he had decided to stay in this area and he needed to get the car north and so I'd be helping him at the same time. He told me I could put the leftover credit from the deposit on my card.

"Only problem was, I didn't know how to drive."

"He taught you, then?"

"Yeah. It took a while before he was satisfied I'd be all right, but he was a good teacher, very patient, and I learned."

It isn't really that hard to learn; I'd learned myself that

morning, in the practice lot the rental company provides. The car had a go pedal and a stop pedal, and you point the tiller where you want it to go. It has a radar system that stops it if you look like you intend to run into something, or slows you down if you're overtaking another car too fast. It has all the gadgets to keep you from hurting yourself, and automatic road-control on the approaches to the cities which guides you in automatically to the garages. It doesn't take long to learn.

"And then you drove up," I said. "To Monterey."

"Yeah. I guess *that* was a mistake."

The warning buzzer sounded; we were reaching the end of the automatic road. If I didn't show signs of alertness and take over the controls the car would automatically stop and park itself. I went through the proper motions.

We were entering the Coast Road, now, and on what I'd been told was The Wrong Side—the ocean side. "Most people go down south and bring cars *up,*" the day manager had told me. "We have a hard time finding drivers going south. Something about driving along that sheer drop for a hundred miles scares them." I could understand why. There wasn't much beach along here—mostly just rocks, upthrust from the surf. The road twisted its way along the cliff face, sometimes climbing high above the water, sometimes dipping down to within a few yards of the booming rollers. Vegetation was sparse and twisted, the trees like gnarled old men reaching in vain for help and safety and shelter. Mist, looking like low-hanging clouds, sent fingers in over the coast, occasionally covering the windshield with tiny droplets of dew which the car automatically cleaned off each time.

Then the road swung inland, around the chin of a low ridge and into a set of deeply groved, heavily forested valleys. High above us the sky turned bright blue, and from somewhere out of sight the sun sent down shafts that set the woods steaming.

"This is Big Sur country," the boy said. "Nice, isn't it?"

"If you go for that sort of thing," I said. The road was climbing now and I had to dodge cars parked on the edge of the road, barely off the pavement. Nature-lovers, I suppose.

We passed odd-looking houses, all detached and on their own acreage, some perched on hillsides of naked rock, others almost lost among the evergreens. They were all stamped with the eccentricity of individuality, and I felt the air of nonconformity, of deliberate oddity, which always alienated me. Some people flaunt it. The people who lived here certainly did.

"Where's the town?" I asked.

"There isn't any—not really, anyway," Tanner said. "Just a cluster of stores and that fake lodge I told you about. They're still up the road a bit."

"You mean the people who live here are all scattered around the place?" I asked, gesturing at a typical house we were passing.

"That's right," he said, his tone a little defensive.

I shook my head and drove on.

"Here it is," the boy said. I swung the car to the left, across the oncoming lane, and felt it brake itself as we crunched over cinders into a parking space. We stopped smoothly, just six inches from the barrier. It had obviously been placed there for exactly that reason. I saw no scars upon its timbers.

"This is where you met Linebarger, is it?" I said.

He said it was.

"Let's climb out and take a look around," I suggested. "If you see him, let me know. But don't be really obvious about it."

"Okay." A little sullen.

The air was still damp and a little cool in the shade, uncomfortably warm in the sun. I made my way into the "fake lodge" with all deliberate speed.

We talked to people, we hung around, we watched the cars that stopped, and we listened to the locals. And we saw and heard not one sign of Linebarger, Mills, Dian or Bjonn. I was beginning to feel foolishly frustrated, a vast sense of anticlimax hovering over me. Finally I decided to use an infomat and check in with my office. Maybe something had turned up.

I keyed in my own office infomat first, for messages. Instead there was a relay-click and Tucker's face filled the screen again. "About time you thought of that," he said.

I sighed. "Okay," I said. "Now, what's happened?"

"It isn't what's happened," he drawled, "it's what *hasn't* happened. Just where are our friends, the Happiness Twins?"

"Dian and Bjonn?"

"I think those are the ones, yes."

"Still missing," I said. "I have them pinned down, though."

"You do? Tell me about it."

I did. Without skipping any important details, but as concisely as possible. I was feeling moderately proud of myself when Tucker snapped, "You mean to tell me you've drawn a big imaginary net around some hundred square miles of undeveloped area on all that flimsy piece of guess-work and circumstantial evidence?"

"Sir?"

"Let's start with point one," he said, bringing his hands into view and ticking off his fingers. "Point One: you have not established the slightest actual, factual link between this Linebarger and the other one—Mills?—much less a link between them and your fugitives. Why, you haven't even found holograms of the two of them for confirmation by your cycle-shop man—and he's the only one who has seen all four of them together, as far as you know. Okay, point two. Without confirming their connection to this Linebarger, you've gone and turned a car-rental agency upside-down. You've spent good Bureau credit on renting a car for yourself, even! And you've operated on the assumption that this Linebarger, in turning his car over to somebody else, must be the party you want. That's points three, four and five, at least. Point Six is that you've assumed Linebarger and party—*if* they're the ones you want—are still in the immediate area of, what is it? Big Sur? If they are your people, do you think they'd lay as open a trail as that? Count on it: if they told your Tanner kid they were staying there, it was so he could pass that info along. By now they could be hundreds of miles away."

"How, sir? Both Dian and Bjonn have no credit—it's been canceled. And I put a Temporary Hold on both Mills' and Linebarger's credit."

"You *what?* On whose authority?"

"On the Bureau's, sir."

"Oh, fine." He smote his brow in a fine gesture of defeat. "Just fine. And how would you like a civil suit slapped on you—on us?"

"I don't think it is that likely, sir—not if they're our people."

"You don't know that."

"I have a pretty strong hunch."

"Totally unconfirmed."

"Okay," I said, suddenly very mad. "I'll *get* confirmation, then!" And I disconnected.

I was still sitting in the infomat booth, figuring out the logistics of my next set of moves—drive down to Pacifica, or back to Monterey and hop down? Speed versus personal pleasure, of which I had thus far enjoyed relatively little. And what about the kid, anyway?—when the infomat buzzed me.

It was Tucker again.

He spoke as if nothing had happened, as if my last outburst had never taken place. "I've sent a local man to that shop, with holograms," he said. "If these *are* our people, what do you plan next?"

"Only one thing I can think of," I said. "Bring in men and conduct a house-to-house search."

He gave me a look of incredulity. "Surely you jest," he said.

"I'm sure you have a better plan," I said.

He said nothing.

"So far I think I've done pretty well," I said. "But I'm just one man, and I have my limitations. I think we've about reached them. I've pinpointed there whereabouts for you to my own certainty. Now I pass the buck."

When he spoke, his voice had none of its former bark and bite. There was no trace of his drawl, either. Suddenly he sounded very tired. "We've reached a dead end," he said. "I'm going to ask you to abandon the case."

"Sir?" I asked, my brain reeling from this abrupt about-face.

"We've pushed it further than I'd expected," he said. I noted that "we" in my mental jotbook. "I've taken it this far on my own authority. I can't buck it higher, and I can't push for anything like what it needs now—what you've suggested. There's no real crime on the books, Dameron. We had very slim provocation for going this far. To take it further—to get warrants for Invasion of Privacy, which is what we'd need to conduct a search—it's just more than I can swing. It's over, can't you see that? You've done an excellent job. But there's pressure from above; you're needed on other work assignments. I can't keep you on this any longer. I had to go out on a long limb with Conners, and it's about to give way." I'd never heard him sound like that.

"What about the man in the cycle shop?" I asked. "What if he *does* confirm Linebarger and Mills? What then?"

"We'll kick it up to the next level, and see what the big boys have to say," Tucker said. "But I don't expect much, and neither should you."

Leroy Tanner was leaning against the side of the car. "What's going to happen?" he asked.

"Nothing," I said, letting the bitterness cut into my voice. "It's being dropped."

"I don't get it," he said. I hadn't told him any of the background—*why* we wanted this Linebarger—anyway.

"You don't have to," I replied. "Get in. Time to go."

"Okay," he said, sounding as though he thought I must be blaming him for the whole thing.

"Relax," I told him. "It's not your worry. It's a nice

day, and you're getting an extra ride out of it—for free. I might even swing that credit on deposit for you, too."

"Yeah?" he said, perking up considerably.

For a moment, I felt a little better, a little happier. I took a deep breath, the air scented with evergreen suddenly alive in my throat, my lungs. I shrugged the weight from my shoulders. What the hell. It wasn't *my* problem any more. I'd done my part of the job—I'd done more than had been expected of me. *I* was okay.

It was while we drove back up toward Monterey that the thought came to me that Tucker had known it would probably end like this all along. He'd known what would most likely happen—and he'd flayed me to get it this far before it stopped. Suddenly I hated the man. Damn his corrosive soul, anyway!

PART TWO

THE FURIES

Chapter Ten

In the late fall the green mountains of Vermont are a subdued brown. In Megayork the skies are gray and bleak, and matched my mood. I picked up Ruth Polonyck at the hencoop in Westport where she still lived, sharing a bunkroom with five other uncontracted girls, and took her to a party in Old Manhattan. Ruth had been brought into our department at the Bureau soon after the fuss over Dian Knight's untimely departure had died down, and I had the feeling that, although she was still a Level Five, she was being groomed to take Dian's place.

I'd had some time to brood about things, and uppermost in my mind had been a question, still unsatisfactorily unanswered, about my boss's motivations.

I'm a civil servant. I put in for the job when I read the notice of an opening, took a battery of tests, and in spite of them I got the job. My advancement since then has been a slow and measured crawl, but it has been largely a function of my own aptitudes, talents, and personality. Which is fine, as far as it goes—and if I never exceeded Level Seven, I would at least have earned the right to remain on that level the rest of my working life, barring disasters of course. (At the time, I'd thought the whole Bjonn-Dian thing *was* a disaster. Perhaps I was right, but . . . a disaster for whom?)

When you rise into the higher levels, however, it is less a factor of your test results and automatic promotions. Up there, in the stratified levels, you come face to face with the fact that a government, no matter how entrenched and bureaucratic, is still a basically political animal. And your job becomes a matter of politics—both polite and dirty.

I always assume everyone I meet thinks as I do, wants

what I want, and does as I do—until I'm proved wrong. If coincidence conspires to shield me from the truth, I will go on regarding my acquaintances and associates in that light for the longest time, blithely unaware of their true natures.

This man, Tucker: I took him at face value. I *needed* to. He fulfilled a need in me that I wasn't even aware of then. I looked at him pretty much as I guess every boy looks on his father—part man, part god, someone you want to impress, someone whose judgment you never question, someone you assume reciprocates your feelings toward him to the extent that he, too, loves you.

But every boy who knows his father after he's six must— I assume—inevitably come to that moment of disillusionment when he finds his father's feet of clay. There comes a time when he can no longer escape the fact that his father is not all-knowing, all-wise, or all-loving. He finds out his father is living a separate life, and one which is not exclusively devoted to his son. He finds out his father is human.

Some sons, I'm told, never forgive their fathers that.

I never knew my father after the age of six. But I had Tucker.

Just what was Tucker's real relationship with Dian Knight? Had there been something between the two of them? Or just the desire for something, on Tucker's part? You can see how my mind shied from the notion: Did Dad have an itch for his son's girlfriend? But of course Tucker wasn't really my father—and there was no real reason he shouldn't have had his own interest in Dian. She wasn't contracted to me or anything.

Tucker had thought a lot of Dian. Hindsight really helps, I've found. Little things I hadn't noticed, like the way Dian rose so readily through the ranks, the way Tucker seemed to be in closer contact with her than the rest of us—the fact that when Dian was upset about Bjonn's initial proposition, it was Tucker (who has his office a thousand miles away) I found with her, in her office. She should have contacted *me*—it was my case. She should've left a message with me, one I'd have gotten upon awaking. Instead she called

Tucker, brought him east on the run, and left the message in my office almost as an afterthought.

Then there was the way Tucker had called me, the next morning. He was still in Megayork. Why? How had he discovered Dian's disappearance so quickly? Had they made arrangements to meet— an arrangement she had not kept?

Had they met, clandestinely, before? Could that explain the apparent lack of men in Dian's life? Had she been seeing her boss on the sly? Or was I starting to build something out of nothing?

There was no mistaking Tucker's reaction at her disappearance. He had betrayed more than just a superior's concern for an underling. If he hadn't punched so many of my own emotional buttons I would have instantly recognized that.

I brooded. And when Tucker brought in Ruth Polonyck, only lately removed from the Public Care rolls, it was a little more obvious to me than it might have been to someone else. Ruth was Dian Knight all over again. Why, Ruth even *looked* a little like Dian: same pert little figure, same bouncy, exuberant personality. She was cute, like Dian— not as bright, maybe, but winsome.

So I sat back with a cynical smile and watched Tucker conduct a new protégée into the department. I sat back for the first month and I watched, brooding all the while.

Then I struck back with a deliberate campaign to take Ruth away from him.

During that first month a number of the men in our department made plays for Ruth. They rarely even got a first date. No one got a chance to encore. Looking for it, I found the whole pattern very obvious. She would go through the motions to a limited extent, but her interests were elsewhere. I knew where.

So I pitched my campaign differently. I found ways to include her in my routine assignments, ways which accented the (ho, ho) glamour of my job, and kept her out from underfoot during the dull (more common) parts. I became a Fun Fellow To Be With, a fellow worker with whom she could share a sense of common adventure. We were Partners In Adversity.

Tucker lived in Great Lakes, and he had a family to look after. He couldn't drop in on Ruth every evening—not even, I decided, as often as once a week. She was chafing for companionship. Young, nubile, and Tucker had gotten her juices flowing; it was inevitable that she would turn to me. At first I was the fill-in man. Then I suspected Tucker and I had reversed roles. I was her primary interest; Tucker was the fill-in.

It wasn't that I really enjoyed what I was doing that much. I felt a cynical pride in my accomplishment—my way of striking back at The Old Man—but I didn't really *like* Ruth that well. The ease with which she had swallowed my line earned for her a certain measure of my contempt. She hadn't even any great loyalty to Tucker! But most important, every time I looked at her a certain way, the light on her face just right, I would see a subtle distortion of Dian's face. And that bothered me.

The party we were going to on this particular night was in a luxury tower in Old Manhattan, down near the tip of the island. The lift ran up the outside of one sheer wall, and the illusion of open space as the city dropped away beneath us was enough to keep Ruth clinging to me all the way up. I wished she wouldn't.

We got off at the 201st floor, most of which belonged to our hostess, Elvira Moore-Williams. She had inherited the largest single share of one of the big private corporations (I don't remember which, and I doubt she does either) and bringing Ruth to her party had been my master stroke. I knew it would get back to Tucker.

"Oh my God," Ruth whispered to me as we waited under the door-scanner, "I never thought I'd be able to walk off. Promise me, please, you won't take me back down in that thing!"

I was saved the necessity of a reply by the opening of the doors. A long, sensual-looking woman stood at one side, a handsome freak with oiled muscles on the other. The woman rubbed her bare belly up and down my hip and thigh, squeezed my arm between her nubbin-like breasts, and breathed, huskily, "I'm Veronica. Please come in."

Ruth, I saw, was receiving similar attentions from the muscle freak, so I abandoned her to her own delights, such as they might be.

Some mildly hallucinogenic gas, perhaps, nitrous oxide, was being circulated through the air-conditioning system, and I found myself laughing along with Veronica as we strolled into one of the main rooms. She had her hand under my loincloth and was kneading my buttocks. "I like the feel of the way they move when you walk," she told me.

"Are you an official greeter?" I managed to ask.

She shook her head. "Haven't you been to Elvira's parties before?" she parried.

I found myself replying in doleful tones. "No," I said, genuinely sad, "I have not been to one of Elvira's parties before."

"Don't cry, dear man. Think how delightful it is that you are here now."

"Yes," I said, immediately brightening, "that's true, isn't it?"

"Elvira likes to be happy," Veronica said. "So she tries to surround herself with happy people. Isn't that lovely? I'm a cat," she added. *"Purrrr."* She rubbed herself up and down my side again. "Are you a tom?"

"I'm sorry," I said. "I'm a Tad."

"Oh. . . . Are you really? Perhaps I'd better keep looking, then." And without another word she moved away, leaving me alone in the swirling mass of laughing people.

I'd heard about Elvira Moore-Williams' parties, but never any details. It had taken me two months to wrangle an invitation, and I had stooped to some politicking of my own to accomplish it. The very pink of fashion, they were, and, I'd been told, a complete world of their own. Now that I was here, I found that easy to understand.

I moved through the people, drifting aimlessly, no real thoughts in my mind—what thoughts I had were curiously elusive—simply wandering, exploring, from room to room. There were people everywhere, most of them fashionably unclothed, some of them doing things which might have shocked or fascinated me on another occasion. But somehow I didn't care just now. I heard the sounds around me as if from down a long and echoing tunnel, a sort of whirling, cycle of repetition imposing itself in a pattern over what I could hear. I recall thinking that time was collapsing, condensing, closing in around me, contracting so that my past and future were both rushing at me simultaneously and—

I groped with my hand on a door button, it slid open, and I fell inside, into an eating cubicle. I let the doors shut without finding the light, and fell forward, my mouth over the evacuation unit, and vomited.

After that I felt a little better, but still unsteady. Everything still seemed to be on a great carousel, moving with ponderous speed past a brass ring. Each time I passed the ring I would reach for it, and one new sound, one new thought, or one new sensation would be added to the overlapping patterns of previous sounds, thoughts, and sensations, still reverberating in my skull. I didn't like it.

Somehow I found the light and turned it on. The universe steadied for a moment. Then I saw that I was not in a normal eating cubicle at all. *I was in a cubicle equipped for two.*

I almost threw up again.

I staggered, and sat down, sitting, inevitably, on the other evacuation unit. I heard myself giggle. "Hey, Dian," I said out loud. "Having a wonderful time. Wish you were here." Without thinking, I fitted the meal tube to my mouth. It felt wrong, tasted wrong. I dialed a flavor which would change the taste of bile in my mouth. I almost choked, laughing, while I ate.

When I was a little boy, I always wondered what it was like in a *girl's* eating cubicle. I knew what it was like in mine, and in the others of boys I knew. But there was something mysteriously and subtly *different* about girls, and I knew it even then. I knew their plumbing was different, and while I hadn't associated it with sex (well, not with the kind of sex an adult thinks about), I had already figured it out that their evacuation processes must be different than mine. Ergo, they would use different equipment, a differently designed evacuation unit. But *how* would it be different? I tried to work it out in my mind, but it was simply beyond my knowledge. My imagination could not cope with it. I was terribly curious.

One day, early in First Form, I saw a girl use an eating cubicle. That is, I saw her go into one, and, later, come out of it again, tugging at her clothing and licking her lips. I was stunned, because *I had used that cubicle myself.*

That was a day of great disillusionment for me. That was the day I learned that girls used the same exact cubicles boys did—that the cubicle at least observed no difference in the sexes. But my old curiosity lingered on. I knew better, but I still wondered . . . could there *be* girls-only cubicles? And even if there weren't, what would they be like if there *were* such cubicles? Had there *once* been separate cubicles for girls? And so on, for the next few years. Then, gradually, I forgot about it. Every once in a long while the old fantasy would return, fleetingly, and I'd ponder the question for a moment before I recalled that I knew the answers, and the answers were prosaic and without consequence.

Now, sitting in a cubicle built for two, that old riddle came back to me, in a shockingly new form: What would a cubicle be like for two people doing it *together?* I had never thought about that one, but here was the answer, again a bit prosaic, if still shocking to one of my morals in its implications: it was simply like one cubicle with twice the space and double the usual facilities. In my bemused and lightheaded state it seemed to me that I was finding answers to questions I had not posed, and that this was a fact of some significance or portent. I wanted to share my sudden knowledge with someone—and in that moment I realized that there was only one person I had any desire to tell it to. Dian.

Damn it all, anyway.

* * *

When I came out of the cubicle, I found Veronica waiting for me. "My, but you were in there a long time," she cooed. "But—alone?"

I started to reply, but a man materialized out of the shadows and elbowed me aside. Veronica disappeared into the cubicle after him. I stared at the closed door for a while, wishing that I was somewhere else, where I could *think*.

"Tad!"

I turned, and there was Ruth. She had less on than she'd worn in the front door, and that left very little indeed.

"Oh," she said, getting a grip on my arm and going limp against me, "I'm so woozy. But, wowee! I'm having *so* much fun. . . ."

"I'm glad to hear that," I said. I could taste the word *liar* right on the tip of my tongue, but I don't believe I said it aloud, because she took no notice of it. "What happened to Mr. Muscles?" I inquired.

"Who?" she asked. She looked up into my face and her eyes wavered, and then crossed and uncrossed.

"The guy at the door," I amplified.

"The door. . . ." she repeated. "Which door? The one in the floor or the door in the door—?" She interrupted herself with laughter.

"Ruth," I said.

"What?" she said, happily.

I was going to say, *You're a drag.* But I didn't. I didn't know what to say. So I said, "There's an eating cubicle right over there." I pointed. "There are two people in it right now," I added. At that moment I was simply imparting a handy piece of information. I could as easily have said, "It's raining outside."

"Ohhh," Ruth said. "This is a *naughty* place, isn't it?"

"This is how The Other Half lives," I told her smugly.

"Which Half is that?"

"What do you mean, which Half?"

"Well, like, is it the Other Half from *us,* or is it—I mean, which Half are *we,* anyway, for it to be the Other Half of?"

"Huh?" I replied.

"Well, you asked me—I mean, you *told* me. . . . Well, there was *something* about this Other Half. . . ."

"Of what?" I asked.

"That's what *I*—"

"What are we talking about?"

"I thought *you* knew."

"I can't think straight," I told her. "Can you?"

"No," she said, giggling. "Of *course* not."

"Well, all *right* then."

"I'll see you later," she said. And the next moment she was lurching off into another room, leaving me still standing in the hall, outside the Eating Cubicle Built for Two. I decided I'd see me later too, and wandered off in another direction.

As I entered the room I'd wandered off into, I heard a burst of laughter from a group of people across on the other side. *"That's* the Other Half," I said under my breath, and mostly just to myself, although a couple of people on the floor whom I was at that moment stepping over did give me funny looks.

As I crossed the room toward them, the group laughed again. When I got closer, I saw that some of them weren't real.

They were watching a life-size 3–D. I didn't realize the fact until several of the people among the group flickered, vanished, and were replaced by others. The sound was off, and they were simply watching the soundless antics of the 3–D holograms. Every so often, one of the voiceless images would do something completely absurd, pulling an extravagant face, or suddenly whirling about or the like, no doubt responding to some unseen voice or sound effect, and everyone would laugh uproariously. It was like watching and laughing at the antics of a bewildered blind man, but it *was* occasionally funny.

I laughed too, especially at the sight of the new images— a man and two girls, all dressed in outlandish costumes and giving each other the most pigheadedly infatuated looks.

Then something about those images jarred me for a moment from my gibbering idiocy. *The man was Bjonn and the girl on his right was Dian!*

Chapter Eleven

I awoke to the discomfiting knowledge that someone else was in my bed. The room was very dark, and I couldn't see. At first I wondered where I was, and thought perhaps I was in a strange bed. Then, as my exploring fingers slid over the smooth warm flesh next to me and I heard a female sigh, I found my memories returning to the events of the party.

Someone had pressed an injectab against my buttock—I'd thought at first it was a stray caress until the sudden freezing sensation reached me—and whatever it had been, it wiped all cares from my mind, completing the job the gaseous air had only begun.

I was still quite dispassionately aware that the two people for whom I'd so futilely searched were cavorting before me in holographic replica, but the knowledge no longer sent jolts of adrenalin coursing through my system. The urgency I'd felt only moments before was gone, dissolved into a spreading sea of bliss.

My own experiences with drugs had been rare. I was even, I must admit, naïve about their use by the upper classes. I have no idea what sort of drug was injected into me, or even its relative strength or commonly defined properties. I know only that its effect upon me was to divorce my conscious mind from the more primal part of me, to subdue my conscious mind into a sort of blasé spectator, and to allow my animal instincts their full flowering. Standing there, watching Dian and Bjonn in their strange pantomimes, laughing as the crowd laughed, I experienced a sudden, unexpected, and entirely spontaneous sexual orgasm, which caught me completely by surprise.

I was shaken by the experience, but filled with a vast sense of wonder and delight. I felt full of Satyr-like power, elemental, a rutting, strutting beast. And the distant *me* could only look on with wide-eyed amazement.

At this point my memories become fragmented. I have lost the sequence of their proper order. But I recall finding the lithe and feline Veronica and dragging her to the floor on that very spot—to which she resisted not at all.

I remember, too (I wish I could be certain it was real, not a later dream, but I remember some of those too), putting on an exhibition with an extraordinarily talented woman before admiring partygoers, and only afterward discovering she had been my hostess, Miss Moore-Williams.

And finally—this is somewhat clearer—I remember the tear-stained face of Ruth Polonyck and her pleading voice as she implored me to take her away from there, to put my clothes on and *please* let's go now—!

We took a pod all the way to Vermont—and I received the credit statement to verify that fact. A blatantly expensive thing to do, and not at all my habit.

The girl made another sound and I leaned closer, peering at her in the darkness. She must have felt my heavy breath upon her face, for she gasped and then spoke.

"Tad—is that you?"

"Yes, Ruth," I said. I put my hand on her belly and let it slowly slide down over the outside of her hip and thigh.

"Ohhh . . . that feels nice," she said. "Do me some more."

I did. She sighed a little, moaned a little, and then reached for me with hungry arms. She was easy to satisfy, as I'd known she would be. Afterward, when I had stopped moving, she giggled.

"Why are you giggling?" I asked.

"Oh, I don't know," she said, her voice coy. "I guess I was just thinking about the party. You know, I've never been to a party like that. Before, I mean."

"Yeah," I said, feeling withdrawn and distant. "Me neither."

"Does that . . . sort of thing . . . go on all the time?" she asked.

"I wouldn't know," I said. "Perhaps."

"What are you thinking?" she asked dreamily.

"Nothing," I said. I was thinking of Dian.

"Will you take me there again?"

I rolled over onto my back. "No," I said.

"Why?" She was disappointed.

"I didn't care for it," I said.

"*I* thought you were having a good time." A pouty voice.

"Somebody was having a good time," I agreed. "But it wasn't me." I'd been lost somewhere along the line.

"I liked it," she said. "*I* had fun."

"You would," I said.

"What?"

"Nothing." *It suits your mindlessness,* I said to myself.

"Maybe I'll ask someone else to take me," she said. "Next time."

"Who?" I asked, not really caring much anymore. "Tucker?"

There was a period of silence. I was starting to drift off again when Ruth spoke: "Who told you about Tucker?" she said. Her voice sliced like fine old steel through my drowsiness.

"It wasn't hard to guess," I said, feeling obscurely pleased with myself.

"How do you mean?" she demanded, voice strident, fingers on my arm tense.

"Did you think you were his first?" I asked sleepily. *Go back to sleep and leave me alone,* I told her with my mind.

"Hey—you, Tad!" she said, shaking my shoulder. "You wake up. I want to know about this. You've got to tell me," she insisted.

"Figure it out for yourself," I snarled. "Who'd you replace in the office?"

"That girl—who disappeared?"

"Dian Knight," I said. "Yeah, that girl."

"What—what happened to her?"

"She disappeared," I said. "Until tonight." My stomach muscles clenched and knotted as I said that. "Until tonight. . . ." I repeated.

"Tonight?"

"I saw her on the 3–D. In some crazy costume."

"What was she doing there?"

I jumped out of bed and groped my way into the other room, where I turned on a light near the infomat. Sitting down before the console, I started pushing buttons, a sudden manic drive seizing me.

A few minutes later I had it all in front of me on a plastic printout sheet.

"What're you doing?" Ruth said.

I looked around. She was leaning against the doorway to the bedroom. Naked, her body looked too short, too chunky. Her waist was too thick, and her breasts, deprived of their under-supports, looked smaller and droopy. The purple rouge was gone from her nipples and her face had a puffy, unfinished look to it. Suddenly I was sick of her, sorry I'd ever gotten involved with her. Some prize! I'd have been smarter to let Tucker keep her for himself. The thought of her with Tucker cheered me a little—at that moment I felt truly superior to The Old Man. This sad creature was the best he could do for himself—and I'd even taken that away from him.

Something in my expression, in my lack of reply, must have frightened her. She suddenly retreated into my bedroom, and the door snicked shut. "I'm going home," came her muffled declaration.

"Fine," I said, and turned back to stare at the printout.

I expected repercussions.

I fully expected the infomat would roust me from my sleep again while Tucker once more chewed me out.

It didn't happen. Instead I awoke—this time to an empty bed, for which I was profoundly grateful—a few minutes before usual, while the windows were still dark. I snapped instantly awake, and quickly performed my morning ablutions, hurrying to be on my way to my office. I took the printout with me. If Tucker wasn't going to call me, I'd damned well call him!

I didn't see Ruth, and I didn't go looking for her. Instead, once in my office, I put through Tucker's office code and sat back to see what would develop next.

I had to work up through his outer defenses, of course, but one secretary (homely, and approaching retirement age) and two assistants later, I was face to face with The Old Man.

He looked older. There was a sag in the skin around his jawline I hadn't noticed before. The weathered face had felt the first touch of winter. His drawl was tired.

"Have you talked with Ruth this morning?" I inquired, very chipper.

His eyes focused on mine and for a single moment I saw naked hate in them. He had talked with Ruth. "Had you something particular in mind," he asked, "or is this just a social call?"

I opened my mouth and he added, "If it is, I'd like to remind you that this is an open line and I have a busy office."

You bastard, I thought. *That didn't stop you when you wanted to ride my back!* "I thought she'd be talking with you," I said, keeping my voice cheerful. "I knew you'd be the first to hear the good news."

That hooked him!

His expression grew more tired, even sadder. "You've called to gloat," he said. "I see."

"I'm afraid I don't get you, sir," I said. "I thought you'd be pleased."

"Listen, you vicious little—!"

I put on a shocked face. "Sir!" I said. "Please! What are you saying?"

"What I'm saying is that I intend to—"

"Sir, I'm afraid we've lost communications," I said, frostily. *"This* is the purpose of my call." I held up the printout. "I have no idea what you have in mind, but I shall terminate this call and wait for you to digest the content of the information I've relayed." (He would be punching for a printout copy of the sheet I'd displayed right now. I saw his eyes track down to his console just as I disconnected.)

It had been a typical public 3–D show called *All Around Town*. The basic format was to present amusing oddities for public titillation while the show's host, Genial Gene, made nasty remarks about his subjects. One of the particular subjects of last night's show was the founding of a new religion, the Church of the Brotherhood of Life. Brother Bjonn, Sister Dian and Sister Rachel had appeared to attempt to describe their Life while Genial Gene hogged the soundtrack to heckle them. The partygoers had been right; it was better with the sound off. I had watched a complete recording of that segment, and had made a printout of what little information I could glean from it.

It had given me real, if fleeting, pleasure to toy with Tucker the way I had, but as I waited for him to return my call I became increasingly apprehensive. I'd stirred him up. I'd done a nice job of covering for myself—a rerun of our entire conversation wouldn't provide him with the slightest grounds for complaint—but we both knew what lay at the root of our little joust, and we both knew that this would hardly be our final round.

I'd just made myself a real enemy.

The infomat buzzed, and Tucker's face flashed on the screen again. "How does Miss Polonyck enter into this?" he asked.

I had to shift gears. "Ah, we were both at the same party when I saw the, ah, 3–D show. I, umm, told her about it afterward. I, well, I assumed she would tell you if she spoke with you, sir," I said. I was Johnny Humble.

"I see," he said. He didn't mention Ruth again.

"It's a real break," I said. "They're out in the open again. It would be no trouble to track them down now."

"And you want to do that, do you?" Tucker asked.

"I'd like to, yes," I said.

"They're still out on the west coast," he said, pensively.

"Yes sir."

"And you want to go out there."

"Yes sir."

"The warrants are null and void," he said. "They expired. I doubt we could get fresh ones. What would you do?"

"Talk to them. Find out just exactly what happened. What really happened, I mean. Find out what's behind this phony religion they're starting up. Get some kind of picture of what's going on." I felt myself tensing and untensing while I wondered what form his revenge would take. Would he say no, simply to chasten me? Or might he send me out, hoping to get me out of his hair with Ruth for a while? I wanted to tell him he could have her, with my blessings, but I didn't dare.

"Any reason why a local man on the coast couldn't do that?"

"I know the situation better," I said.

"Umm," he said, cupping his chin with one hand and absently stroking his jowl. "Very well, then. Go." The screen blanked out.

The "Church" had its headquarters near a sleepy little town in northern California called Cloverdale. To reach it I took an HST to Oakland, and a tube to Santa Rosa, which is as far north as the tube goes. There I rented a car—they hadn't said I couldn't, when I'd received my cost clearance for the trip—for the drive north of Bay Complex.

North of Santa Rosa the city drops away almost immediately, and the road begins climbing. This was an automatic road, and a far cry from the old Coast Road on which I'd last driven. As I went up into the hills I looked back down into the city and saw that it was one long finger that extended up the Napa Valley from the south, tapering almost to a point that terminated with Santa Rosa. Unlike the other megacities I'd seen, however, Bay Complex did not flow over every natural formation of land like an inexorable tide. Here and there strong greens still thrust up into the cold damp air, and most of the valley itself was rich with the vineyards and orchards for which it had been famous for centuries.

It wasn't a long trip. Soon I was heading the car down an exit-ramp from the roadway and into Cloverdale itself.

There wasn't much to see: tree-shaded streets, a few local shops—most needs could be taken care of in the city—and here and there low (less than twenty-story) coops interspersed among older dwellings. Despite its closeness to Bay Complex, the town had a smugly rural appearance. I cruised along the main street, past four blocks of commercial shops, an entertainment palace, three resort hotels, looking, without luck, for some sign of the "Church." Finally I turned around and headed back, stopping at the local fire-control station.

A raw-looking youth looked up from behind a desk half-hidden by consoles. "What can I do you for?" he asked, grinning.

"I'm looking for a group of people," I said. "I thought somebody here might know of them."

"You're an easterner, aren't'cha?" he said.

I nodded.

"Thought so. Who you looking for?"

"Group calls itself 'the Church of the Brotherhood of Life,'" I replied. "Saw something about them on 3–D last night."

"Come all the way out here to join up, did'ja?"

"You know where I can find them?"

"Yeah, you just—wait a minute. Got a fire to take care of."

Something had lit up on his console; I couldn't see it from where I was standing. His hands flew over the keys of the console with practiced fluidity, faster than I could follow. There was a traditional blast from a siren somewhere outside and above us, and then I heard the shriek of turbines revving up.

"You wanta' watch?" the kid asked. "Come on over here." I followed him over to a bank of screens which were apparently monitors. He punched a couple of buttons and several screens came alive.

One showed the interior of a garage. Just as I'd realized what I was looking at, the picture zoomed up on the garage entrance and swerved out onto the street. I thought I recognized the car parked at the opposite curb, and I turned to look out the front window of the fire-control office just as a big red truck swung past, obliterating in a mass of articulated machinery every view but that of its side. The other screens showed bits of sky and trees, a blur of shopfronts and sidestreets, and even the pavement of the street flashing by. It was obvious that all the broadcasts originated from the big truck.

The kid gestured at the screens. "This is just for my amusement, really. So's I won't get too bored in here."

"They monitor the firefighters?" I asked.

"In a manner of speaking, they do," he agreed. "Whole truck is remote-controlled by our boys up in Ukiah at Fire-Control Central for this area."

We watched the monitors as the big robotruck careened along some back road toward a reported fire. "Uh, listen. . . ." I said. "Any chance you could tell me—?"

"Oh yeah—that church group," he said. His eyes never left the monitors. He had a greedy expression on his face. "You go on through town—north, that is—on the old road, the street out front, you know? About two miles out you'll see this big old house up on a hill; that's it."

"Any way I can know for certain that's the house when I see it?"

"Only one around for miles that old, that big," he said. "Can't miss it. Local landmark. Old Benford House—ask anybody."

I thanked him and went out. The last I saw, in one final glance over my shoulder, he was still plastered to those monitors. *Have a nice fire,* I thought, as I climbed back into my car.

Chapter Twelve

He was right, I didn't miss it. The house belonged to another century. Vast, rambling, many-winged, it was a monument to some long-dead owner's vast ambition and lamentable taste. It stuck up on the hillside like a sore thumb.

I had to park the car down on the road; there was only a narrow, winding white gravel pathway leading up the hill.

Someone had recently planted shrubs along the path, and some were late-bloomers, showing tiny starlike blossoms. The path twisted back and forth among these shrubs, forcing one to a slower pace and probably adding 50 percent to the length of the hike. The sun had broken through the overcast and the back of my shoulders grew hot. Small insects, no doubt attracted by my sweat, buzzed around my head and kept striking my face and neck. I slapped at them, but without diminishing their number greatly.

"Hello, there."

I raised my eyes from the path and saw a young man sitting on a bench that had been placed among the shrubbery. He was small, features close-set, hair very dark and skin quite light. He returned my stare and as our eyes locked I felt my old atavistic hair-bristling response. *This man was one of them.* It was there in the way he held himself, the way he spoke, the way his eyes rested so calmly, so certainly on mine.

"I'm here looking for a couple of people I know," I said. He smiled and rose to his feet and I wondered why I had immediately felt so defensive in his presence.

"Certainly," he said. "Won't you come up to the house? I'm sure they would be pleased to see you." He didn't ask me who I had meant.

As I trudged up the gravel path behind my guide, now

and then giving my neck a random slap, I asked myself just exactly what I hoped to accomplish by this confrontation. It had been three months since I had last seen Dian and Bjonn, although I'd hounded their trail for days after. I had nothing concrete to say to them, and not much I could threaten them with. What was the point of it all? Was it just that I couldn't let it go without seeing them again, without talking to them one last time? As we approached the big house I felt the muscles of my stomach tense and a small knot of pain begin to spread through my abdomen.

The young man ushered me in through the door, and a wave of cool darkness washed over me. For a moment I imagined I really stood in an ancient church, a place of vaulting ceilings and stained-glass windows, all silence and majesty. In actuality I was in a vestibule, rich with stained-wood paneling, flanked by massive inward-hinged doors and leading through an archway into a large room.

The room beyond enhanced the feeling. The ceiling was not high, but its white stucco was crossed by heavy beams of dark wood; the walls were wainscoted in more dark paneling, and the windows set above the wainscoting fitted with leaded glass. The floor was bare of furniture, with only a richly hued rug at its center, and few cushions scattered about. Dian was sitting on one of the cushions, facing me. She was the only person in the room.

"Tad," she exclaimed, executing an intricate maneuver that put her on her feet. She crossed the room toward me— I still stood near the door—her hands extended to me. "How wonderful to see you here," she said.

I looked around, but the young man who had brought me here had vanished. The room was dry and cool, but I felt sweat running down my back.

Dian's toga-like robes swirled about her as she moved and she had an ethereal presence, almost as if floating, gliding above the floor. Her hair was its natural color and it formed a halo about her face. Her smile lit her face like a torch.

I couldn't keep my eyes on her. "Hello, Dian," I said, moving to one side to evade her touch. "Where's Bjonn?"

I asked. I turned away from her and walked over to a window.

"He's here," she said, and her voice lost its first glow of warmth. "Would you like to see him?"

"Yes," I said, keeping my back to her. I stared through the window, but in my mind I still saw Dian. I wanted to crouch over to diminish the pain in my gut. As I heard her move away, I slipped my hand over my belly. It didn't help.

No time seemed to pass, but suddenly I was aware that someone had entered the room behind me.

"Tad," came Bjonn's resonant voice. "Will you tell us what brings you here?"

I turned at last and saw him in the shadows of the opposite side of the room. Dian stood next to him, her tiny figure somehow no longer dwarfed by his. Bjonn was also in robes.

"I saw you on 3–D," I said.

"And so—?" he probed gently.

"I came out here to see you," I said.

"As now you do," Bjonn replied. "But surely you did not travel all this distance merely to confirm the sight of us you beheld on 3–D?"

"No," I said, trying to put steel into my voice. "No, I came out here to get a few answers from you."

"Ah!" he laughed warmly. "Bravely put. I had not expected it. We should be pleased indeed to share our answers with you."

Something twisted in my stomach and I felt my knees shake. "I think you're deliberately misunderstanding me," I told them. "You're evading the subject."

"What subject?" Bjonn asked.

"The subject of—look! Are you aware of the mess your disappearance caused? Why the hell did you run out like that? What led you out here to—to this Godforsaken place?" I waved my hand at the window. "What're you up to out here?" I felt my voice dissolve and with it some of my anger. "Just tell me what's going on, will you?"

"Tad—" Dian, solicitously—"is something wrong? You look ill."

I swayed, dizzily. "I—could you?—an eating cubicle?"

I wasn't aware of him crossing the room, but suddenly Bjonn was at my side, holding my arm, supporting me. I felt a cold sweat cover my face. "We have no eating cubicles here," he said.

I fainted.

They revived me only seconds later. I was sitting propped on cushions, Bjonn still holding me. Dian held something sharp and acrid-smelling under my nose.

"There," she was saying, "does that help? Are you feeling any better?"

"That stuff. . . ." I said. "It gives me . . . a headache."

"All right; we won't use it any more," she said, doing something with it that removed the smell. She was using a tone of voice on me which I recognized. My den mothers used to talk that way to me.

"Lean forward," Bjonn suggested. "Put your head between your knees. It will help."

"The sun. . . ." I said, doing as he said, "climbing up that hill. . . ."

"I can understand," he said soothingly. "You'll get over it."

But I still felt sick to my stomach.

"Why are you so concerned about us?" Bjonn asked, after I felt well enough to sit up and talk. He sat facing me on another cushion. Dian had disappeared into another room. I'd seen no one else.

"In case you've forgotten," I pointed out, "you're my responsibility."

"Nonsense," he smiled. "I am my own responsibility."

"It's my *job*," I insisted. "I was responsible for you."

"I'm afraid," he countered, "that I have been responsible for you. I apologize to you."

"Why'd you run away?" I asked.

"We didn't," he said.

I sat there and glared at him, while he smiled in return. I wanted to get up and hit him. I'd never hit another man in my adult life. But at the thought the pain in my gut redoubled. I leaned over a little more, clenching my stomach a little tighter, and gritted out:

"Let's not quibble over words. You ran. You grabbed Dian, made the 21:00 HST to Pacifica, took a tube to Santa Barbara, rented a tandem cycle, and hunted down a man named Linebarger, spent the night as his guests, and the next day the four of you—you, Dian, Linebarger and a girl named Mills—took a tube north, rented a car, and drove it as far as Big Sur, where you turned the car over to a kid named Leroy Tanner, and then you dropped out of sight— the four of you—until now. Until last night. On 3–D. Why? Just tell me that, will you? Let me close the damned books on you, huh? Tell me why!"

He waited me out. Then he nodded, slowly. "You've compiled an interesting dossier on our activities, haven't you? None too detailed, but in keeping with your dark suspicions. 'On the run,' I believe you put it. I 'grabbed' Dian. We 'hunted down' Bob Linebarger and 'a girl named Mills.' We 'dropped out of sight,' you say. I can understand why you feel that way, Tad, but it isn't true. None of it's true."

He raised a hand to forestall my angry interjection. "Oh, I'm sure you have the bald facts," he said. "But a collection of facts is in itself no guarantee of truth. The omission of a fact can certainly cast other facts into a different shade entirely. Would you like the truth?"

"That's what I'm here for," I said flatly.

"I see. You *think* you're here for the truth. But are you? If it contradicts what you think—what you believe? Will you still want the truth then?"

"Look, Bjonn," I said. "It would be a pleasure—a distinct pleasure!—to hear just a little straight talk from you. Yes, *I'd like the truth!*"

"Very well," he nodded, Buddha-like in the shadows.

"To begin with, Dian and I did not 'run away,' as you seem to believe. After Dian had confided to me the truth of your assignment it seemed to us both that the necessity of our mission demanded a less hostile setting. Dian knew that a friend of hers was vacationing in Santa Barbara and we determined to visit her."

"Her?" I interjected.

"Karilin Mills," Bjonn said.

"This was in the afternoon of that day," he continued. "We wanted you to join us, but Dian feared you would not—that you would attempt to stop us if you could. I confess she understood you better than I. It was her plan— it struck me then as a pointless stratagem—to visit her roommate and switch credit cards with her. It would gain us credit, she told me, if you tried to have ours stopped. Which you did." His gaze seemed accusing.

"She committed a crime," I said.

"The card she exchanged for her roommate's was far more valuable than the one she took," Bjonn replied. "This may be a crime by your standards, but I find your standards irrational.

"In any case, we next arranged to meet you to ask you to join us. Your answer was to flee in blind panic. Where-upon we simply proceeded without you. We went to Santa Barbara in the manner you discovered, found Miss Mills without difficulty, joined her and her friend, Bob Linebarger, and shared our sacrament with them. Then we spent a peaceful night, arose the next day to travel about the town for a short spell—it seemed a shame not to enjoy so beautiful a place for at least a little while—and then, since that was to be our companions' last day in Santa Barbara, we simply moved on with them. That had been the reason for our haste, you know; Dian knew they would be moving on the next day and she had no further address for them. We drove up to Big Sur, where Bob had friends, Bob made arrange-ments to return the car, and we spent the next month in Big Sur, meeting many wonderful people and sharing our life sacrament with them. One of them owned this beautiful old house, and he gave it to us, so we came up here. And here we have been ever since. Never hidden, never 'out of sight,' Tad, and never unavailable to those who seek us. To be truthful with you, Tad, I had not expected to see you among them."

"You were in Big Sur a month, you say," I repeated, tasting the gall I'd swallowed when Tucker had ignored my suggestion and all but told me I was a fool for thinking they were still there. A full month! We'd have routed them in less than a week. In one part of my mind I was already composing a memo to Tucker, a memo that would resound with the full tones of my indignation.

Bjonn was nodding again. His expression was strangely sad. "That is the truth, Tad. Can you accept it?"

"Accept what?"

"That you have fabricated a pair of fugitives in the dark recesses of your mind, that no one was fleeing you, no one trying to evade you, that we have been in the open all the while."

"But carefully avoiding the use of your credit, or any other tipoff to your movements, your whereabouts," I suggested cynically.

He shook his head. "*You* cut off our credit, Tad. Do you think we had any choice?"

I stood up. The pain had subsided a little. "Who owns this place?" I asked. "Is he here?"

"No," Bjonn replied. "What do you wish to know?"

"I'm just wondering if he knows what's going on here."

"He knows. He is one of us."

This time I sought out Bjonn's eyes. They seemed full of pale blue electricity. "*One of you*," I repeated. "You haven't told me about that. About your crazy religion. About the—the *difference* between you and your, ah, converts and normal people. You haven't told me the whole truth. You've left out a few facts yourself."

The sadness seemed to fill his eyes and I couldn't look at him any longer. His voice seemed haunted with melancholy, when he spoke. "Your heart is so filled with hatred, fear and vituperation, Tad Dameron. Have you no room for your own feelings?"

I looked back at him and smiled, and it was my own

smile and not one of his sickly saccharine creations. "Indeed I have, Bjonn, and my feelings have warned me about you from the start."

He came to his feet then, towering up over me, and I thought he was angry until he spoke.

"I think you'd best go now, Tad," he said. His voice was very quiet.

"You won't tell me any more?"

"No."

"You won't tell me about this religion gimmick of yours?"

"No. If you were to share our sacrament, you would learn of it. There is no other way. And you are not yet ready."

"What's this 'sacrament?' What would I have to do?"

"You'd have to eat with us, Tad," he said, and at that moment it seemed to me that his words were tinged with almost curdling pity.

"A neat trick," I said. "You've all but talked me into it. I'll say goodbye." My legs were stiff and aching, and my stomach still uneasy, but I went quickly toward the outer door.

It *was* a neat trick. He'd trapped my curiosity, built my desire to know, my *need* to know almost to the point beyond which I would have succumbed. He had almost succeeded in seducing me.

When they'd first put it to me, this idea of sharing a meal together, I'd been purely and simply revolted by it. Now it was no longer a matter of my revulsion to the basic idea—I was more than certain that when Bjonn *shared a meal* with someone, when he administered his "sacrament," he was inducing that person into a transformation of some sort. I could not distrust my senses to that extent. I *knew* that every person Bjonn had touched, he had corrupted into something like himself. And every person he had corrupted had become his follower. It was subtle, insidious. But it was as I'd first believed; he was a point of contagion.

He spoke of being "in the open," as though he actually

had been. And all the while he had been bent on giving his "sacrament" to as many as he could, converting them into followers, into a buffer ring around him, capable of protecting him, certainly shielding him, donating their credit to him, ultimately giving him this house and grounds in all its isolation, all designed to shelter him until he had sufficient power to come out into the open—as he had done at last, on the 3–D.

Sufficient power to come out into the open . . . for what . . . ? What was his ultimate purpose? Just what was his "mission" here on Earth?

I felt a chill run down my spine as I stepped out into the afternoon sun. He *was* accomplishing *something* in this subtle expansion of influence over the people around him. He was demonstrably *changing* them.

As I strode down the path to my car, I found a girl, robed in the now-familiar uniform, staring at a flower on one of the bushes. She looked up at me, smiled, seemed to take from my expression a clue to my intent, and let her smile slip.

He was *changing* people, in some specific way. I decided it was time to see if the method or the result of that change could be scientifically established.

"You," I said to the girl. "You belong to this, ah, church?"

The answer was recorded plainly upon her. She nodded, wordlessly.

"You're coming with me," I said, and I seized her wrist and pulled her down the hill after me.

No one saw us. No one stopped me.

But all the way down to Santa Rosa, she regarded me with sad and compassionately knowing eyes.

Chapter Thirteen

I took the girl, whose name was Lora, into our Bay Complex office. I'd called ahead; they were expecting me. I led her into an unused room and told her to sit.

"There are two ways we can do this," I told her. "We can take you apart, muscle filament by muscle filament, until we have you laid out all over a laboratory. Or you can tell us what you know about the changes your, um, sacrament brought about in you."

"Why have you waited until now to tell me this?" she asked. "Is it because you feel more safe here?"

Every time I spoke with one of these people, I ran into the same disconcerting feeling that we could only talk at cross-purposes. I wanted to slap the girl. Perhaps it showed; she shrank back from me. "All right," I said, turning my back on her and pacing across the short floor to the opposite wall, turning, and pacing back. "We'll take you apart, then."

"You can't," she said. "I am aware of my rights. As a matter of fact, I am a Lawyer, Class D, and I am licensed to practice before the bar in Bay Complex." She gave me a sweet smile. "My license number is A2MHX-6910CK-alpha-alpha," she added. This is an office of the Bureau of Non-Terran Affairs and can claim absolutely no jurisdiction over me."

At that I felt genuinely happy. I gave her my warmest smile. "Not directly over you, perhaps," I admitted, "but definitely over your body, which has been isolated for testing for suspected alien plague." I removed a printout sheet from my hip pouch and presented it to her. "This is an order, granted in Geneva, for the isolation and quarantine of your body"—I'd had her name filled in when I'd called to make my initial report from Santa Rosa—"for the purpose of biological tests." I flourished the plastic sheet and then thrust it at her. I loved meeting lawyers.

She paled a little. But she accepted the sheet and read it thoroughly. At least she wasn't a bum lawyer. Finally, she looked up. "I can't tell you anything," she said. "Will you really have me destroyed?"

They took her to Lima, and I went back to Megayork. I had the flat feeling of anticlimax, of a confrontation that had somehow misfired, aborted. When I replayed the events in my mind, when I dictated my prelims on them, I found them fuzzy, indistinct, and somehow unreal. When I tried to pin down a specific memory—what color was Dian's robe? Which direction did the windows of that church-like room face? How long had I actually spent in that house?— I found my thoughts squirming out from under my scrutiny. Had I succeeded in my specific mission? I felt I hadn't— and yet Tucker had been almost warm in his praise for me (a reflection, I was certain, of the praise he had received from *his* superiors). Sharp-eyed young Level Seven Agent spots fugitives on 3–D show (who watches 3–D anymore?) in new roles as religious leaders. Quietly pursues his mission to West Coast, where he tracks them down to hillside retreat. Sure, I even kidnapped an innocent girl and turned her over to the X-T biolabs. I must certainly be in line for a medal and a commendation. If not promotion.

I needed a break. I hadn't seen or spoken to Ruth since the night (morning?) she'd stormed out of my apt. And I had no real desire to. That ploy was finished, dead. It was stupid to begin with. But thinking about it started a chain of associations going. . . .

I had to use a little push to get into the restricted part of Directory Assistance—first names aren't much to go on—but I got a make on Veronica. Her last name was Mullins. I suppose that explained her reluctance to use it.

She lived not a mile away from Dian's old residence, but, mercifully, much closer to the pod line. Her studio occupied the top three floors of another ancient building very much like the one in which Dian had lived. But at least this building had been modernized; the doors were new and slid back as I approached them, and the lift took me up to the tenth floor in about three heartbeats.

Veronica produced sensuals. The entire time I was in her studio I was aware of the vibrations overhead, and the impression of heavy machinery above me made me want to hunch in my shoulders and drop my head between them. I cannot understand why she chose to live on the lowest of her three floors instead of over her production plant, but it seemed of absolutely no concern to her, and she laughed the only time I mentioned it, waved her fingers distractedly, and dismissed the whole subject. I didn't bring it up again.

"The whole private-enterprise thing is just a myth, you know," she told me almost immediately after I entered her apt. "Anybody can play—if you can supply something for which there's a demand."

"And there's a demand for you?"

"Always." She glanced upward. "All twenty-four."

"Perhaps I should have subscribed, instead of coming here," I said.

"How did you find me?" she asked.

"Persistence," I said.

"How nice. And why?"

"I remembered you from Miss Moore-Williams' party."

She laughed. "You became quite the stud, I recall." She mock-pouted. "And you told me you weren't a tom."

"That was earlier," I said.

"—And then you weren't," she agreed. "Now . . . ?"

"You intrigued me. I wasn't sure how much was memory and how much—"

She laughed. "Elvira's parties often produce that effect!"

"—how much I dreamed. I decided to check it out."

"You're very dogged."

An infomat buzzed and claimed her attention, so I turned slowly around, surveying the room she'd brought me into. It was long, perhaps the combination of two smaller rooms with the dividing walls taken out, and stylishly decorated with hue-shifting walls and the Roman-style couches which seemed to mark the latest fad among the well-to-do. The far end of the room was dominated by a lifesize pornographic hologram of my hostess, which invited my closer attention, and from which I quickly shifted my eyes. Instead I wandered over to one of the low couches and sat down on it.

A moment later she was back, dropping quickly to a seat beside me. "The one drawback," she said lightly, "business. As long as I'm here, I have to put up with it." She sighed. "I go out often."

"Tell me something about yourself," I suggested.

"What's to tell?" She shrugged.

"You didn't always produce sensuals."

"No." She seemed to look inward for a moment. "But I try not to think about that."

"Oh."

"You're not really used to this sort of thing, are you?" she said.

"What do you mean?"

She smiled, self-deprecatingly. "The, oh, call it the life of the idle rich—even if I'm not exactly idle all the time."

"It's above my touch," I confessed. In point of actual fact, I had crossed a subtle but sharply defined class-barrier, first in taking Ruth to the party and again in coming here. It had seemed less so when I decided to come here, but that had been beforehand.

There is no law, no rule even, that says a man of my credit standing, a government employee, cannot enter the high-credit life. It is not even difficult, as far as the mechanics of it go. Class distinctions exist far more as attitude-barriers than anything else. To enter this world I had to cross over into a world of alien attitudes, of differing mores. It was uncomfortable. I felt like a fish out of water. These people did not think as I did. The gulf tat separated us was the one most difficult to bridge. For most people the notion of crossing it was unthinkable. We tended to think of ourselves, each of us in his own class, as the only sort there was; we rarely even acknowledged the existence of other classes, either above or below us. Their thought processes were too alien.

I rarely watch 3-D.

"It bothers you?" she asked. "Our life style?"

"I've never even subscribed to a sensual," I admitted.

"How would you like to make one?" A wicked smile teased the corners of her lips.

"Me?"

"I'll even give you a share of the royalties."

"What appeal would there be—for your customers?"

"Oh, novelty, perhaps. . . ."

"I don't know. . . ." I hesitated.

"Isn't that really what you came here for?"

"No, not to become a—a performer."

"We all perform; life is just one continuous show—*live and in solid color*, you know? Why not hook in to it?" She got to her feet and moved lithely across the room. Again my gaze was attracted to the hologram on the far wall. *Could I climb inside that hologram?*

She came back, something in her hand. "Have you ever been outside yourself?" she asked. "Really outside, I mean?"

"That night at the party. . . ." I said.

"That's not what I mean. Have you ever thought of making a sensual, and then *experiencing* it?" She leaned forward, lips pursed, and kissed me.

The shock of oral contact was like ice and fire, alternately scalding and numbing my nerve ends. I never even felt the injectab against my neck. She leaned back and smiled a lazy smile. "There," she said proudly. "Now I know you'll want to."

I shook my head a little stupidly. "I don't get you," I said. My lips felt puffy and slightly anesthetized; I had trouble speaking clearly through them.

She stood up again, her movements seeming jerky to me. "Come—on," she said. "This'll be—fun now."

Deep inside myself, I wailed with self-pitying anguish. *What am I doing here?* my buried mind screamed helplessly. *Why did I get into this? What's this woman* doing *to me?* But I climbed readily to my feet, feeling as if I was on a sudden swift lift that catapulted me into the air. Then I was dancing, feather-light, on the balls of my feet, frisking after Veronica, who beckoned and led me into another room.

It wasn't like the party. I wasn't disassociated from myself. My sensations seemed, if anything, more immediate, more acute. Reality was more *real*. But I had very little self-will; I initiated nothing.

I followed her into a small room where she was already disrobing. "Hey," I said, "I'm incompetent. You know that?"

"It's all right," she said. "Just take your things off."

I did, and then she began smearing a colorless but strong-smelling paste over my body, avoiding only my genitals and those areas where my body hair was thick. It was a highly gratifying sensation, and I became lost in it, only to be jerked back to awareness when I realized she had stopped.

She put me in a 'fresher then, removing the paste from my skin. This made no sense to me until I noticed that my body hair was now also gone. I realized the paste had been a depilatory, and I said, proudly, "Hey, that stuff took my hair off, right?"

"It'll grow back soon," she said. "You'll never miss it— and it won't really show."

I nodded in agreement. I was pleased with my powers of ratiocination.

She smeared a thin jelly over my smooth skin, and then had me don a very lightweight skintight suit of sorts, the crotch of which had been cut out. I expected her to attach connections of some sort to the suit, but she explained— very patiently—that the micro-sensing circuits of the suit included extremely short-range broadcast units and that wires would only get in the way. "Here," she said. "Let me test you." She ran one fingernail slowly down my left side, over my left nipple and across my hip. The suit transmitted the sensation to me like a second skin.

"The suit picks up what you do?" I asked.

She'd gone over to an inconspicuous console set in the wall of the room and appeared to be checking it. "No," she said over her shoulder, "it picks up what *you* experience. It's keyed into your nervous system. It plays back *everything* you experience, you know."

"Oh," I said happily. "Well, I'm ready to start experiencing now."

She laughed, an honest, open laugh. "All right," she said. "I guess we're all set."

Afterward she let me experience the sensual. The drug had worn off by then, and I felt almost bitter with embarrassment.

"This will travel all over the world," I said.

"You should hope so," she said. "Think of what it'll do to your credit rating! You're a businessman now, you know."

"I could lose my job," I responded.

"I doubt it. The only way anyone could ever know it was you would be to ask me. And if I'm honest enough to give you royalties, you can trust me to keep your little secret safe."

I stared at her. "Have you any private feelings left?"

She tossed her head. "I don't know what you mean."

"You're a public commodity—for those who can afford you."

"So are you, now. Do you feel any different?"

"I don't know, yet. How can I tell?"

She shook her head. "Tad Dameron," she said. "You live in another world. Do you know that?"

"I'd just about figured it out," I said.

"You look wrung out," Ditmas told me the next day. He had the office cubicle next to mine. He was just back from his accumulated six-month vacation, and looking very fit. "You need to take some time off the job, fella'."

I gave him one of my weaker smiles. "It's the off-the-job moments that leave me looking like this," I told him. I felt hollow and exhausted. I hadn't slept much that night, and my digestion was off.

He laughed, and popped back into his own office, no doubt convinced that I was living it up on my offhours. Ruth had leaked the Word about the Moore-Williams party, and it was common knowledge now. It didn't give me a whole lot of satisfaction to note that she was also a free agent these days, and spending her time with anyone who asked her. Tucker had let her go and probably realized himself to be well off by now.

I did routine work for the next few hours, and caught myself making only a dozen or less errors. I did a lot of intermittent staring out my window, but the sky was a leaden gray, the water of the Sound two shades darker, and the whole scene of no great emotional uplift.

Finally I did something I had been putting off for years. I made an appointment with a shrink.

Her office was furnished like a particularly homey apt, and I felt a sense of instant *déjà vu* when I entered it. She was seated on a comfortable-looking couch, facing a second couch across a low table upon which a parasitic plant of some sort was growing. She was looking at a sheaf of printout sheets, and looked up almost guiltily when the door snicked shut behind me.

"Hello, there. You must be Tad," she said. Her face was soft and warm, dominated by a large nose and two deep brown eyes, which regarded me a little quizzically. She'd had no cosmetic surgery, and her age showed, despite the current mode of her lightly silvered hair. "Won't you sit down," she added. "I'm afraid I was just checking out your file just now. I've been so rushed," she said apologetically.

I eased myself down onto the couch facing her. The cushions were hydraulic, and heated. They adjusted to my body and soothed some of the tensions from my muscles as I sat there. She had returned to my file and was flipping quickly through the remaining sheets. I wondered what I was doing here and what I would say, but did and said nothing.

She was a large woman, unabashedly matronly. Her clothing made no attempt to hide that fact. I found myself watching her hands as they flexed and gripped the plastic sheets; the play of muscles under the loosening skin, the furrows of tired flesh, the age and the strength they showed in her. Long fingers, curiously graceful. One ring: a single platinum band; anachronistic. No timepiece on her fingers. She looked up again, and this time, it seemed to me, a little sharply.

"It took you a long time to come to me," she said. "Do you have any idea why?"

"I don't know why I'm here now," I admitted. "Why don't you tell me? You're the shrink."

"'Shrink,'" she repeated. "Why do you call me that?"

"What else should I call you?" I asked. The couch was very warm, very comfortable. It nestled me.

"Why don't we be honest with each other," she suggested. "Why don't you just call me Mother?"

Chapter Fourteen

"It wasn't coincidence, was it?" she said.

"No," I agreed. "I checked a directory. The name caught my eye—not many of us Damerons around. I had a check run."

"So you came to see me."

"I wanted to know."

"And I," she nodded. "My son." She shook her head and repeated it: "My son."

"What did my file tell you?"

"You've read it yourself," she pointed out. "What does it tell you?"

"Not much that I didn't already know."

She nodded. "You decided you needed therapy," she

said. *"Then* you found my name. Did you think you could find valid therapy with me?"

"I don't know," I confessed. "I don't like the ways things have been going lately. I had to do *something*. And I've tried just about everything else."

"I think I should disqualify myself," she said.

"For God's sake, *why?"*

"I am your mother. Are you relating to me as a therapist, or as your mother? The distinction is important. How could I ever be sure?"

"Look—you've set up this whole office like an apt, and you present yourself as a mother, as an earth-mother type. Isn't it a little disingenuous of you to disqualify yourself just because you really *are* my mother? If I was somebody else, you'd want me to pretend you were my mother, right? So it's a little easier, isn't it? Because, I know you really are."

"But—"

"Look, *Mother*—I last laid eyes on you more than twenty-five years ago. I don't even have a good *memory* of you! I walked in here, wondering, trying to remember, and I looked at you and *I didn't even know!* That's how much my mother you are. Why, I remember my *den* mothers, for God's sake, better than you. Don't you think you *owe* it to me to try to help me?"

She shook her head as if confused, tears that looked real glistening in the corners of her large, soft eyes. "I don't know, don't you see? That's just it. What if it's *my* fault— that you're . . . the way you are . . . ? How could I help you then?"

"Why don't you tell me why you gave me up?"

"I've been listed all these years," she said. "Why didn't you ever look me up before?"

I shrugged. Standoff. "I'm here now," I said, finally.

We regarded each other. Her eyes dropped first. I was making her nervous.

"Well." She shuffled the printout sheets. Then she raised her eyes again, almost as if imploring me in some way. "Your father and I," she said, and stopped. "It was a question of priorities," she said, backing off and starting again. It didn't appear to take her where she wanted to go. "Tad," she said, "I'm sorry. I had to do what I did. Perhaps it was wrong." She stared down at the plastic sheets she was still gripping. "It turned out to be wrong. But nonetheless, it had to be done, then. Your father and I were not happy with each other. We decided to revoke our contract. You were a problem. Contracts are nonrevocable where children are involved—I guess you know that. We discussed it. Your father decided to abandon us. Under the law, an abandoned contract is null and void after one full year of absence. I went on Public Care, and you were taken into a public den; it was automatic."

"And you went on to become a therapist."

"Yes. It was a matter of years, Tad. It took me twelve years to earn my license. During those twelve years I could not have been a mother also."

"So you became a counterfeit mother, you earned a license to become an ersatz mother for profit? Did it ease your conscience?"

"How can you talk that way to me?" she cried. "Is *that* why you came here? To confront me and revile me for abandoning you?"

"No," I said. "But can you blame me for being bitter?"

She shook her head. "No," she said in a low voice. "No, I can't blame you."

"So," I said. "Here I am." I gestured at the file in her hands. "And there I am."

"Thousands of children," she said, slowly, as if picking out the words one by one, "maybe millions, are raised in public dens. They don't all turn out as you have."

"No," I said. "Some are worse."

"Don't you *see*, Tad, I can't—I just *can't* handle this situation properly? How could I be your therapist when you already have me feeling so guilty about you, about your problems?"

"I didn't give you that guilt," I said. "You did. How are you going to get rid of it? By throwing me out and never seeing me again?"

"I couldn't do that," she said.

"Maybe you should take me on as a charity case," I suggested.

Her eyes blazed angrily, and then subsided, a sudden spark of flame from dying embers. "You didn't come here with that in mind," she said.

I shook my head.

"I have an enormous overhead," she said. "The rent on this office—you have no idea the amount they get for space like this now. And the taxes—! Private enterprise"—she snorted—"is far from what it's supposed to be. I work here all day, every day of the week, just to keep my accounts straight."

"I've checked your credit rating," I said.

"I'm not going to give you a free hour every day," she said.

"I didn't ask for it," I said. "I merely suggested a sop for your conscience."

She frowned and straightened herself on the couch. I found myself sprawling even more indolently on mine. It was a very relaxing couch; no doubt a tool of her trade. "If we are not going to waste the rest of your time—?" she said briskly.

"Okay," I said. "You're the therapist."

"I can't seem to become involved with people," I said. "I try, but. . . ."

"In what way do you try?"

I told her about my visit with Veronica, minimizing what we'd done. "I wanted just to, well, get to know her. You know what I mean?"

"How do you mean it?"

"Well, hell. She's a girl."

"You seem to have taken care of that aspect of her," she observed dryly.

"I wanted something, umm, less physical. I wasn't a real person to her; I was an object. She treated me like an object."

"Does that surprise you?"

"What do you mean by that?"

"How do *you* treat people?"

"Like people."

"I don't think so. Think about it."

It went on like that. Back and forth. I tried to explain myself. She forced me into word games, kept me on the defensive. I never seemed to get to the things I wanted to talk about. Finally she told me, "Your problem seems to be that you have difficulty relating to people."

And I said, angrily, "That's what I've been trying to tell you, dammit!"

It was not a very productive session. And I wondered if future sessions would be any better. I'd always distrusted shrinks; why should I expect more of my mother? What reason had she, of all people, ever given me to trust her? As I left the session I turned black thoughts over in my mind, and wondered how a mother could make money from her own son's psychological problems, when she was undoubtedly at their root.

I had to skip the following day's appointment. I was called to Geneva.

Tucker and I took the same HST; he'd come to Megayork the day before, although I hadn't known it. I found my seat, settled in and prepared to doze off when someone sat down next to me, and a warning bristled in the back of my mind. I turned my head casually, and found myself staring into Tucker's slate-gray eyes.

"Greetings," he said.

"I guess you're coming to Geneva too," I said brightly. I had not actually confronted him in the flesh since the episode with Ruth. Now he was strapped into the twenty-four-inch slot immediately adjacent to mine. His knuckles grazed mine as he laid his left arm on the armrest that separated us. The recirculating air suddenly made my forehead icy.

He chuckled, and I knew he was enjoying the situation. "That's right," he agreed, saying nothing.

"Have you any idea what is going on?" I asked. The

demand—or maybe command—for my appearance in Geneva was unprecedented, at least to me. All my previous dealings with the home office had been by infomat.

"Ayup," he said, volunteering nothing more.

I didn't want to give him the satisfaction of asking more questions, so I shut my mouth and kept my silence. He chuckled once or twice more, and then became quiet. Maybe he was becoming bored by his own game.

The seatback cushions inflated, pinning us into our seats, the warning lights flashed, and in short order we were rising into a low orbit which would carry us outside 82 percent of the atmosphere, and drop us almost a quarter of the way around the world. The acceleration was brisker than on the west-coast hop, but, because we had a more favorable ballistic curve, the trip took no longer. Soon enough the flash of the sun on the waters of Lake Geneva heralded our touchdown into the late afternoon of another continent.

We were met by couriers and taken by private pod to the Concordat, wherein our Bureau's offices occupied a secluded niche (although no less grand to my eyes for that fact). We were ushered across an interior lawn under an artifical sun, to an office framed by a living wall of flowering vines. Several men were reclining in sun-deck chairs there, and I felt absurdly out of place in my North Am clothes. I didn't feel a lot better when I noticed Tucker seemed similarly disconcerted.

We were seated and ignored, while the others conversed in low voices. I was wondering why we had been brought here, if not simply to humiliate us with a better knowledge of the insignificance of our roles in the Bureau, when a man with a young face, but tired, old eyes and dead-white hair turned his chair around and addressed us.

"Gentlemen, the Bureau is indebted to you for your forthright perserverance to your duties as you saw them. I am going to tell you something, and I am going to state it for your ears only—because you have earned the knowledge.

"The girl brought in by Level Seven Agent Dameron has been exhaustively examined by our labs in Lima, and we have definitely established the fact that her body has been entered—invaded—by an alien parasite."

He spoke in a dead flat tone, almost wearily conversational, as if repeating a common fact for the thousandth time, but the small chill that had been crawling slowly up and down my back suddenly spread its icy fingers and clamped them tight in my intestines.

"We have established," he continued without pause, "that this parasite has created a second nervous system, directly parallel to her own, with its own nervous center at the base of her neck. The filaments of this parasite not only penetrate her ganglioplexus at many points but also along her spine and her brain. The relationship appears symbiotic. She is in excellent physical health. She claims voluntary control of many body functions, such as ovulation. She also claims that the effects of this parasite in her body are entirely beneficial. This, of course, remains open to doubt, inasmuch as she could easily be under its mental domination." *I'd sensed it all along.*

"Sir," Tucker said. "You're suggesting this girl has been taken over by an alien parasite? Via Bjonn, the colonist from Farhome?"

The man shifted his gaze directly to my superior and seemed to examine him as coolly as he might have a minor insect. "I *stated,*" he said, coldly, precisely, "that the girl's body and brain have been invaded by an alien parasite. I infer that the parasite was brought to Earth by the colonial emissary, Bjonn. This is not a known fact, although it seems very likely."

"Has—has the girl said anything about how she was given the parasite, sir?" I ventured to ask. My voice sounded shrill in my own ears, but the man appeared to give my question due consideration.

"She spoke only of a religious ceremony," he said.

I nodded. "The 'sacrament of life.'"

"Exactly." He seemed on the verge of thawing a little.

"Then," I said, a little more boldly, "it's reasonable to assume that Bjonn established this religion of his for the purpose of spreading his parasites."

"That is our assumption," the man agreed. I noticed the others were also watching me now, and I felt suddenly very conspicuous and dangerously out of my own level.

"Exactly our suspicion, all along," Tucker said, throwing his hat into the ring. I kept a straight face and didn't risk any sidelong glances at him. "I'm sorry we had to lose a valuable agent to them."

No one was looking at Tucker. They were still watching me. I felt suddenly apprehensive. *They hadn't called us all the way to Geneva just to tell us this.*

"You said this was for our ears only," I said, surprising myself a little. But what the hell; I was already on the spot. "Why? What do you plan to do with Bjonn and his Church?"

The man smiled and nodded; it was like the sun breaking through a winter overcast. "You're right," he said. "We are not going to interfere with Bjonn at this time. Religious freedom is always a touchy issue. Instead, we want you, Agent Dameron, to join his Church."

It sure sounded easy—on the surface. That's why I had cramps in my stomach and strong misgivings about the whole plan, all the way back to Megayork. They'd rather carefully outlined the whole plan to us. I was to infiltrate Bjonn's Church, but *without* becoming a host to one of those parasites. I had a valuable talent: my intuitive sense of situation and my ability to grasp by hunch the key to nonapparent problems. I was to exercise my fine talent— which had, after all, been the first to alert the Bureau to the problem—to get in deeper and decipher the colonist's motives and purposes. You bet. It made a certain amount of sense, if you didn't ask yourself certain key questions, like *What more is there to find out?* and *How will this help contain the spread of these parasites?* and also, *Why aren't they acting against Bjonn* now? I had the distinct feeling that I was being neatly maneuvered, that I was a rather minor pawn in a much larger game. You can record it officially; I was less than pleased with my new assignment.

The girl was to be brought to Megayork; I was to ferry her back to the Church. I spent an hour in my office staring at the dreary Sound, and then went down to the office lounge. My time-scale was shattered by the intercontinental hops and I had another hop upcoming. I decided on a brief nap.

The dimly lit lounge looked deserted when I went in. The odor of marijuana incense floated in the air, and I flopped on a couch and let my mind loose. I rarely used the lounge, despite the fact that everyone in the office is urged to take a break here at some point in his day. I've never liked the idea of artificial relaxation; I preferred to take my tensions home with me and sleep them off. Just now, however, it seemed like the easiest way to kill time.

"Say, hey there, Tad." It was Ditmas' lazy voice, still full of vitamins, from a couch on the far wall. I rolled my head and saw a vague shape sprawled out there.

"Didn't see you when I came in," I said, feeling a minor irritation at this intrusion on my mental privacy.

"I figured you didn't," he said.

I said nothing more. It was my profound hope that Ditmas would reciprocate.

"That guy from Farhome," he said, breaking the silence after what may or may not have been a long time. "Wasn't he your baby?"

"What about him?" I asked, tightening my fingers into fists.

"Just wondered, that's all."

"I was in charge of him," I admitted. "Why?"

"No real reason," he said. His voice was distant. "They're setting up the next run out to Farhome, and it just occurred to me he was your baby, that's all."

"What's that you said?" I asked, suddenly alert.

"It just occurred to me, you know, when I was thinking about it, that he was your man—the fellow from Farhome, I mean."

"Not that," I said, sitting up. I felt dizzy. "Before. What you said about a run to Farhome."

"What about it?"

"*What* run to Farhome?" I demanded. I felt like screaming. "There's no return expedition planned for another year, yet."

"They changed it," he said, dreamily. "They changed it around."

"How do *you* know?"

"Gave me the assignment," he said. "I'm going out with them. How about that, huh? Next time I see you, you'll be a lot older, ol' Tad."

Ditmas was Level Eight. He didn't have a black mark in his files. No one had classified *him* "unfit for space."

Chapter Fifteen

I met the girl at the terminal. She was accompanied by a grizzled-looking woman, who spoke in an incongruously sweet voice as she said goodbye to Lora. Lora clasped the woman's hand for a moment, and it looked as if they'd become genuinely friendly. I wondered how she'd receive me. I made a small noise in my throat to signal my presence.

She turned confidently, and said, "Hello again, Mr. Dameron."

"Hello," I replied, feeling a little awkward. "I know it's not part of the schedule, but I wonder if you'd mind sharing the last leg of your trip with me?"

"Back to the Church, you mean?" She was calm, very calm. Her escort had already vanished into the crowd. She knew her business, that one did.

"That's right."

"Why? Why should you want to come back with me?"

"I guess it's, well"—I did a figurative toe-scuffle in the nonexistent dust—"I guess I just feel responsible for you. I mean, for grabbing you like that, and all."

"They didn't hurt me, you know. They didn't take me apart and string me out over their laboratory."

"I know. I mean, I knew they wouldn't really do that. I was trying to scare you."

"Why?"

"It seemed to be what was called for—then, I mean."
She wasn't making it any easier for me.

"Now you regret it?" she said.

"It was my job." I shrugged my shoulders, unhappily.
"Where does it say I have to like my job?"

Her eyes seemed to pierce mine, and for a moment I felt
she was looking directly into my mind. "I can see that,"
she said. "You *are* unhappy, aren't you?"

"Yes." No lie.

"What good do you think it would do to go back with me?"

"I—I've quit my job," I said, pitching my voice into an
awkward impulsiveness. "I can't go on with it."

"You feel guilty? Is that it?"

I nodded gratefully. "Yes."

"You want to join the Church?"

I looked at the floor and made myself sheepish. "I
. . . don't know. I mean, *eating*. . . ."

"It still bothers you? That much?"

"It's not something I can accept overnight."

"But you want to?"

I couldn't meet her eyes. "I've got to see. I've got to
find out."

"Whether you can go through with it, you mean?"

"Yes. That's it."

She reached out her hand and touched my wrist. The
significance of that gesture was not lost on me. "All right,"
she said.

It was a strange sort of conversation; it reminded me of
sessions spent with shrinks. I kept my guard up, since it
had occurred to me the girl might be looking for flaws in
my story. But at the same time I felt a need to talk to her.
It had been a long time since I'd been with someone I knew
I could talk with—since Dian, in fact. My need to talk
didn't sit too well with my fear of becoming trapped in an
inadvertent lie; I was pretty uncomfortable, all through the
trip.

We talked about what had happened to Lora; I'd wondered how she felt about it. "What must happen will hap-

pen," she said, philosophically. "We all play the roles assigned us."

"Yeah?" I wondered. "Did Bjonn assign you that role?" I was wondering if she'd been planted there, waiting for me to leave the house and find her. Had I been goaded into nabbing her? Or had Bjonn—warned by Dian's knowledge of the Bureau—simply guessed I would take someone, and made her handy?

"No one *gave* me the role," she said, smiling a little. "It simply became mine by necessity."

I shook my head. "Tell me something I can understand," I said. "That sounds like dogma of some sort." Actually, it sounded a lot like something Veronica had told me. *We all perform; life is just one continuous show.*

"You have to come to terms with yourself," Lora said, a little enigmatically. "You'll see."

"You think I will?" I wondered that myself, half fearfully, half hopefully. I was starting to believe my own phony role.

"You need to," she said. "You're groping. I can *feel* it in you. But you're—you're fighting it."

I changed the subject. "How'd a lawyer like you ever get hooked into that Church?" I asked.

She laughed. "It *is* absurd, isn't it? I was a serious young lawyer, you know. My speciality was Tax Credit Deductions for members of The Guild of Plastic Artisans. I spent five years, buried in printouts from the files of the tax courts of Bay Complex, and came out of it with what I thought was a permanent squint, a positive aversion to sunshine, and a specialty that would serve exactly two hundred and thirty-seven men within my licensed area." She shook her head and wrinkled her nose. "What a ninny! However, it just happened that one of my clients was the son of old Dr. Benford, and when his father donated his house to the Church, Jim Benford—my client—decided I should handle the tax-credit declaration. So I met the old man, talked to him, and decided that if the Church was responsible for the way he glowed with good health, then just maybe it could do something for me. Which it did—including a free trip to Lima!"

"You were waiting for me, though, weren't you?" I said.

"No. It was all your idea, Mr. Dameron. You can't shift responsibility to someone else."

"I was upset," I said. "Bjonn was pretty nasty."

"I don't believe that." She put her hand on my arm to forestall my interruption. "That's just the way it seemed to you, that's all. You *were* very upset. I gather, from what I've heard, that you were involved with Bjonn, and with Dian too, earlier. I can understand the emotional undertones which must have been involved. But when you came storming out of the house, I had no idea you were there, or who you were even. Nobody *put* me there just for you to find."

"I'm sorry."

"Don't be sorry. I'm not. I was worried, but I needn't have been. They were very nice to me; they didn't hurt me at all. Oh, I see! You still feel guilty about it—about what happened to me. Don't you?"

I massaged my temples with my fingers. "I guess I do," I said. "You were pretty cool to me when I approached you, back there in Megayork."

"I was unsure of you."

"You aren't now?" I held my breath unconsciously.

"No," she smiled. "I know what you are, now."

I wondered how she meant that.

Another rented car took us on the final leg. It was dusk when Lora gestured at the glowing windows of the house on the hill, and I pulled off the opposite side of the road and parked. Two other cars were parked ahead of mine this time.

We climbed the path, our way lit by tiny glowing lamps, like fireflies frozen in stasis. It had a strangely magical effect, as if by climbing this crooked path we were leaving behind the mundane world and entering a new world of seclusion and mystical contemplation. *Complete rot,* I kept thinking, and yet the feeling haunted me. The autumn night was growing chill, and we'd shivered a little when we'd crawled out of the cocoon of the car, but up here where the winds should be pushing the damp cold even more readily through our scant clothes the air was quiet, scented with summertime, and if it weren't for the throb of fear I felt in anticipation I might have become completely a part of the other-worldly atmosphere.

The door was an open invitation, the interior of the house warm and beckoning. I followed Lora hesitantly, dreading the confrontation that must come.

Perhaps twenty people—all ages, both sexes—were sprawled in robes upon the cushions of the church-like room where I'd met Bjonn and Dian before. But neither Bjonn nor Dian was there now.

A stocky young man with short, curly blond hair rose from a cushion near the door, and extended his hands to Lora, smiling all the while. They said nothing that I could hear, but embraced, almost passionately. I turned away from them and let my eyes wander slowly around the room while I waited for the prolonged greeting to end.

As my eyes met those of others seated about the room, they seemed to look up at me and then nod a silent greeting. But no one else rose; no one else said anything at all. I turned back to Lora and the young man to find them engaged in a long, mutual oral kiss. I felt the heat of the blood which rushed to my face, and turned away once more.

"Tad.".

The voice was very low, very soft, but it startled me as much as would have a tap on my shoulder.

"Dian!"

She had come up from behind me. Now she reached out to tug at my arm with one hand, a raised finger to her lips. Still gesturing for silence, she led me out of the big room and down a long hall. My last glance back at the doorway of that room showed me Lora and the other still locked in each other's arms.

Dian led me into a small room that had once served a previous owner as a study; most of its old furnishings still remained. She seated me in a comfortable chair and took another. "They're in meditation," she said, nodding back the way we'd come. "It's best not to disturb them."

I shrugged.

"I'm surprised to see you here again, Tad," Dian said.

In the soft light she seemed to glow, almost as if from within. "Did you wish to see Bjonn again?"

"I suppose so," I said. "But that's not why I came back."

"Why did you come back, then?"

I leaned forward. "I quit my job," I said.

"They sent you here?" she asked.

"No, no, I quit the job," I repeated. "The Bureau. I walked out. Like you did." I shrugged again. "Well, less dramatically."

"Did you?"

"Don't you believe me?" I worked hard to get a throb of honesty into my voice. *Infiltrate the Church—sure! Easy as—what? Breaking a leg?*

"I'm not sure I do, Tad," Dian said. Her voice seemed less controlled, a little less certain. "Why should you quit the Bureau? It was your whole life, wasn't it? The Bureau— and space?"

I screwed my face up into a grimace of sorts. "Yeah, but if you know that much, you know the rest."

"They wouldn't let you into space," she said, nodding. "And finally . . . you gave up?"

"Things have changed since you left, Dian," I said. "You don't know how Tucker chewed me out about your disappearance. He's still burned about it."

She sighed. "I can imagine. Poor Arthur. It must have been a blow. . . ." She stared past me, her eyes distant, reflective.

"Well, anyway, there was a lot of friction," I said. "I could have stayed on—hell, I could've held out to retirement—but it would have been bad, every single day of it." (One corner of my mind spoke up about then: *And you think you're making this up? It sure wasn't much to look forward to.*) "So I quit."

"Why did you come here, Tad?"

I stared at her. "You know that," I said.

She dropped her eyes and I thought I saw her blush. It might have been the lighting. "Will you join the Church, Tad?" she asked, low-voiced.

"I . . . don't know," I said. "You know why."

"The ritual," she said. "You're afraid to eat with us."

I nodded.

"There's no way to avoid it, you know," she said. "Not if you want to join us."

"I *know*," I said. "But—well, could I just hang around for a while? You know, just to kind of get used to the idea a little more?"

"Perhaps you should not try so hard, Tad," she said. "We don't ask people to overcome basic objections to our ritual; not when they are as strong as yours. Perhaps you should try something else, somewhere else."

"Don't you even *want* me to join you?" I asked.

She gave me a grave smile. "Of course I do, Tad. But some things don't happen just because I'd like them to. I wanted you to join us a long time ago. Do you remember that?"

I did. "I couldn't help that—my reaction, I mean," I said. I didn't even like to think about it.

"Just so," she said, nodding.

"But maybe if I, you know, hung around for a while, I could, umm, overcome my reactions some. I've been fighting it you know. I *have* thought about it."

She sighed. "I can't throw you out," she said. "I don't know what to do."

"Ask Bjonn, " I suggested.

"I can't. He's not here just now."

"Oh." If he wasn't here, could they hold their Sacrament of Life without him? "Will he be back soon? Could I wait?"

She nodded, slowly. "He'll be back in two days," she said. "I'll have a room made up for you."

My room was on the third floor, up under slanting eaves, and had an unpolarized dormer window that looked out upon a starry night. Down the hall was a curious little room which Dian pointed out to me on our way to my room. Inside was an anachronistic old evacuation unit, a bowl with faucets for running water, and, a more recent addition, a 'fresher cubicle. It was a curious mixture of inappropriate appliances. I experimented with it after Dian had left me in my room, sneaking almost guiltily down the hall, and carefully locking the door. (Dian had said meditation would continue for another two hours, leaving me with very little to do during that time, so I wasn't really worried about someone walking in on me. I'd asked about the meditation, too—since it really didn't fit with what I knew to be the facts about this alien-parasite cult. She'd told me only that it was a necessary cleansing process for new recruits.)

I found myself unable to use the evacuation unit, since I had no food tube with which to replenish myself, and my body had been well trained never to relinquish what it could not replace. That reminded me; there were no eating cubicles here. Just what was I supposed to live on?

But I used the 'fresher to good advantage, ran the water in the bowl over my hands just to enjoy the sensation of openly running water, and went back to my room, falling asleep on top of my bed, fully clothed.

I had weird dreams, and in my dreams I found myself constantly arguing with or fighting a strange female whose identity was unfathomable. At times it seemed she was my mother, but then again she seemed to be manipulating me as Vernoica had, while yet again she was, perhaps, Lora or Dian. When I saw her face, it was a face I'd never seen before. My final and most lasting memory was that she had drugged me in some way and was dancing about me, unwinding a bolt of cloth in her hands and wrapping it around me. It grew tighter, more constricting, and I was struggling against it, sweating, and—

Something—I didn't know what it was at first—woke me up. My clothes were twisted around my body and were tight and uncomfortable. My face felt sweaty and greasy. My feet were very hot in their bootlets.

Then I heard a board in the hall creak, and I realized I'd heard a similar sound before—that it had been what awakened me. The door rattled as someone turned its knob, and then it swung open, the light from the hall silhouetting a slender body in half-transparent robes.

I sat up as she came into the room. I reached out and fumbled and found the old light switch.

"Hello, Mr. Dameron." It was Lora, and she was carrying a covered bowl of some sort.

"Uh, hello," I said. "Must have dozed off, I guess."

"Did I startle you?"

"No. That's all right, you didn't wake me up." Well, not precisely. "I didn't intend to fall asleep," I added.

She nodded, very seriously, and sat down at the foot of the bed. "I brought you something," she said. "It occurred to me that since you don't—wouldn't—umm, eat with us, that, well. . . ." She flushed. "Maybe it would be easier for you here."

I stared at her with surprised gratitude. I'd been wondering how I'd be able to eat, and she'd brought some food up to my room. "Thank you, Lora," I said. "That was very nice, very thoughtful of you. I *am* hungry. . . ."

"It's mine," she said earnestly. "I wanted to do it."

I didn't understand her. Not yet. "I'll take it down the hall," I said, intending to create an impromptu eating cubicle out of the little room with the appliances.

"I'd rather you did it here," she said. Then she uncovered the bowl.

She thrust the bowl at me and I took it automatically, my fingers closing over it before I'd even noticed the smell, like dry earth and musty, or my eyes had registered the obvious fact that this was no bowl of algae gruel, soup, or stew.

Then I looked at it. Then I saw it.

It was alive.

Dead-white in color, amorphous in shape, jelly-like, moving, pseudopods forming and dissolving in it. Fetid-smelling. *Warm.*

I dropped it. The dish fell to the floor and the—*thing*—flopped from it, squirming. "Oh my God, my God!" I said, leaping to my feet in shock and horror. "Oh sweet God!" I brought my bootheel down hard on the squiggling thing and felt it *squish* slimily underfoot.

"*Oh, no! Oh, stop.*" the girl cried. "*Oh, don't*—please *don't!*"

She threw herself on me, sinking to her knees, her arms

tightening on my legs as I stomped the alien parasite, shock still erupting in my stomach, bile thick in my throat.

"Get off me!" I shouted at her as I ground the white slime into a paste on the floor, still kicking at it. I grabbed a bunch of her hair in my hand and yanked her head back. "Get away from me!" I screamed, tears running down my cheeks.

"Killer!" she cried hysterically, *"murderer!"*

I kicked her in the face, and she fell away from me with a low moan.

Chapter Sixteen

I'd blown it.

In one moment of blind panic, I'd thrown out all my chances for infiltrating the damned church.

I stared at the girl, lying on the floor, her hair loose in the drying chalky film that had been the parasite, blood trickling from her nose. Yeah, and I'd blown it on the parasite, too—on my chances for taking out a live parasite, free of its host. My pulse hammered in my head, and I had trouble seeing clearly. I'd blown it and all that mattered now was to get out.

I went to the door and peered out. I didn't see anyone. If nobody had heard us, me stomping on the floor and Lora screaming at me, if nobody was curious enough to check us out, maybe—just maybe—I had a chance.

I wondered if they might know when a parasite was killed. Hell, I didn't know anything about the damned creatures—just that they extended their own nervous system through the body. Were they telepathic? Did they stay in communication directly? Or was it all through the host-creatures? It seemed important to me, right then, to know. It would give me some idea of the odds on my escape.

I tiptoed down the old hall, keeping to the side, where the boards seemed to creak less. Then I went down the stairs. The top flight was narrow and walled in and turned corners. The lower flight was wide, bannistered, and straight. I made both of them and was in the main hallway before I had my first encounter.

It was the blond guy who'd greeted Lora so passionately. He came out of the meditation room just as I was abreast of the door—we almost collided.

"Oh, hello there. You're the new fellow, right?" He thrust out his hand. "I'm Jim Benford."

I didn't want to take his hand. I didn't want to touch him. In the half-light of the hallway his posture, his expression, even his words seemed titled and odd: *alien*. Somewhere inside this man a white blob the size of my fist had anchored itself, spreading ganglion-thin pseudopods throughout his body. I might even be touching the ends of several such nervelike white threads if I shook his hand. My mind recoiled.

But I did it. I took his hand, giving it only the most minimal quick squeeze. I nodded, and told him my name.

"Stepping out for some air? It's lovely out on nights like this—so crisp-smelling, you know," he said. He gave me a shrewd look. Had Lora told him what she planned?

"Umm, yes," I said. "I have, umm, a decision to make."

It was the right response. He gave me a nod. "I know it can't be easy for you, Tad. But I want you to know, we're all pulling for you." What lurked behind his transparent sincerity?

I mumbled a few appropriate words and pushed out the front door.

The air was chill. "Crisp" has been a euphemism. A wind had come up, and it cut through my thin clothing. The night had a rawness.

My panic ebbed a little. The necessary caution involved in making my escape had quieted it, and my chance encounter—or was it chance?—with Benford had demanded a veneer of calm. But the chill air, and the shivers it produced, soon had me agitated again. Halfway down the path I glanced back up at the house. I couldn't see the window of my room from this side; most of the others were dark. I wondered if everyone was asleep—and how long it would take to spread the alarm among them. By the time I hit the bottom of the hill, I was running.

I started the car and then glanced up through the transparent bubbletop—now completely unpolarized in the absence of sunlight—to see three lights suddenly wink on from the second floor of the house. It seemed to me for a moment that the lights were like the beams of searchlights, probing for me in the outside darkness. I felt a moment of *déjà vu,* and the panic came back, hard. I swung the car around on the empty highway in a tight arc that brought screams from the tires, and accelerated the vehicle like a manned projectile into the night.

The darkness enclosed me on all sides, the wide beam of my driving lights a bar of light that shone down a narrow rectangular tunnel through which I raced. A red light began flashing on my dash, and a buzzer sounded. The car leapt and bounded like an earthbound missile struggling to become airborne. I kept my foot down flat on the go pedal until the red light remained steady and the buzzer was a constant keening sound in my ears. I kept my eyes on the road ahead, flicking them to the rearview screen for only split seconds; it was all I could do to keep the car on the obsolescent highway. But I saw no pursuing lights behind me.

Then I was in Cloverdale, its dimmed lights and sleeping buildings passed in a clangorous jangle. I had to slow as I went into the curve at the south end of town, but at that I'm sure I left long black ribbons of rubber on the wrong side of the road behind me.

When I got up the entrance-ramp and onto the automatic highway, the car slowed itself to half its former speed, the red light on the dash vanished, and the shrill buzzing stopped. I'd done all the running I could. Now all I could do was wait.

It was 02:40 when I turned the car in at Santa Rosa, but Bay Complex was as alive as it would be twelve or sixteen hours later. I found an infomat and placed a direct call to Tucker, in Oldtown Chicago. I wasn't surprised when he came on looking fully awake and functional.

I had to explain my flight from Cloverdale, and the reasons for my call, and it was difficult to put into words the feelings, premonitions and intuitions I'd had. I had to justify the fact that, after less than twelve hours among the aliens, I had left them. I did not go into details about what I'd done; I simply described the parasite and let it go at that.

Tucker sighed, spoke a few mild expletives, and told me to get a room in a local hostelry. Call in my whereabouts to the local Bay Complex office, and he'd have a man out to see me the next afternoon. He seemed calmer than I'd seen him before; the sarcasm was missing, and with it his drawl. He acted almost human.

I found myself a room in a quiet hotel in San Rafael, called in to the local office, and went to sleep. It wasn't easy getting to sleep—I had to resort to ten minutes of public-channel 3–D for a soporific—and when I did, I had long sequences of disturbing dreams each of which culminated in nightmares which jerked me awake, usually in an upright, sitting position, my heart racing as if I'd just run the two-minute mile.

I don't remember the earlier dreams—only that I had them—but the final dream was quite enough for me. It concerned me as a small child, back when I still lived with my real parents. I recognized my mother immediately, but the man who was my father remained caught in the shadows until I followed him, deliberately tagging along after him, to where he could no longer hide his face.

It was Tucker's face.

I screamed when I saw who he was, and the knife-edge of fear sliced through my heart, because I knew, suddenly and certainly, that this was a secret I was not meant to know. Tucker turned and looked at me and his eyes were glowing, rays of light streaming from them, pinpointing me, paralyzing me, holding me.

I wanted to run. I was only a frightened boy and I wanted to run away. But he wouldn't let me. His gaze pinned me down and while fear climbed into my throat and choked my breath, he *smiled* at me. It was a terrible, knowing smile, inhuman—*alien*.

Then he opened his mouth, reached up his hand, bent forward as if to regurgitate into it, and then stood up again, impossibly tall, towering over me.

He held his hand down to me.

In it was a pulsing, living object of translucent white jelly.

It formed a mouth and smiled at me.

I woke up to find myself sitting up in the middle of the bed, my heart pounding and my face streaked with running sweat. The images were still fresh in my mind, the sense of shock still immediate. I thumbed on the light and staggered over to the 'fresher. My mind was confused; I could not distinguish fully between what had really happened and what I had only dreamed. I knew I'd been offered one of those alien slugs—and it seemed at that moment as likely true that it had been offered me by Tucker as that it might have come from Lora.

Why?

I stepped from the 'fresher in the eating cubicle—the reverse of my more usual procedure—and after I had restoked my body I found myself better able to think again.

Item: dreams are commonly understood as a man's attempt to deal with the emotionally unacceptable—or, alternatively, to understand something which he has not yet fully admitted to himself.

Item: I am gifted with a remarkable sense of intuition. Intuition is simply another word for deep-consciousness reasoning powers—for the ability to encompass a wide variety of data and process it unconsciously, receiving the results of that processing as a "hunch" or a "feeling" without conscious reasoning to back it up. I always play my hunches and I'm rarely wrong.

Item: my intuitive powers sometimes work best when my conscious mind is laid low by shock, fatigue, or the like. As it had been, the night before.

Conclusion: I'd observed more than I'd realized. My

deep-consciousness was doing its best to push an emergency response up to where I'd notice it and act upon it. And just what *was* it I'd noticed?

Tucker had been taken over by the aliens.

I had to think of them as aliens now—not simply as human hosts to alien parasites. That notion was too unwieldy. Their behavior was alien, their goals alien. Forget what they *had* been—a *flash of Dian perched on my office console, swinging one leg*—they were *aliens* now. Inhuman, presumably hostile, and incresinngly dangerous.

I'd sensed this all along. Or, more properly put, my deep-consciousness "computer" mind had noticed this quality of *alienness* all along, and had started ringing bells to bring it to my attention as soon as it could.

It was as I'd first told Dian. I'd recognized a quality in Bjonn—a defining quality in all the aliens—which distinguished them from normal humans. A sort of too-intense quality, a behavior which seemed a little out of kilter, responses which didn't seem to quite fit the situations. Their gaze was too direct, too obviously in violation of one's privacy. They spoke too directly, as well—while at the same time usually evading the very questions one asked. Lora—I'd almost come to think of her as human again, on that trip back. She'd made it easy for me to talk to her, or to *want* to talk to her. But—she'd been the one who came at last to seduce me with her alien offering. It made me snort a little at my own naïveté; she'd made me want to talk to her, indeed! She'd probably all but plied me into confessing everything. Who knew what alien mentality directed her now? Who knew what roles she was being manipulated through in order to charm and disarm me?

And now Tucker.

I'd seen it the night before, when I'd spoken to him: the unreasonable calm. The wakefulness at an hour when he, of all people, would be sleeping. The direct gaze. (The infomat diluted the intensity of that direct gaze, but it had been enough to perturb me, somewhere deep.) All the signs were there, but I hadn't been looking for them then; I'd had no idea they'd reached *Tucker*. It had been there, before my eyes, and I had not understood it, not then.

But now I did. And cursed myself. I was a fool.

There was a tap at my door.

I glanced at my chronometer: 13:30, local time. Afternoon. (The room had no windows; the day, therefore, was arbitrary in its divisions. My timepiece said afternoon, so it was afternoon. Had it for some reason stopped hours earlier, I would have found it to be morning.)

A man from the Bureau, then.

I slid back the door and found myself staring into Ditmas' smiling face.

"Hi yuh, Tad," he said.

"What are *you* doing here?"

"They sent me out to see you—to debrief you."

I waved him in and closed the door. "I was expecting a local," I said.

"Sure, I know. I think they figured it would be better to send somebody you knew—know what I mean?" He settled himself on my bed.

"Why here?" I probed. "Why not down at the office?"

"Hmm?" he looked up as if he hadn't heard me. "Why what?"

"Why debrief me here? Do you have a recordomat?"

He shrugged. "You can just tell me," he said. "We'll get the prelims down later."

"No good," I said, shaking my head. I stalked around until I was directly in front of him, looking down at him. Deliberately, I looked him in the eye.

He stood up, suddenly decreasing the distance between us. I think he expected me to step back. I didn't. We were uncomfortably close.

"What's gutting you, Tad?" he asked. His tone was deceptively quiet, deceitfully pleasant. It might've worked, had I not already looked into his eyes and seen the truth.

"You," I said, matching his tone with my own forced calm. No warnings. "You, Ditmas." Then I hit him.

This time there was no panic involved; this time I knew exactly what I was doing.

I was dealing with an alien. That had been a foregone conclusion. Tucker had set me up. I knew too much. If they'd reached Tucker, they'd be all through our Bureau by now, and it was a cinch they'd have the local office.

Ditmas had been a surprise, though. I hadn't been expecting him, and he threw me off for the first few moments—no doubt as they'd expected. *Ol' buddy Ditmas. Pleasant surprise.* Sure.

My fingers were stiff and straight, thumb in, wrist straight, fingertip to elbow one smooth line, as I drove my hand into his upper belly, just under his left rib cage. The nail on my middle finger caught in the fabric of his blouse, and later I found the nail was ripped and torn and it hurt some. Just then he was jackknifing over, his face meeting my updriven knee, the cartilage of his nose smashing into his skull. Something—maybe his jaw or chin—struck the nerve on my knee and strummed it like a hot wire. But I followed through with my other hand: a swift finishing chop on the back of his neck. When I stepped back, he crumpled lifelessly to the floor.

I learned to fight in the den. There were twenty-seven of us, ranging in age from five to twelve. I was not yet seven, and small for my age. I learned that in my position a kid had two choices: either accept the beatings and squeal a little to make the older kids happy, a self-perpetuating sort of misery which one or two of the other kids almost seemed to enjoy—or make it a point to get back at my tormentors so that they'd learn to leave me alone. I opted for the second choice. One of the eleven-year-olds picked a fight with me the first night I was there, while I was lying on a bunk over two other young kids and crying to myself. He grabbed one of my legs and before I had any idea what was happening the floor came up and hit my face. My nose bled and I dripped all over the floor and myself, all the while crying, while the sadistic eleven-year-old worked me over. He was fat, had pimples, and seemed to think it was important to impress upon me the pecking order of the den. The way he saw it, I was bottom man on the list.

I cried myself to sleep that night, and my bunk was filthy with dried brown stains of my nosebleed the next morning. But I waited for my chances, and caught the fat kid in the 'fresher the next afternoon, after calisthenics. I jammed the catch on the door from the outside with my shirt, which I'd taken off for that purpose, and I opened the maintenance locker and changed the setting on the 'fresher controls. I damn near burned that kid alive in flesh-dissolving enzymes, and when I let him out he was missing not only the largest portion of his epidermus—his dermus very shiny and pink—but most of his arrogance toward me. Just to impress the fact on him, I tripped him—an easy task, since he still had his eyes screwed shut—and had the pleasure of watching him smash his own face against the tiled floor.

After that I didn't have too many fights to worry about. Occasionally we'd get a new kid, and if he was older or bigger, he usually felt he had to beat up on someone with a reputation in order to establish his own. Mostly he'd pick me, and usually he'd lose. I was a pragmatic kid and I'd learned in a few easy steps that it wasn't how you played the game; what counted was winning. Don't get me wrong. I wasn't a bully; I was a loner. I let the others alone and all I asked was to be let alone in turn. Since I had to earn this right the hard way, I'd learned the proper methods. And I've never forgotten them.

I stared down at the still figure of Ditmas on the hotel-room floor. I hadn't wanted to kill him. I hadn't realized my own strength.

The last time I'd hit someone else was better than seventeen years ago. I'd still been a kid, then, fighting to keep my own against a bigger kid. I had not raised my hand against a single person since.

It wasn't the same now. I'd reacted as I had years before, but with the power, the muscles, and the frame of a grown man and not a half-grown boy. I'd had sixty pounds additional weight behind my blows, and, truthfully, any one of them might have been enough in itself. Driven deeply enough, and at the right upward angle, a single thrust of the hand under a man's rib cage can rupture his heart. The splintering of a man's nose, if the blow carries bone and cartilage back into his skull, can penetrate his brain. And a precisely placed blow to the nape of the neck can break it. Any one or all, the result was the same. Ditmas wasn't breathing anymore.

Chapter Seventeen

I stared down at the man's body and knew real fear.

This time you've crossed the line, Dameron, a voice inside my head told me. *This is murder.*

I stared down at the man's body. Somewhere within it lurked a white jellied lump of protoplasm, its ganglious pseudopods shriveling at this very moment.

Ditmas was an alien. It wasn't murder; Ditmas was an alien.

Sure, fellow, but he *looks* like a human named Ditmas who worked for the Bureau of Non-Terran Affairs, and you can bet that's the way the police will look at it.

I thought about cutting him open and looking for the parasite. I didn't have the nerve.

I was shaking. I stared down at the man's body and I couldn't see it clearly and then my knees began to buckle. I made it to the bed, sat down on the edge, and then threw up. On Ditmas.

I killed him. What can I do now?

I stared down at the man's body, and I shook with fear.

My body rebelling, I stripped the alien of his identification as Ditmas. I was nearly sick twice more as I moved him about, turned him over, and breathed in the stench of my own vomit and the discharge from his bowels. Once as I shifted him his jaw sagged open and I thought I saw something white in the back of his mouth. I let him fall back as he'd lain before, his face to the floor.

I'd had time to think a little, to turn over the possibilities in my mind. Hotel rooms are cleaned only when the room is unoccupied. If I left the body here, it would register as occupied. Therefore, no cleaners. And probably no discovery of the body for days.

That might give me some time. I'd need it.

I used Ditmas' credit card when I took the tube to Oakland. I used Ditmas' card when I took the HST to Hawawii to the shuttleport. And I used Ditmas' card and Bureau Clearance for the hop up to the Moon.

I'd put a few of the pieces together, you see.

Ditmas had already told me he was going out with the next expedition on the *Longhaul II*, and that it was leaving soon. That meant he'd be expected on the Moon, and that clearance for the trip up was prearranged. What was simpler, then, than for me to take his place?

Farhome.

Everything pointed back to Farhome. The aliens came from Farhome. I had to go there. Farhome was where the answers lay.

Simmons wasn't there this time. My identification as Ditmas took me through the Bio-Customs without delay, however. Then I was on my own. On the Moon.

Did I say Lunaport was small? It had always seemed that way to me: small, cramped, almost provincial. Man's major outpost on the Moon. But Lunaport exists in three dimensions, like some of those new cities they're carving out of nowhere in Africa. Conceived as a cube, rather than a flat map, Lunaport exists almost entirely beneath the lunar surface, twenty levels deep. That doesn't mean much when you stack it against the average city building, Earthside, fifty to a hundred stories high. But Lunaport is a *cube*—more or less; I doubt its perimeters are that geometrically precise—and there are no open avenues, no parkstrips, malls, or canyonlike streets. It's packed densely with little cubiclelike rooms, narrow institutional corridors, and boxlike lifts. It's twenty small cities packed on top of each other.

And me without a native guide.

Fortunately, I didn't have to go blundering into the heart of the city. I was on the surface-level, just below the actual lunar surface, somewhere immediately under the Earth-shuttle landing area. Not too far off would be the interplanetary field, and the *Longhaul II*. I tried to remember the way Simmons had taken me, and how we'd escorted Bjonn from there to here. The day I'd met Bjonn seemed long ago and far away; my memories were flat and sepia-tinted and hard to believe. Had it been only a few months?

I must have shown my indecision. A girl in Bio-Customs uniform stopped and gave me a curious look. "Can I be of help?" she asked. Her smile was warm and concerned.

I gave her a tired smile in reply. I really *was* tired; I hadn't been able to sleep on the hop up. "I want to get over to the *Longhaul II*," I said. "I've been assigned. . . ."

"Oh, yes," she nodded, "you'll be Mr. Ditmas."

I agreed.

"I'll take you over," she said. "It's not far away, but for newcomers it *is* complicated to explain."

"Thanks," I said. "That's very nice of you."

She gave me another smile, her eyes leveling with my own. "I'm glad to," she said. I was too tired to care.

It wasn't far. I vaguely remembered the way, once she had me firmly in hand and led me there. Memories of the sort which pop back up the instant after they're no longer needed; useless for anything but confirmation. I was running on reserve energy, and it felt like I didn't have much left.

We skipped the room where I'd met Bjonn, took a different corridor at that point, and then went through a curious double chamber. Then we were in the interstellar ship.

The knowledge hit me with a jolt of adrenalin.

"This is the ship, isn't it?" I asked. It wasn't exactly a stupid question. The corridor we were now in was of about the same dimensions as the one we'd left, its walls plastic instead of tiled, the floor underfoot no different to tread upon—but the *smell* was different in a subtle way. The air no longer had that almost antiseptic, vaguely ozoned odor. It smelled of men and machines and, yes, even plants. And I knew, because space had always been my dream and I'd studied the published plans for this ship just as I'd heró-worshipped its captain, that this ship carried a mixed crew of fifty-eight, a hydroponics section wherein alga were grown and supplementary oxygen generated, as well as the life-support machinery for the entire globe of the ship. Right now the *Longhaul II* was resting in its cradle, the cradle lowered below the lunar surface, its exit-port (or ports; there were others on other levels and other quadrants) aligned with and sealed to the life-system and corridors of Lunaport. I'd expected something more, though, the first time I stepped aboard an interstellar ship. A subtle throb in the decks under my feet, I suppose, and the patina of journeys between the stars. It was, somehow, mundane—anticlimactic.

"That's right," my guide said. "I'll show you to your quarters, and then I'm sure the Captain will want you to report to him."

"That's it?" I asked. "No more red tape? No additional Bio-Customs check? I'm *here?*" It was at once both more and less real than I'd imagined.

"You just checked through Bio-Customs; didn't you?" she said with a brief laugh. "And I brought you directly here. What more could there be?"

It all seems too easy, I thought.

"Here," I said, echoing her. "Which deck are we on?"

She pointed at an inconspicuous letter on the wall of the intersection we'd just reached. A tightly coiled stair led both upward and below. "This is E Level," she said, confirming the point she'd made visually. "Your quarters are up two levels, on C. You'll find the Captain on A Level, I believe."

I followed her up two levels. E Level is the business level of the ship. The mysterious engines of the Feinberg Drive lurked somewhere beyond the unbreached walls of that featureless corridor. Below were the shops, gardens, and kitchens, as well as the small-craft docks and additional quarters. And above. . . .

It was easy to follow my guide up the tight spiral of the

stair—she was built to be followed upstairs. But you can climb sixteen feet in lunar gravity very quickly, even under such constraining and distracting circumstances. I wondered if the brief climb had put the slight flush in the girl's cheeks.

She showed me to an empty cell with a number on its door. Inside was a double bunk, a mirror on one wall, a set of drawers under it, an audio-only ship's phone, and a prison-like sense of cramped confinement. I wondered if I could live for a period of weeks—hell, months—in that tiny room. I doubted it, even then.

She pointed out the phone. "You'd best call up; I don't know when the Captain was expecting you."

I threw my bag on the lower bunk and nodded. I didn't know either. "Thanks again," I said.

She gave me a wistful look that said she was open to an invitation to linger, but I was too tired to intercept it. I let her innocent green eyes gaze unblinkingly into mine for a moment, and then turned and picked up the phone. I heard her expelling her breath as I punched the code thoughtfully listed on the wall for Captain Lasher. When I turned around again, she was gone.

I was tempted to do a little exploring first. The memory of the plans I'd studied as a boy were sharp in my mind, the different colors that coded the different sections of the ship were as vivid now as they'd been those many years before when I'd translated them into one of many scale models.

But maps do not the territory make. My model was just a thing of plastics and thermal joints; *this* was the *Longhaul II*. As I went back out into the corridor again, I felt something of the old thrill seize me again.

I was walking the decks of an interstellar ship.

But I had the time to do my exploring later. Right now I was up to see the Captain, to officially check in. For a fleeting moment while I'd spoken to him on the phone, I'd wondered if he might remember me from that day when Simmons and I had been part of the reception committee. But there was no good reason for him to recall my face.

I'd been one of a horde of greeters, lost among the men from the media. I'd never even spoken to him.

I swarmed up the stair to the A Level and found myself in a large, almost dark room. Directly overhead were stars; for a moment I had the heart-stopping fear that I had somehow blundered out onto the lunar surface. Foolish, of course; I was in the control room of the *Longhaul II*. The A Level was but a single vast room. Somewhere nine levels below was the torch of the Feinberg Drive, aimed at the Moon's core.

I glanced around. Consoles and recliners rimmed the gloom of the vast (or so it seemed, after my tiny bunkroom) room. The viewport overhead was immense, a transparent dome through which I could see not only the starry night above—incredibly rich blackness punctured by a million pinpoints of colored light—but also the distant rim of the lunar crater with Earth beyond it, either just rising or just setting. It was a jewel in a priceless setting.

"Quite a sight," commented a dry voice from somewhere behind me, Captain Lasher's voice.

"It is," I said. My voice was hushed, involuntarily. This was *my* church. Reluctantly, I turned.

The glow of his console unit was a spot of light in the darkness of the deck, and I saw his figure silhouetted against it. He was leaning toward me from a recliner. I moved across the deck toward him almost like a man in a trance. I was lucky there was nothing in my path. Had there been, I would have stumbled over it. I was conscious with every step of the tapestry of space hanging so closely over my head—and also of the immediate confrontation with Captain Lasher, my boyhood idol.

"Ditmas reporting, sir," I said, when I approached him.

His expression was hard to read in the dim light. The console's lights behind him seemed to cast a reddish halo around his head. He looked stern, "Ditmas, is it?" he said.

"Yes sir," I said. "Bureau of Non-Terran Affairs." I expected something on the order of "Glad to have you aboard, Ditmas," from him. Instead:

"I think not, Mr. Dameron. I think this charade had played itself out."

My mouth went dry, and my tongue felt glued to my palate. "I, uh, Dameron, sir?"

"Let's don't run a bluff, Dameron," Lasher said. "You have an old friend here." He gestured.

A shape peeled itself loose from a recliner I'd thought empty; it had been facing three-quarters away from me. It was still too dark for me to make the man out, but I recognized his voice, of course.

"Your journey to the stars is over now, Dameron," Bjonn said. "This is as far as you go."

PART THREE

REPOSSESSED

Chapter Eighteen

In retrospect it was easy to see; I'd been blind to miss it.

Of course Bjonn had spread his parasites among the ship's crew. He'd had months in which to do it: months in which to win them over, subtly, insidiously, starting first with just one of them, the weakest and most easily swayed. Possibly it had been a woman. Then with the help of his first convert, another, and then others, pairs perhaps, and then larger groups. The ship was a microcosmic society. Once he had won over the important people, or perhaps just the bulk of the personnel, his battle was won. The rest was easy—perhaps even a matter of simple force. I wondered why I hadn't seen it.

And then Lunaport. When Bjonn came to Earth, he left behind fifty-eight men and women who were now controlled by the alien parasites. Lunaport too was a closed system, a somewhat larger microcosmic world from which there was no escape. Perhaps they started with the Bio-Customs Department. Their aid would be helpful, after all.

I looked back on the memory of the girl who had so efficiently guided me aboard the ship. They'd been expecting me. She was one of them. *Why hadn't I seen it then?*

Because I was tired, and the girl was too distractingly female. I'd misinterpreted her looks at me. *Where's that much-vaunted talent of yours now, Dameron?*

They took me into custody. Bjonn had a hand-weapon, a device which fired a chemical spray. I recognized it as part of the ship's stores. The chemical, he assured me, penetrated directly through the skin. It would paralyze my nerves. If it struck me in the wrong place, it might kill me. He pointed this out more in tones of regret than anger; he told me he hoped I would not cause him to use the weapon.

"So why threaten me with it?" I asked. "You've got me; isn't that enough?" He was marching me back to the cell-like cubicle in which I'd stowed my bag and briefly considered home.

"You're a dangerous psychopath, Dameron," he said. "You've already killed one man—yes, we know all about Ditmas—and we don't propose to let you try it again." He ushered me back into the bunkroom.

"You've got your way of looking at it," I said, the nervous, physical and emotional exhaustion all crowding into my voice, "—I've got mine. Don't call me names, *alien*."

He gave me a strange look and started to slide the door shut.

"Wait a minute," I said.

He paused, the weapon still directed at me through the half-closed door. "What is it?" he asked.

"What are you going to do with me?" I asked. I was wondering why they were putting me into this cell—*aboard the ship*. For a moment, my heart leapt with wild surmise.

"We're taking you back to Earth," he said, dashing my last hopes.

I felt exhaustion sweep over me. "I'm surprised you aren't disposing of me here," I said. "It would seem to serve your purposes better." *They weren't going to let me make the trip, after all. I wasn't going to see real space.*

"Your mind is an endless source of melodramatic claptrap," Bjonn said. He looked about fed up, probably with me. "We're holding you here until we can get clearance for a special shuttle back to Earth. Then we'll be taking you down. Is that all you wanted to know?" He began sliding the door panel shut again.

"A special shuttle?" I said. "You bastards must have worked your way all the way up to the top."

The door closed shut.

I passed the time in dreamless sleep. I slept for fourteen hours, by my chronometer. But I still felt drained and exhausted when they opened the door again and took me out. There were three men—Bjonn, and two who were strangers to me. All carried the same weapons. All looked deeply annoyed with me. They answered my few questions in monosyllables, and didn't pursue the topics I'd raised. Mostly I wanted to know what they were going to do to me, and mostly they said I would find out soon enough.

I had passed beyond fear to a kind of exhausted stoicism. I moved like a puppet in another person's dream, going through the motions demanded of me. My curiosity remained, but it was a blunted emotion, rather like that of a bewildered child. The last time I'd felt that way was when they'd taken me away from my parents. This time I was dry-eyed, though—if that was any improvement.

I had been caught, well and fairly caught. I had penetrated to the core of their conspiracy, and now they had me. I wondered what they planned for me, but it was an abstracted, intellectual curiosity. There were only two things they could do to me now: either they could kill me or take me over, turning my body into a host for one of their jelly-like parasites. Either way, *I* would be dead. It wouldn't matter much.

Oh, I'd thought brave and heroic thoughts, back in that cell before I'd fallen asleep in the midst of their jumble. I'd thought of somehow dramatically warning the world, or bursting into the Executive Session in Geneva to herald the parasites and the doom they brought—but it was all public 3–D nonsense, and a little beyond even that. Daydreams: thriller stuff. It was all of a piece, I realized bitterly, with my dreams for a career in deep space; in the end it was only nonsense. I wasn't going to warn anyone, because, first *they* wouldn't let me—and, second, pretty soon now there would probably not be anyone left to *warn*.

I'd done a little elementary math, and it frightened me.

One man brings one parasite. God only knows how fast the things multiply, but I could assume no less than one a day. Bjonn had given one to Dian one day, and two to her friends the next. (Although the second of those might have been Dian's contribution—how fast did the pasty little slugs settle in before they started to breed again?) So work it out. One man the first day. Two the next. Four the next. Keep doubling. Do it every day for several months. The sum gets astronomical pretty fast; no wonder they'd gotten to Tucker. I wondered if anyone over his head was still human yet.

Oh, sure, there must be millions—even billions—they hadn't gotten to yet. People exist in pockets, and the recruitment program wasn't flawless. There had to be delays and snags. The whole world wasn't gone yet. Just the best part of it.

Heroics are for the 3–D. In real life I'd be lucky, unbelievably lucky, just to keep my own personality alive.

Simmons was there to see me off. He stared at me with alien and unwavering eyes, his face devoid of expression. I felt sorry for the poor son of a bitch. At least he'd been a prig before—when he'd been human. I felt real pity for him. Anything was better than this.

The shuttle was empty except for me and my captors. I suppose I should've felt honored, but I didn't.

We took seats in the public lounge—no nonsense about the private berths this time. A shame, despite my lack of any real appetite, it had been a long time since I'd eaten.

"You're treating a plain old Level Seven Agent pretty special, aren't you?" I asked Bjonn. Mostly I was just jabbing in the dark. I didn't expect to get much of a rise from him.

"Oh, you are special, Tad," he said somberly.

"Tell me about it," I suggested. *Talk to me, alien.*

"What made you think you could get away with it?" he said.

"With what?"

The gymballed seats swung gently from horizontal to vertical. I glanced at the narrow viewport. Soon the Moon's arid surface would come into view. Just now there was nothing but lights and darkness; the lights swung past in a blur.

"With this Farhome nonsense," he said. "Passing yourself off as Ditmas. How long did you plan to keep the impersonation going?"

"It wouldn't have mattered, once we were underway," I said. "They wouldn't have aborted the trip."

"I see," he nodded. "Ditmas—Farhome—it was all just an excuse."

"An excuse?" I echoed.

"To get into space. Into *real* space." He seemed to be sneering at me.

"I figured that maybe on Farhome. . . ." I let my voice trail off.

"Yes? What? What did you expect to find on Farhome, Dameron?"

"Some answers," I mumbled.

"I didn't hear that." A vibration had started up in the shuttle rocket. I felt it more than I heard it.

"Answers," I said, more distinctly. "I was looking for answers."

"What were your questions, Dameron?" Bjonn asked, his voice relentlessly probing at me.

I turned my head away from him and stared out the viewport. I'd never watched during a liftoff. Now I could.

"I asked you," Bjonn repeated, "what were the questions you thought you'd find answers for on Farhome?"

I ignored him. Beyond the port the distant ridge on the strangely close horizon was a sun-washed slate-gray. A black needle shadow pointed directly toward the ridge, its broad base disappearing beneath the viewport. It divided the pocked lunar landscape neatly into two equal sections. As I watched, the ridge seemed to shift position, to fall back a little, and I realized that what I was actually seeing was the point of the black shadow racing across the flat moonscape toward the ridge. For a moment the shadow stood free and I could see it in its entirety: exaggeratedly long trunk, stubbed wings at nose and tail; stretched out but shrinking by the moment. The ridge dropped suddenly away, no longer anywhere close to the horizon, the shadow over it in one ripple and darting out of the sawtooth shadows of the ridge to race over the floor of the Moon as an ever-tinier splinter of darkness. Beyond, the Earth rose sharply in the deep blackness of the sky, and then disappeared above my vision. We passed over into the nightside of the Moon.

"You don't know, do you?" Bjonn said, breaking the silence. "You really don't know why you wanted to go to Farhome."

I tore my eyes away from the viewport. "I know," I said. "Tell me."

"You're an alien," I said. "Your body is possessed by an alien slug, a parasite. It's taken over your nervous system. *You*—Bjonn, the human being—don't exist. The *you* I'm talking to is an alien creature—like everyone else aboard this shuttle. So tell me why I should tell you anything?" Did I have the creature just a little worried?

Looks passed between Bjonn and my other captors. I didn't attempt to translate them.

"You were going to Farhome, then, because that's where you figure it all started?" he asked.

"That's right," I said. Did he look relieved? What else was he afraid I might have thought of?

"Dameron," he said, "you're one of the most mentally unstable people I've ever met—and, believe me, I have met a few other extreme cases on Earth besides yours. Is your rampant paranoia so strong—are you so completely compulsive about space?—that rather than travel a few miles to ask your questions, you'd make a trip of many light-years? Do you realize that if you'd made that trip, the earliest you could have returned here would have been a matter of some thirty years? Did you expect events to stand still, to wait for you those thirty-odd years?"

Oddly enough, what flashed through my mind when he said that was an image of Dian; I could not imagine her thirty years older. "Is that your line?" I asked. "I'm a nut? Is that the way you plan to handle your opposition? By classifying me mentally unstable? How very pat for you, and you're not even a licensed shrink. Are you going to have me put away somewhere, worked over chemically, electrically, and all the rest? Or will you simply force one of those slugs on me and lobotomize me that way?"

Bjonn gave me a patronizingly pitying look, and turned

away. I was just as happy; it gave me a little more time to gaze out the viewport at space. I wouldn't have another opportunity and I wanted to make the most of this one.

Time passed, and yet more time. I stared out the viewport and saw nothing—a nothing that extended across the infinity of the known and unknown universe. Scattered like glitter across the black and empty nothing were tiny and incredibly distant stars, pumping their energy out into nothing: slowly, infinitesimally, inexorably running down. Entropy. Out of nothing: something. And out of something, a return to nothing. One day the universe would run down and stop. Well, at least I'd never see it. I'd starve first. Much sooner.

I complained to Bjonn, and his reply was typical of him. "You're the most compulsive man about food that I've ever met," he said. "If the world was populated with nothing but people who thought as you do, it would come to a quick end."

"It wouldn't become dominated by *your* types," I said, bitterly.

"Tad, do you honestly think that mankind always ate its food in the rigid, obsessive manner it does today? Or even that a man *should?*"

"Eating is a private and personal act," I said. "There's nothing more private and personal than eating."

"Not even elimination—umm, 'evacuation' I believe is your word?"

I felt the blood leaving my face and hands. "You have a filthy mouth," I said.

"Do I?" he replied. "I wish you'd think about that—about your choice of phrases."

I did. When the implications sank in, I decided I'd been even more appropriate in my choice of words than I'd first thought. I said as much.

Bjonn sighed. "You know," he said, after a pause. "I wonder if you realize that there is not one eating cubicle on all of Farhome. Had you thought of that?"

"No," I said. "How could I know?"

"You could have asked. You might even have inferred it, from what you knew of me."

"I should have realized," I said, only half seriously. "You aliens never eat."

He didn't see the joke. "You're a fool," Bjonn said. His face was flushed and he looked more angry than I'd ever seen him. "You've lived from infancy on a diet of tasteless, tube-fed pap. You've never left the teat. You connect yourself to an 'evacuation unit' and your entire alimentary tract is plugged in, part of the circuit of an obscenely sterile machine. You're a product of conditioned reflexes, of compulsive habit patterns. No wonder you're so deeply neurotic! The wonder is that *everyone* isn't as sick as you are.

"You think yours is the only way! You have the audacity to suggest that if we don't eat as you do, that we must not eat at all. And that from you—from an algae-eater who has never tasted fresh-cooked meat, never chewed crisp raw vegetables, whose palate has never known flavor, never savored the delicacy and the vigor of real food, of anything but homogenized pap! Your food, Dameron—do you know what it is?" A vein throbbed on the side of his forehead. His eyes were burning with intensity. "Your precious food is grown in algae vats. And you know what nourishes those vats, Dameron? Your own feces—your own wastes. Sewage: that's what you eat, Dameron, and that's what you are—you're a closed circuit, *a sewer!*"

One of the others reached out a hand and touched Bjonn's arm. He said something too low for me to hear. Bjonn stopped himself, and I watched him brake his emotions to a shuddering halt. Slowly the violent color left his face, and the vein receded. His expression softened. He laughed a weak laugh, a timid bark.

"Sorry, Dameron," he said. "You've just had a concrete demonstration. I'm as human as you are. It just takes me a little longer to get wound up." His voice shook a little.

"No," I said, shaking my head. "I don't think so. But it was a nice try. You almost had the part down cold."

His eyes, when he locked them on mine, were as gray and cold as a winter sky.

Chapter Nineteen

There were two men waiting for us when the Shuttle landed. One was Tucker. *The other was—Ditmas.*

Both gazed at me as a scientist might at a misbehaving guinea pig: condescendingly, but with annoyance and concern.

I couldn't take my eyes off Ditmas. "You said I killed him," I breathed in an undertone at Bjonn. The alien from Farhome was standing closely at my side. *"You said he was dead."*

"You *did* kill him, didn't you, Tad?" he replied.

"I *thought* I did."

Ditmas stepped forward. "Hello, Tad," he said. His voice seemed choked, and I had the fleeting thought that this was not Ditmas at all, but a ringer brought in to confuse me. In the next instant, however, I knew with chilling certainty that the man was indeed Ditmas, whom I'd killed and left without ID in a San Rafael hotel room. His nose was pink and purple: pink where new flesh had somehow grown, and purple tinged with yellow-green where the bruises remained. Somehow he'd been brought back to life and carefully repaired.

"Ditmas is another little advertisement," Bjonn said, "for our way of life." He accented the last word a little to underline the intentional irony of what he'd said.

"Hello, Ditmas," I said. I wondered what else I could say. "I—I'm glad you're not dead."

"Yes," said Tucker, joining the conversation, "it takes a certain responsibility off you shoulders, doesn't it?"

It took a while for that one to sink in. I'd been living with the thought of myself as a murderer for a matter of what my chronometer assured me had been days, now. I hadn't liked it, but I accepted it. I had killed a man. I felt no pride in the accomplishment, but I accepted it as an additional fact in my internal reference file on Tad Dameron. Along with the statistics of my height, weight, spectrum, age, and so on, next to my other achievements to date, I'd entered the notation *struck and killed Ditmas,* along with the hour and date. And, lurking in the back of my mind all the while, the unspoken correlative of *apprehended for murder on the ——th day of the ——th month of the year ——*. The blanks had just been waiting to be filled in.

But Ditmas wasn't dead.

I felt a weight lifted from my head and shoulders, as I processed and assimilated the new data. *Ditmas wasn't dead.*

"You're right," I told Tucker. "It makes it a little easier for me to live with myself."

I surprised a startled look on Bjonn's face, a look that spread in ripples of relayed reaction to the others, Tucker last among them, his eyes momentarily widening a little as he noted it.

Then I added, "It's nice to know that, in addition to your other talents, you can't be killed. Makes world conquest a little easier, doesn't it?"

Tucker narrowed his eyes at me and resumed his once-characteristic pose of shucks-now cynicism. The only difference now was that he was better at it, and it fit him less well.

They took me to Bay Complex in an official aircraft. I didn't try to talk to them. I felt surrounded by my personal demons: Bjonn, the original alien, the one who'd taken Dian; Tucker, the father-figure I hated; and Ditmas, the good buddy who had everything going for him where I didn't, the one who had turned death back into life. Once they'd been human beings—or at least there had been a time when I'd thought of them that way—but now they were alien figures, the symbols of my torment, and they had me boxed. I tried not to think about what they'd do to me, at journey's end.

We were met by an official Bureau car, big and black

and built to seat eight. Counting the driver, my captors and the two guards who'd accompanied me from the *Longhaul II*, we were seven. They let me have the back seat all for myself.

The day was drab and dreary. Long banks of fog rolled against the mountains, higher clouds scudded low across the sky, and above them hung a dismal overcast. Someone had put a gray lid on the world, and all the color was draining out. I felt gray myself.

It started to rain while we were still heading north on the automatic highway. The front spoiler buffeted most of the rain up and over the car, but the windshield still picked up spray. The side windows were useless, streaked with water on the outside, misted with condensation on the inside. It didn't change the view much; the grayness just became more blurred. The men on the seat facing mine— my two nameless guards—stared past me at the back window as if they might somehow see something beyond it. Their eyes grew fixed and unfocused.

The tires sang monotonously on the wet pavement, somehow counting each tiny drainage groove as it was crossed, and adding it to their soprano tone. The air inside the car was close and a little too warm. It wadded up in my head. I felt life and purpose draining out of me, leaving me a husk, an empty shell, a zombi-creature waiting for its jelly-like new tenant.

Then the tune dipped and deepened, the car slowed its head-long pace, and we were rolling down the exit ramp. Cloverdale. Again.

It came to me then, how close I was—to total and utter defeat. I had already given up—it was hard to know when I'd first given up—but always I'd sensed a grace period, a little time yet before the end.

Now the time was running out.

I did not shift my position, but I felt myself growing alert. From somewhere deep inside me nerves were drawing taut, muscles coiling. My brain came awake. I felt myself poised on the edge of eternity. Below was a bottomless black gulf. There was no other side. I was all but balanced on that edge. Could I cheat eternity? Could I move back again without losing my footing and falling?

The blackness seemed to rise up, like a thing alive—like no thing alive—totally empty, totally devouring.

A part of me accepted it, and was willing to meet it. I felt at once supercharged with energy, and very weary. Things had to break soon. The balance had to shift—in one direction or the other.

And we were already through Cloverdale.

The big car jounced and swayed on the old road, but its tires still keened to themselves, and the distance grew quickly shorter. A couple of miles? A mile? Half a mile?

The driver swore out loud. The car slowed, went into a momentary skid that threw the rear out across the road and then swung it back in again, and then stopped. I peered forward. Both my guards angled in their seats for a look.

"This damned rain," the driver was saying. "These cars aren't built for such slow speeds; the rain-shield doesn't work." The front windows were heavily beaded with water.

"Use your manual wipers," Tucker said. His voice was peevish. "That's what they're there for."

"That's just it," the driver complained. "They're not working. I've gone this far, but now I just can't see well enough. I'll have to get out and clean the windshield myself." His tone indicated that this was not his job and it was a damned shame someone else hadn't volunteered to do it.

The guards were still looking forward. I took my chance. With one foot on the crumbling edge of the black abyss, I made my leap. I was out the door and into the roadside drainage ditch in one quick jump. The ditch wasn't part of the plan—but then, I hadn't much plan. I stumbled, rolled over, and was on my feet again without pause. Behind me I heard exclamations and a heavy grunt. Doors were popping open.

A hand closed on my ankle as I was scrambling up the low embankment beyond the ditch. Fear clutched my vitals in the same moment. I kicked backward with my free foot and felt the solid connection. The hand let go; the fear did not.

I didn't look back. Rain was falling all around me, and the light was muted, as at dusk. The palms of my hands were gritty with mud and my legs were streaked with it. I ran.

Tall dead grass whipsawed at my legs. My feet stumbled over the hidden furrows of the uneven ground. I was running blindly, without any backward glances, but there was some sense in the course I'd picked. The land fell away in a downward slope, and no more than forty yards ahead trees threw up a barrier against the broken field. There, at least, I might find cover. Beyond that I had no idea.

A sharp pain started lancing my chest with every gulp of air I took through my open mouth. My gasps were a roaring noise in my own ears. I felt doomed to ineffectuality, like a runner trapped in a nightmare.

I crashed in through the trees, ripping my thin tunic on a shrub of some sort. It was already wet enough to fall apart. I kept on running, blundering between the trees as they grew thicker, caroming from one to another, heedless in my panic. Then I tripped, and fell headlong.

I let out a cry—half a sob of anguish, half a forced exhalation—and then lay silent. Around me, water dripped in random patterns from leaf to leaf. I was lying amid the curled brown leaves of summer. They were soggy. It was almost winter now.

The woods were quiet. As I subdued my heavy breathing and tried to force my mind out of its desperate panic, I heard no sounds of pursuit.

Carefully, fearfully, I rolled over onto my back and sat up. When I was a boy in the den they used to kid me about the bottom bunk. You had to look out for the things that lived under the bottom bunk, they said. It sure was too bad about the guys who had to sleep on the bottom bunk. I had the bottom bunk. I knew there was nothing under it. Nothing but tile and plastic and maybe dust. But when the lights were out I had to steel myself to reach over the edge with my hand. Things *might* lurk in the dark unseen.

I felt that way now.

I didn't want to see what was behind me. I was afraid

to look. I was afraid that when I turned over the first sight I would see would be Bjonn's impassive face. Or, worse, a grinning Ditmas, just standing there. Right behind me. Right over me. I didn't think anyone was there—I hadn't *heard* anyone—but I had to steel myself to roll over and look.

Nobody was there.

I felt like laughing, but I didn't laugh. I had the idea I was on the verge of hysterics. Putting my hand out on the wet trunk of a tree, I climbed cautiously to my feet. As soon as I put weight on it, my right ankle protested. In shooting spasms it informed me that I'd twisted it, and pulled or sprained it. I told it to shut up.

Where were they?

They wouldn't just let me run off without doing anything about it. They couldn't. They had to be planning something. If they weren't chasing around after me, playing this wet game of hide and seek in the weeds, it had to be because they had a better way of catching me. An easier way.

I wondered what it was.

I thought of going out to the edge of the trees for a look, and that's about as far as I went in that direction; I gave it a thought. Then I started hobbling in the opposite direction, still downhill, deeper into the woods. Overhead, the rain made pitter-pattering noises on the leaves that sounded like hundreds of tiny animals scurrying this way and that. I wondered for a moment if they were running messages, keeping tabs on me. I wondered if there was any reason why the alien parasites had to restrict their jellied presence to human hosts. But that was a dark and alarming fantasy, and I shut it out before it had me believing in it. The rainy woods were too dark, too gloomy, for thoughts of tiny scampering spies to be at all amusing.

The land dipped, suddenly, into a narrow fold through which a stream ran. I made my way down to its bank, old and mossy, knit together by gnarled and naked tree roots, and stared at the rushing water.

It was neither a broad stream nor a deep one. But the

bed was at least four feet below the overhanging bank in most places, and sometimes more. I looked down and thought about the mud and dirt with which I was covered, but I had no very strong inclination to clamber down that bank and wash myself in the stream. Romantic notions from the 3–D aside, the water looked cold, even colder than I felt, and I was already chilled to the bone and wet through. The thought of jumping down on my sprained ankle didn't encourage me either.

I had the choice of turning upstream or down.

I turned downstream, to my left. That meant north, away from Cloverdale, and somehow that seemed backward to me. North is *up* on the maps, and rivers flowed south. But nobody ever told this stream that.

The way along the bank wasn't difficult. The leafy trees—almost equally divided between those which held their leaves and those which hadn't—thinned out and were mixed with and almost replaced by evergreens. Here and there the mossy bank was carpeted with a spongy layer of needles.

I hadn't gone far when I glimpsed a building through a gap in the trees ahead. I stopped and peered at it for a better look. I couldn't see much, however, so I went on.

The stream twisted, made a deep bend, and then I found myself staring at a rustic sort of dwelling which might have come right out of an earlier century—maybe even pioneer times.

It was built of weathered wood in a small clearing just above the stream, its uncovered siding silvered and warped by age and exposure. Its roof, low and peaked, was shingled with splits of a darker wood. It stood on stubby footings that looked almost like the stumps of felled trees; its underside was open. Cut firewood was stacked along and just under one side. Blue smoke drifted lazily from its stone chimney, curling slowly up and then flattening into a layer of thin haze only yards above the gable.

Someone's refuge in the country. I debated approaching it; I feared taking the chance of going inside it. But I did. I climbed the wooden plank steps to its porch almost furtively, and pushed against the old hinged door. It moved open.

The house had no electricity; the large single room was lit by a burning lamp of some sort. There was also a fire in the fireplace, but it was half coals. A woman was sitting in a chair, doing something with her hands and moving her shoulders rhythmically. She had her back to the door, and to me.

The fire in the fireplace sprang up, and the lamp guttered. But she must have already heard me, or felt the breath of cool damp air against the back of her neck. Her face in shadow, she half turned. "Who is it?" she asked in a curiously muffled voice.

"I'm sorry," I said, hesitantly. "I didn't mean to intrude—I mean, to just walk in, but I saw the smoke from your chimney, and. . . ."

"Come in, then, Mr. Dameron," she said. She turned the rest of the way. The light silhouetted her puffy lips, and cast a highlight on a livid bruise that ran along her jawline.

"Hello, Lora," I said. An elevator in my gut began to sink.

"Come in," she repeated, her swollen lips blurring her words. "Close the door, please. It's damp and growing chilly out."

I closed the door and moved further into the room. I could feel the heat from the fireplace, but it was like an unreal phantom, nibbling at the edges of my chilled reality. It didn't warm me. I was very cold.

She saw me better then, as I entered the pool of light shed by her lamp, and her expression seemed to melt and change. "What's happened to you?" she asked. The softness had returned to her voice.

I shrugged. "I was in the woods. In the rain."

"I can see that. But your clothes—they look like you ran into an old barbed-wire fence! And you're covered with mud and dirt! You look like a wild man. Have you been in the woods all this time?"

"All which time?"

"Since . . . since you ran away."

"No," I said. "That was—days ago." I couldn't tell how many days. I always lose my sense of time when I leave Earth. I glanced at my chronometer. It was broken. It had stopped at 15:52. Hours ago.

"Well, you *look* like you've been out there for days," she said.

"Just a few hours," I said. "But it felt longer." I sidled up near the fire, putting my back to it. "I didn't expect to find *you* here," I added.

"I can understand that," she said. For a moment anger flooded her eyes. Then it washed away. "But now," she said, "we're both here. Full circle, you might say."

"I—I'm sorry," I said, "about what I did to you, I mean." I couldn't keep my eyes off her face. "I didn't want to hurt you."

"No, but you did," she said. "Why, Mr. Dameron? Why did you hurt me?"

I felt my shoulders sag. I was losing my last dregs of energy. "I don't know exactly," I said.

"Tell me about it," she said. Her hands had returned to her lap and a peculiar garment which she seemed to be weaving with two thin sticks and a ball of heavy thread or twine. Her hands moved with a rhythm and life of their own. She seemed to ignore them.

"I'd like to," I said, "but how can I trust you?"

She looked up and her eyes met mine. "Don't you think that's a peculiar question for *you* to ask, Mr. Dameron? Who, after all, has trusted whom? And who has broken that trust?"

Chapter Twenty

"You're an alien," I said.

"I'm not," she said.

"Somewhere inside your body," I said, "an alien parasite has nestled itself. It has extended itself in ganglionlike threads throughout your body . . . including your brain. And it controls you. It thinks for you. It *is* you. And it—you—the others, they're starting to take over. . . ."

"No," she said. "You're wrong. You're completely wrong. I am myself, the same person I always was. I'm just better now, more whole, more complete. I'm a better person; I'm not a different person. Don't you know that yet?"

I wanted to believe her. I wanted, desperately, to understand her and to believe her. And I wanted the warmth of the room and of her own personality to displace the terrible cold that inhabited my body. I shivered a little as I spoke, and I bit my words out: "How can I believe you?" I asked. "How can I trust you, knowing what I do?"

"What do you know?" she asked in turn. "Lab tests, medical reports? Do you even know all that was in them?"

I shook my head. "But I know what I saw. . . ."

She shared my memory for a moment and her face paled. The bruise was very ugly. "You killed it," she said. "I made it and gave it to you, and you killed it."

"Can you blame me?" I cried out. I felt my own guilt, my own anguish, tearing loose from me. I felt hysterical. I was shivering uncontrollably.

"Tell me *why*," she demanded. "Tell me *why* you did it."

"I—couldn't help myself," I said. My teeth were chattering.

She shook her head as if to clear it from a bad dream, then looked up at me again. "You're still cold," she said, as if surprised.

"Y-yes," I said. I was shaking badly.

She rose from her chair, neatly placing her work on it. She came closer to me. "You're still wet," she said. "Wet and filthy," she added, in an aside. "We've got to get you out of those rags and cleaned up." She reached out and before I could stop her, she ripped my tunic right off me. It was already in soggy tatters; it all but fell apart in her hands. "Come on," she said. "Get the rest off."

I turned to watch her as she went to a cupboard of some

sort and took down a large plastic tub. It was three feet in diameter, and at least two feet deep. She put it on the floor next to my feet. "You can help," she said. "Get those things off your feet and take off your kirt."

I bent over and slipped loose the lacings on my bootlets. They were wet and caked with mud. My feet, when I touched them with my fingers, were dead cold, and numb. I couldn't wriggle my toes at all. My ankle was swollen and bruised.

Lora reached inside the fireplace and swung out a metal arm, from which hung a steaming kettle. At my questioning glance, she said, "I keep water hot. It's nice to have; you never know when you'll need it." She gave her words an ironic emphasis.

Strangely, the chill had already lessened its hold on me before she finished undressing me and had me stand in the empty tub. She dipped a towel of some sort in the kettle and wrung it out. I watched her do it, and although steam drifted up from the mouth of the kettle, the fact that she'd handled the towel left me unprepared for the scalding heat of it. She threw it over my shoulders, and I almost screamed.

She paid no attention to my reactions, but began rubbing and sponging me with the towel, starting with my head and neck—all but suffocating me in its steamy folds while she cleaned my face—and then working down. She did it swiftly, competently, and without apparent emotion, pausing only to frequently rinse and wring out the towel again. Water trickled down my legs and collected in the tub at my feet.

At first the wet warmth only penetrated my outer layers: a stinging heat, it became gradually a deeper, more relaxing warmth. Blood returned to the shell of my skin and left it pink and flushed. Electrical pins kept pinching at my feet as the water rose around them.

She washed me, scrubbed me, and rubbed me, and somewhere along the line the chills left me, and I became very drowsy, almost stuporous. I have the vague memory of being told to lift my feet, and then of setting them down on something dry. My next memory is that of lying in a

bed. It was warm and cosy in the bed, and when I shifted
my weight from one shoulder to the other, I encountered
another warm body. It felt soft and comfortable, and I felt
no alarm as I drifted back again into sleep.

I had a dream. It was long and involved, and most of
it I can't remember, but I do recall that it concerned my
mother. I was very young, and yet, as is the way with
dreams, I was a grown man at the same time. My father
did not appear in the dream, but I had a sister. We shared
a room and slept together, in the same bed. The part I
remember is this. We were lying on our sides, facing each
other, and we were kissing. Long, slow, oral kisses. Our
tongues were touching and I felt at once very wicked and
very delighted. My sister's tongue pulled back from mine
and I knew she was going to do something. I didn't know
what it was, but I was feverish with anticipation. Then,
suddenly, our mother entered the room, throwing on the
lights and confronting us. She was very angry, and she
shouted at us and called us names. We'd jerked apart of
course, and I felt disappointed and angry because my mother
had spoiled it—whatever "it" was to have been. I wanted
to scream back at her, but then she told us that we were
evil and that because of that she was going to give us away.
She was going to give us to a den.

I woke up tense and rigid, Lora's hand on my arm.

"What is it, Tad? What's wrong?"

Across the room the gray dawn looked wan in the un-
draped, unpolarized windows. The room was cold. I pulled
the heavy covers back up over my shoulders. "A—dream,"
I said. "That's all. Just a dream." I felt as if something had
happened to me—or was about to happen . . . something
profound. Somewhere deep inside me, something had been
resolved. I'd made a decision.

"What were you dreaming about?"

I couldn't look at her. "You, I think. You were my sister.
That doesn't make any sense."

"Maybe it does." She yawned and stretched, raising her
arms over her head, then quickly slipping back under the

covers. "Maybe you've made a decision," she said. Her words came so close to my own thoughts that they startled me.

"What decision is that?"

"That you can trust me. Did you feel that way about me in your dream—when I was your 'sister?'"

"Yes," I said reluctantly.

She rolled over and stared at me. Our eyes were on a level when I turned my head toward her. We were separated by only a foot or so. "I didn't betray you, Tad," she said. "I had plenty of opportunity if I'd wanted it."

"Betray me, how?" I asked, feeling deliberately obtuse.

"However you expected me to," she replied, the corners of her mouth turning up in a brief smile. "However it was you thought a—*an alien* would betray you."

I felt a sense of *déjà vu* as I turned over to lie on my side and face her. I was coming too close to acting out my dream—and I had no mother near now to put a stop to it. "Maybe," I admitted. "But tell me what it means."

"Come on, now," she said. "You're the man with the talent, remember? You're the man they send out to take an intuitive measure of circumstances. Don't tell me your intuition doesn't work on your private time as well."

"What're you driving at?"

"Just this: Do you really think I'm some sort of alien demon, bent on world conquest? Really?"

"Well, I—"

"Forget the diagrams and schematics and lab-test reports you've heard about. Forget everything except *me*. Just me, Tad. Am *I* alien?"

I moved my head against the pillow. "No," I said. "You're not."

"You *know* I'm not, don't you?" It wasn't really a question; she was driving the point home.

I agreed. "I guess so."

"Well, then. Maybe you'd better rethink some things."

"Tell me."

"Maybe you've got it all wrong. The whole setup, from

beginning to end, Bjonn and all. Maybe you've been completely wrong. Could you accept that?"

I closed my eyes. "I don't know," I said truthfully. "I just don't know. How *could* I be completely wrong?" I felt painfully naked, and I clutched at the covers for protection.

"Think about it; that's all," she said. "Just think about it. Think it through again. New data. Integrate it."

My clothes were shot. She'd cleaned my bootlets, and they were about all I had left. I put them on, and put on the coat she gave me. It was several sizes too small, and despite the belt it kept coming open in front. I decided it didn't really matter.

She dressed as I did, slipping easily into a lightweight robe. The fire in the fireplace was roaring, and the room had lost its chill. It was easy to watch her, easy to admire her smooth and economical movements as she dressed and tended to her chores. But in some strange way I understood the truth of my dream; she felt like a sister to me. There was a bond of affection between us, even an easy intimacy, but it had the familiarity of a close brother-sister relationship—nothing more. That seemed both strange and marvelous to me. I'd never had a sister before.

Some time the previous night she'd put new water in the kettle. Now she ladled out the steaming hot water into two bowls, and then added a powder from a canister. The powder seemed to soak up the water and expand, and as it did so, a strange smell rose from it.

"What's that?" I asked.

"Breakfast," she said. "High protein corn meal, with algaetes added for familiarity. Come and get it."

I stared at her without moving.

She carried both bowls to a table on the other side of the room. One chair already stood at the table; she dragged another over to it and sat down. "Come on," she said. "It's time you lost a few prejudices."

"I—can't," I said.

She sighed, pushed herself away from the table, and stood up. Then she came to where I stood and put her hands on her hips and looked me up and down. "For a big bold world-saver," she said, "you certainly are a coward." She seized my hand and tugged at me. I let her drag me over to the table and put me in the other chair. Sitting at the table's edge, so close it was almost under my nose, the bowl of "breakfast" steamed its strange smells at me. I felt both dizzy and weak.

"Here," she said, picking up a narrow utensil with a cupped end. She dipped it into the bowl and raised it to my mouth. "Try it," she said. "Come on, open up." As if in sympathethic pantomime, she opened her own mouth wide.

I opened my mouth, and her hand darted forward. The next instant, the food was in my mouth.

It was more granular in texture than the food I was familiar with, and its flavor was at once stronger and more subtle—as if many different flavors of varying strengths were competing for my attention. At first I gagged a little, but I closed my eyes and pretended for a moment that I was home, safe, in my own eating cubicle, and that did the trick. I swallowed.

"There; that wasn't so bad, was it?" she cooed. "Try some more."

Obediently, I opened my mouth again, and she quickly shoveled in another load. This time I didn't gag, and I found it easier to swallow.

"Try it with your eyes open, this time, why don't you?" she said. I opened my eyes to see the third mouthful of the food hovering before my lips. Without thinking I opened my mouth. "Good boy," she said, smiling.

"Why don't you try it now," she suggested. She handed the eating object to me, and I turned its handle over in my fingers. "It's called a 'spoon,'" she said. "A very ancient eating device, I'm told."

"It seems inefficient," I said, dipping with it into my bowl. "A tube would be faster, easier."

"Yes," she said, "but have you noticed anything different about the taste of this food?"

I nodded.

"Well, that's because it *isn't* in a tube." She dipped her

own spoon and took a mouthful from her own bowl. I watched covertly, from the corners of my eyes. "You taste with your nose as much as you do with your mouth. That is, smell is as important as taste, really. You can only taste four things: sweetness, saltiness, sourness and bitterness. Everything else is really in the odor—in what you smell. But—" she continued to eat while she talked, pausing occasionally "—but, when you get your food from a tube, you never really have a chance to see it or smell it, and besides which, it is deliberately made to have very little flavor. A big-deal change in the 'menu' is just a slight change in flavor and texture. They never really change what's really in your food; it's always the same thing. Unless you're rich, of course. But who's rich?"

I could think of a couple of people. But I didn't feel like mentioning them. They belonged in another world.

"It's *unnatural*, eating from a tube, anyway," Lora said, nodding in agreement with herself. "It perpetuates the infantile instincts, I think. You get used to sucking at a plastic teat for your nourishment, and since you're completely plugged in, it's like you're still a baby, un-toilet-trained. You just react to the stimuli. You—".

I was squirming. I'd finished most of my bowl of breakfast, and her words had thrown a mental switch somewhere inside me.

"Oh!" she said. "It's, uh, outside. A little house by itself, around the corner."

I barely made it there in time.

What was it Bjonn had called me? Compulsive?

I felt foolish striding up the path in my bootlets and Lora's ill-fitting coat, but Lora assured me it would not matter. "Besides," she said, "I'm sure one of the guys up at the big house will have some spare clothes you can wear, if you decide you still need regular clothes."

I felt even more foolish when I realized that the path up which she was leading me was a direct route back up the hill to the highway and across it to the old house. All my struggles in the woods yesterday seemed silly and pointless. I was beginning to understand why I hadn't been pursued.

The sun was a dim red disk in the morning haze and jumbled welter of the trees. When we came out of the trees into the field, I saw the mist still rising from the ground like low banks of miniature clouds. The world seemed very empty and still, and I found it hard to believe that several billion people lived only a few hundred miles to the south. From somewhere behind us a bird called mournfully, as if despairing the full warmth of the sun. Overhead, as if in answer to both the bird and my lonely thoughts, an aircraft trailed a sonic boom: a sudden whiplash of sound from the empty sky. A reminder that the emptiness was illusory. It made Lora jump. "It always does that to me," she said. "You'd think it wouldn't bother me, now. But it still does. I guess I have a ways to go yet before I can take over the world."

I felt like the butt of a bad joke. "Forget I ever said that, will you?" I said. But she only grinned at me.

"I'm going to rub it in, Tad," she said. "You're getting off lightly, you know."

I hoped so.

The sky overhead was blue by the time we climbed the meandering walk up to the big house. I turned to stare back down the hill and across the highway in the direction from which we'd come. The field was golden; the woods below were still hidden by the blue-white table of mist over the valley. I couldn't see the path, and there was no sign of the cabin.

As if reading my mind, Lora said quietly, "I went down there to be by myself for a few days. I was hurt, and I needed to be alone, to heal." I knew she didn't mean just her face. She looked up at me and reached up her hand to touch my cheek. "I'm glad you found me there. Now I can come back."

Now we'd both come back. Something shifted queasily in my stomach.

"You're still just people, right?" I asked. I needed re-assurance.

"Just people, Tad," she said. "You'll see."

We went in through the big front door and the weight of the house closed down over my shoulders. Unconsciously, I felt myself slumping, hunching my shoulders inward a little. I'd come here twice before. Third time—for keeps?

Chapter Twenty-One

"Why did you come back, Dameron?" Bjonn asked. I stood at the entrance to the large room which I had labeled in my mind "the chapel." Lora hugged against my arm. The room beyond Bjonn appeared empty, but I couldn't be sure; it was unlit and gloomy with shadows. I couldn't even read Bjonn's expression in the dim light. "You had a chance to run away. Why did you come back?"

"I changed my mind," I said. It was hard not to let the old belligerence rise. There was something about Bjonn which challenged me, challenged my manhood, my very right to existence. It made me bristle. "I don't have to explain myself to you."

"That's true," he said surprisingly, "you don't. But don't you think you owe it to me?"

"What do I owe you, Bjonn?" I asked. It was hard to keep the bitterness from my voice.

"You owe me a great deal," he said. His voice was somber. "You owe me your second chance at life. In more senses than one. Do you realize that?"

"I'll have to think about it," I said. But I knew.

"So tell me why you came back."

"It—it's not easy."

"I know that," he said. "But lots of things aren't easy. You will still have to face them, you know."

"I know."

He waited.

"I—was wrong," I said. It was hard to say the words.

"Wrong?"

"About—you. About—the people here. About—about, Lora."

"How so?"

"Do you have to ask?"

"I want to hear it from you, Tad."

"I—I saw conspiracies where there were no conspiracies."

"Why, Tad? Why do you think that happened?"

"I—don't know."

"How do you know you're wrong, now? How can you be sure you weren't right all along?"

"What's the idea? Are you trying to argue me out of it?"

"No. I just want to know the footing for your new position. I want you to explain it to me."

"Why you?"

"Because you owe it to me—and to yourself."

"Could I sit down?" I was feeling very uncomfortable, even with the silent Lora beside me in the doorway.

"Come on in and sit down," he said. "You'll have to use the floor; there are cushions for the purpose."

I took a cushion and let myself down on it, facing Bjonn, who took another. It felt uncomfortable; I didn't know what to do with my legs and I couldn't lean back. I was relieved to be sitting, and yet I could not relax. Lora sat somewhere behind me. I found myself wishing she hadn't; I missed her.

"Now then," Bjonn said. "Let's continue."

"What do you want me to tell you?" I asked.

"What do you want to tell me?" he countered.

I shook my head. "I don't know where to begin."

"Begin with Dian," he said. "Isn't that why you resent me so much?"

"Because of Dian?"

"Isn't it?"

"I don't know. I hadn't thought of it that way." I had, though. It inkled at the back of my mind.

"I took her away from you."

"Yes."

"But, did I?"

"I don't understand."

"Was she 'yours,' Tad?"

"Well, no, not exactly, that is, I mean—"

"You thought she was Tucker's mistress, didn't you?"

"Yes. I think so."

"Well, that's between you, Dian, and Tucker. I don't believe she was—not in the sense you regarded it, anyway. But you thought I seduced her from you, didn't you?"

"You did, didn't you?"

"No."

"No? I can't believe that."

"That's your problem, Tad, not mine. I am not in the habit of lying; I never have lied to you."

"You—seduced her with the, the alien whatever-it-is."

"No. You're wrong. I offered it to her, and she accepted it. I don't believe she has at all regretted that, but it was her free choice."

"It *has* to be, Tad," Lora said from the darkness behind me. "It has to be your own choice."

"Dian wanted to offer the sacrament to you, just as I did," Bjonn said. "But she was afraid for you. Do you know why?"

"She knew I'd reject it."

He nodded. "And do you see why you rejected it?"

"I was—am—too compulsive. Too much the creature of my—habits."

"You can see that now?"

I nodded. Moisture stung my dry eyes. "Now," I said, "yes."

"What brought you back?"

"I had to come back."

"Why?"

"I—I couldn't just turn my back on it. Not on—the chance for something—something better."

"I don't know whether or not we can help you, Tad," he said.

"*What?*"

"I'm impressed by what you've told me. I'm even more impressed by the fact that you've come back again." He lingered on the last word. "But you're a convincing dissembler, Tad. You're skilled at lies and half-truths. I don't know whether I can believe you."

I felt as if he'd kicked my stomach in. I clutched at it despairingly. "You're not being fair," I whispered. "I came back. I ran away from you and I came back."

"Yes," he said. "I can see that. But—"

"That's enough," came Lora's suddenly forceful voice. "It's not necessary to subject him to some sort of ordeal."

"—but," Bjonn picked up where he'd been cut off, shifting the thrust of his words from me to Lora, "Dameron has proven himself dangerously psychopathic. You don't know, Lora. He only kicked you in the face, but he killed someone else."

"That's not entirely true," I said, feeling my voice turn sick. "Ditmas isn't dead."

"No. Fortunately, his *arapad* lived, and was able to restore his life to him. But that is hardly to your credit, Dameron. And," he added, returning to Lora, "he took the identity of the man he killed and went to the Moon. He tried to pass himself off as his victim in order to join the next voyage of the *Longhaul II*."

"Back to Farhome?" Lora asked. She breathed the planet's name as if it was Heaven; maybe it was.

"Back to Farhome," Bjonn agreed. "His only explanation was that he was seeking the answers to the conspiracy he saw to be taking over Earth. *He has yet to admit to himself that he murdered a man and stole his identity solely to satisfy his long-standing compulsion to enter deep space.*"

The words struck me like hammer blows, and I tried to defend myself against them:

"No, that's not true," I cried. "But where else could I go, when I saw the very agents of my own Bureau being taken over? I killed him by accident, but once I'd killed him, what could I do? I had to escape. I had to escape Earth entirely."

"So you ran away to the Moon. To a veritable nest of those of us you considered your enemies. You came straight to *me*." Irony was thick in his voice. "What *could* you have done? Did you ever think of giving yourself up? Of turning yourself over to the local authorities? The Bureau of Security was your obvious answer. You could have pleaded—oh—self-defense, if you'd wished. You might even have told them your conspiracy theory. That way you might have gotten some worthwhile therapeutic help."

"You know why I didn't," I muttered.

"You thought they were in on the conspiracy."

"Weren't they?"

"*What* conspiracy, Tad? You told me you'd been seeing conspiracies where there weren't any conspiracies. Isn't that right?"

"I *thought* there was one, then. At the time, I thought there was a conspiracy. What do you want me to say, Bjonn? That I was out of my head the whole time? But that I'm still responsible for everything I did?"

"Weren't you?" he replied. "Aren't you, Tad?"

They left me alone in the heavy darkness of the room, closing the doors behind them. "You have a lot of thinking to do, Tad," Lora told me before she followed Bjonn. "You have a decision to make. I—I pushed you too fast, that other time. I didn't understand then. Now I do." She stooped and gave me a chaste kiss.

Then I was alone with myself.

I had a decision to make. I'd known that. I'd known it for some time. And I'd done everything in my power to avoid facing it. Now I couldn't put it off any longer. I'd recognized that this morning, when I'd decided I could trust Lora. Now I had to follow through on that decision with another—with the Big One. In a strange and subtle fashion they'd made it clear to me; no one else was coercing me. My battle was with myself.

When had I first started fighting that battle? How long ago?

I had so few memories of my childhood. When I thought

of my mother, it was the face of the woman in the shrink's office that I saw in my mind—not the face of a younger woman, the woman who had mothered me. My father— why couldn't I remember him at all? Why had I so flatly rejected my memories of the man? I'd known him for the first six years of my life. By then I'd learned to read, write, code and punch. I hadn't lost *those* memories. . . .

. . . sitting on a chair that was too low to be comfortable, pulling my legs up and squatting on my feet before the infomat, hesitantly poking my fingers at the standard keyboard. *How old? Three? Four?*

"Hello, Tad," said the disembodied voice of the infomat's special voder. "Will you play a game with me? I'd like you to spell your name for me. Can you do that? Let's start with 'Tad.' Look at my screen. What do you see? That's right—a 'Tee.' Will you find the 'Tee' on my keyboard and punch it? . . . Very good. And now an 'A.' . . . That's right. You're very fast; that was an 'A.' And now, 'Dee ' . Right. And what do they spell when we put them together? Look at my screen. 'Tee,' 'A,' 'Dee.' That's 'Tad,' isn't it? Will you *say* the letters with me, and punch them as you say them? 'Tee' . . . 'A' . . . 'Dee.' That's very good. And now for your last name, 'Dameron.' This is a longer name and it has more letters. . . ."

Sure, I could remember my lessons, sitting on my legs until they cramped, day after day. But where was my mother? Where was my father?

I remembered the public shrink. They'd sent me to see him when I was ten. "Tad doesn't relate well to the other children," my den mother that year said. *The other children*—I could still hear the patronizing tone of her voice. We were little aliens to her, a race apart. They called us "children." I never thought of myself as a child. I was a person, denied my rights to existence as a person by the bigger people, the so-called adults. I was surrounded by other persons, closer to my age, who contested me for those somehow unquenchable rights every day of my youth. It was a state of armed truce which often erupted into momentary war. Who "related?" That was a word the grownups used to cover up their ignorance.

"You're something of a loner, aren't you, Tad?" the shrink had said. He seemed old and used up to me then. Defeat crowded the features of his face. "Why do you suppose that is?"

I'd just stared at him without bothering to answer him. It was a stupid question. We were all alone; I knew that and so did he. That was obvious. The only difference between us was that he was still going through the motions; he still hadn't admitted the truth to himself yet.

He reached out a hand and put it on my bare knee. I let it rest there for a single moment that stretched for too long; then I removed it. I broke his wrist.

He screamed, and leapt to his feet, fear and anger fighting for control of his expression, and he cursed me very fluently, very expressively. And threw me out.

I never liked shrinks. They sent me to others, and they seemed cut from a common pattern—even my mother, as I thought about it: they were all failures. Each and every one had failed at his own life and given it up. Now they wanted to try again—on someone else. While I was in the den I had no choice. I went to whom I was sent. And I endured them. The silly women who wanted to "break through my shell," either to seduce me or to mother me. The men who saw "an interesting challenge" in me and wanted either to seduce me or to father me. I endured them all, stoically, and as silently as possible.

Later I tried going to shrinks of my own. I knew I'd only seen the worst, the ones who worked for Public Care. I knew they were the dregs, and I hoped, stupidly, that if I invested some money I might have better luck.

All that happened was that I met a higher class of failure: the ones who lived on others' troubles, feeding purse and soul from their victims. They hid it better, but it was there if you searched for it. There was no sense relying on such people. It only made you their property. I preferred to remain my own, for better or worse.

Then there was the opposite sex. There were girls in the

dens—but in dens of their own. We boys knew about girls, told jokes and stories about them, sniggered about them, long before we had any idea of what we were talking about. Some of the older boys boasted about the girls they'd known. Their stories were flamboyant lies, and I'd realized that at the time. Our only real contact with the female race was our den mother—and the older boys would snort behind their cupped hands whenever we had a den mother under the age of forty, remarking on her legs, her breasts, or whatever might be her outstanding characteristic.

They introduced us to Girls when we were twelve. We attended formal social gatherings which followed a ritualistic plan, the origins and sense of which were both long lost in antiquity. The girls hated it, and so did we.

Then we were transferred, at thirteen, to mixed dens, given a sex education and sterility shots, and left to cope for our own with our peers. I remained a loner.

It seemed to me then—as it still does—that we were herded together like animals to breed with each other, that we were supposed to act out some ancient rutting rite for the vicarious benefit of our supervisors (we didn't have den mothers by then). We had rooms—tiny cubicles, really—of our own, and were assured privacy. I never tested it. I never invited a girl into my room. I never invited a boy, either. It was *my* room—my own room. I kept it that way. And then, suddenly, before I was quite aware of it, the other boys had learned something, some sort of behavior, which I had not and which I didn't understand. There was this shared knowledge, this knowing way, they had. And the girls seemed to have it too. It formed a barrier, and I found myself on the outside. That bothered me, but less because it excluded me than simply because it represented a mystery I couldn't plumb.

The year I graduated the den I met a girl. Her name was Vivianne. We both had cubicles in a Public Building. Mine was tiny because I insisted on living alone; she shared hers with three other girls. I was nineteen. She was a little older.

We saw each other in the halls. She was pretty, and she stirred up an ache in me. I started making a point of running into her on her way into or out of the building. Soon we were going places together, doing simple, banal things together. I dreamed about her all the time. I thought of marrying her.

One night she stayed in my aptroom, and initiated me into the mysteries of sex. It was thoroughly unpleasant. She was impatient with me, with my clumsiness. When I told her I'd never done it before, she laughed at me. She didn't believe me. She instructed me in the mechanics, and we both professed our satisfaction with the coupling, but I never tried to see her again. I changed aptrooms and buildings the next day. And the day after that I took the tests for a job with the Bureau.

It was a spiraling trap. I could see that now. I'd never been close to other people. Through the years I'd picked up the veneer of experience; I became adept at the so-called social graces. But they only widened the gap. I distrusted other people.

I sat in that darkened room for many hours. A great many thoughts ran through my head. Most were old and familiar. But many required fresh examination. I stood a few on their heads and observed them critically. For so much of my life I'd acted upon unspoken assumptions. It was time to speak them and see if they still held up.

Too many of them did not.

When I rose from the cushion my legs were stiff and numbed and my mind felt much the same. I went to a window and pulled back its heavy drapes. It was the same window from which I'd peered on my first trip to this house. The light was pale and yellow and the hour was late. I glanced at my chronometer, but it still said 15:52; it was still broken.

I felt exhausted, and yet oddly stronger. I hadn't put all the pieces together yet, but I knew now that they all fit. Locked in my head was a vast jigsaw puzzle. I'd never tried to work it this way before. It was comforting—genuinely comforting—to know that it *could* be worked.

I'd made my decision.

Chapter Twenty-Two

It was a simple ceremony. "We place no great value on ritual for the sake of ritual," Bjonn said. "That which we do is meaningful in its own right. It is as simple and as important as a lovers' kiss."

The simile was appropriate, I discovered.

I sat in the center of a circle of people. We were in the chapel once more, and it was again only dimly lit. Among those grouped around me were faces I knew: Lora, Jim Benford, Bjonn, Dian, Tucker, Ditmas, and others which I recognized as having seen here before, but whom I did not yet know. There was a solemnity to the occasion, but at the same time a certain warmth and cheerfulness. These people were *together* in a way still alien to me, and still a little frightening. As I waited, the last vestiges of the old arguments fought against the new:

This is outside my experience; it frightens me.

Nonsense. You've been conjuring up demons and monsters, but these people are offering to share paradise with you.

Paradise? What sort of paradise can they offer me? Curious, but still fearful.

The paradise of self-realization. The paradise of being a whole man.

Is it? Or is it a delusion of wholeness given to a puppet on mental strings?

Don't be afraid; they won't take anything away from you. They only add to what you've got. Judge for yourself.

Well, that's why I'm here.

"We're here today to celebrate life," Bjonn said. He spoke conversationally; he didn't orate. He addressed the entire circle of which he was a part. And he spoke to me. I felt the attention of the circle focus on me. It was an uncomfortable feeling. I felt pinned down.

"Life is so precious," Bjonn said. "We are given only a finite slice of it, and when it is gone we are finished. Yet, so many of us try to ignore this fact as we let our lives slip heedlessly through our fingers.

"We're here to celebrate life," he said again, "but in celebrating life we must also celebrate death. The two are one, the *yin* and *yang* of existence. We must all die. Only when we can accept this can we fully utilize our lives.

"We're here to celebrate the life and the death of Tad Dameron, who sits in the center of our circle. He has passed through a third of his life—perhaps only a quarter" (he smiled) "—and he has made many mistakes with it. These are not for us to dwell upon. He comes to us now to celebrate the Sacrament of Life with us, to join with us in the life that precedes death. He comes to receive his *arapad,* that which will catalyze his life into joy and self-realization. Who will offer him his *arapad?*"

I recognized the question to be more than idle. Once before someone had made that offer, and I had spurned it in blind panic. Who would make the offer this time? I felt myself tensing. I wanted to twist around and scan the faces behind me. But I did not.

"I will," Dian said softly. She was on my far right, just within the periphery of my vision.

"How do you choose to make your offer?" Bjonn asked.

A pink flush spread across her face and she hesitated for a moment. "By the Kiss," she said.

I flicked my eyes back to Bjonn, to find his own staring directly at me. I couldn't make out his expression. "Very well," he said, "come forward, please."

Dian knelt in front of me and reached out her hands to take mine. Her body blocked Bjonn from my sight, and I wondered if that had been deliberate. I felt suddenly shy and embarrassed, as if about to perform some very intimate act before strangers, and she seemed to sense it. "It's all right," she whispered. Our eyes locked. It seemed to me then that she had never been more beautiful; she looked so beautiful that I wanted to cry.

She tugged me up onto my knees, and then drew my

head down to meet hers. There was something asexual but very personal, very tender in her actions. I had never kissed Dian. I had exchanged mutual oral kisses with very few women in my life. It had always seemed far more intimate than genital coupling.

Our lips met. It was as if a charge of built-up static electricity was exchanged between us on that first contact. Her lips were full and very soft. They trembled slightly against mine. Then they parted. Hesitantly, I opened my own.

Something probed between my lips and against my teeth, and I thought it was her tongue. I thrust forward my own to meet it and brushed instead against—it—

The alien parasite. The dead-white blob of living jelly. The *arapad*.

I could not help the shudder that passed through my body. My tongue recoiled. I started to clench my teeth. Dian squeezed my hands in her own, her nails biting into my flesh. Her eyes blazed at me.

This was my last chance. There would be no recourse if I turned down the wrong path now.

A zombi, controlled by an alien puppet-master?

—Or a free man?

Which?

I could only place my trust in my intuition. Sometimes I had read its signals wrong, but it was the only part of myself I completely trusted—perhaps the only thing I'd ever really trusted.

I forced my teeth apart, made my mouth open and receptive. And tensed myself as something at once warm and cool, slickly slimy and furry-dry thrust a questing pseudopod into my mouth.

It seemed to balk for a moment, as if sensing it might not be welcome. Then, so quickly I could not follow its movements inside me, it *inflowed*, like sudden liquid.

I felt its weight pass over the base of my tongue and I began gagging, but then it seemed to melt and disappear. I couldn't breathe for a moment, and then I could, as though through cold-stuffed sinuses. A heaviness weighed at my face, spreading across under my cheeks and disappearing. Then all sensation of strangeness was gone, as if it had never been. There was not even an aftertaste in my mouth.

Dian slowly relinquished her kiss and leaned back on her heels. Her expression was soft and caring, and it seemed to me she hadn't really wanted our kiss to end just yet. The pressure of her lips still lingered on mine, and I wanted to taste my lips with my tongue, but I refrained.

"Is—that all?" I asked. "I don't really feel any . . . different. . . . "

She smiled. "It takes a while. Come! Join our circle now!"

They made a place for me, and I found myself sitting between Dian and an older woman I didn't know. We all linked hands.

"I touch you and I am touched by you," Bjonn said. Lora was sitting next to him and she repeated it. Benford, next to her, repeated the statement. Each person said the words, and with each repetition they sounded sillier and more meaningless. And so it passed around the circle to the woman on my left. "I touch you and I am touched by you," she told me. I felt awkward and strangely embarrassed. I felt no different than I had before. Nothing seemed to have happened to me. I was unchanged. I was still an outsider, a loner. It made me feel at once melancholy and cynical.

But when that woman—a stranger to me, someone I had never met before—when she said the words it seemed as if they took on meaning for the first time since Bjonn had said them. They became literal. She touched me. Her hand held my hand. Her fingers were coarsened by age and labor. The back of her hand was veined, its skin a little loose. Her grasp was firm, warm and dry. Her touch seemed to communicate in that moment her words. She touched me— and was she also touched by me? Did my return of her handclasp communicate something of me to her? Was it something more than just the linkage of two body-shell appendages? Was there something of *me* in my hand's grip?

An alcoholic tingle seemed to be moving over my body.

I felt a rush of blood to my capillaries. It heightened the sensations in my fingers, in my fingertips.

I turned to Dian. "I—touch you," I said, feeling the warm, gentle caress of her clasp. And in that moment a shell seemed to burst open in many marvelous colors inside my head. I stared at her, dumbfounded. Suddenly, it seemed I could *see* her as I had never seen her before. She radiated beauty. Her soul shone through her face like golden sunshine. And linked with her I realized the presence of another—a moon to her sun, silver to her gold—twin to mine own. Her *arapad*. A shining presence, alien but beautiful too, in its own right. "And," I said, "I am touched by you." It was at that moment a gross understatement. I was overwhelmed by her.

Her smile was a shivering tinkle of wind-chimes. Her eyes were pure and loving. Her hands told me it was true, all of it, all true.

My *arapad* was starting to acquaint me with reality.

"They're not true parasites, you know," Bjonn told me later. "Rather, they are symbiotes. They give as much— maybe more—as they receive. And, as you've now learned, the *arapad* has no consciousness. It doesn't 'think' at all. They have only one function, and that is to stay alive. In order to do this, they require a host body. An *arapad* can live outside his host only in a dormant condition. It dehydrates, forms an outer shell of dead matter, and continues to dehydrate until, ultimately, it is reduced to a sort of spore. If it is ingested by an living creature of cellular complexity, it reverses the process."

"Is the *arapad* then a single-celled creature?" I asked.

"Yes and no," Bjonn said, smiling a little. "It appears to be made up of a cooperative of cells, each serving a different function, each capable of producing the others to complement it if separated from them. However, the entire *arapad* is capable of cellular fusion, at which time the entire organism, umm, *mixes* its cells—they flow together to form one unicell—and then fissions, dividing into two organisms, each of which returns to the multi-cellular condition. In any case, it is a very simple creature; an adult *arapad,* weighing almost two ounces, contains only six cells. Most of the weight is in water, of course.

"They appeared to be native to Farhome," he said. "They lived in conjunction with the native animals. One of the original colonists had killed a native animal and cooked and eaten it. His child, a boy of three, had taken a scrap of raw meat to chew on. It contained a section of broken-off ganglion from an *arapad*. The child had grown his own, and then, when it fissioned, given *aparads* to his friends. The adults were shocked when they discovered the *arapads'* existence, but quickly became convinced of their beneficence.

"As I was saying, an *arapad* wants to stay alive. In order to do this, it requires a healthy host body. And an *arapad* is willing to do all it can to maintain the upkeep on that host body.

"It *polices* your body. It clears out the hostile bacteria and viruses. It accelerates the healing process—it can 'read' the DNA information in your cells and recreate damaged parts. That's what happened to Ditmas, you know."

"Doesn't that all but bestow immortality upon a host?" I asked. I was recalling Bjonn's sermon on life and death.

"Apparently not. The *arapad* is immortal. I suppose the original mutant creature that became the first *arapad* is still around as a component of all the ones we have—they are all byproducts of it by fission. But while the *arapad* can lick a lot of the so-called diseases of 'old age,' it can't stop the aging process itself. Or, if it can, we haven't yet found the way to tell it to. We live long and healthy lives, Tad, but we're still human. We still die at the end."

"I understood we *do* have some conscious control over them," I objected.

"Well, again, yes and no. The *arapad* allows us certain degrees of conscious control over ourselves. It allows us to function more optimally. It functions in some senses as a second nervous system. It give us much better control over our emotions, for instance. As you yourself must realize, our mental states are intimately influenced by the chemical nature of our brains. Minute chemical changes can have profound results. That's the basis of the last several centuries of drug therapy. The *arapad* 'reads' from our genetic heritage the proper chemical balances, and restores them. That's automatic. But one of the things we learn to do in our group sessions is to work *with* the *arapad* so that we can ourselves by conscious will effect those changes in balance. We also learn to control other aspects of our hormonal system and our metabolism. But in many senses this is gilding the lily and tampering with perfect health. Let the *arapad* alone and it will uncripple you in mind and body. To ask more is to be arrogant." He smiled. ". . . But also human."

The first twenty-four hours were full of unfolding wonder for me. I felt as if my eyes had always been covered with film-like filters, and now the films had been removed . . . as if my ears had been plugged with wax, and the wax had been taken out . . . as if my nose had been permanently burdened with the effects of a low-grade viral infection that had deadened my sense of smell—which event Bjonn assured me was quite likely—and that this too was now gone. Colors seemed bright and vivid, deeper and richer, their interplay more subtle and complex. I saw hues and shades I'd never noticed before. Bjonn had an art object which looked like a square of brown until one examined it more closely. Then the reds and oranges, purples and greens appeared, delicate traceries, subtlety among subtleties. One could dwell upon it for hours of discovery.

The wood of the old house seemed to whisper to me, while its scents told age-old stories. I found myself running my fingers over things, tracing their contours, their curves. Dian had something she called her "feelie," an abstract sculpture of compound and complex curves, folded into and upon itself, which she offered to my touch. I was on a jag, a voyage of discovery through my own senses. Someone brought in a leaf from outside and gave it to me. It was a maple leaf, tattered, a faded gold, already musty from its communion with the soil. It occupied me for two hours.

I didn't sleep at all during those first twenty-four hours.

It didn't seem to be necessary. "Sleep is often the refuge of the copeless," Benford told me with a grin. "Things look bad, so you cop out, you escape into sleep, hoping everything will be better by the time you wake up. People sleep a lot more than most of them need to." That rang the bell of truth.

I couldn't be bothered with sleep. I'd been asleep all my life and I'd just awakened. The world was my toy and I wanted to experience every bit of it.

But, finally, I returned to the room on the top floor and lay down on the bed. I'd been enjoying all my exterior senses; now it was time to go inside and see what it was like in there.

At first I noticed my breathing. The pattern seemed self-conscious, rigid. I broke it into a relaxed syncopation. That amused me, and I laughed to myself. Something gurgled in my intestines. At first I tensed against the pang, and then I let it go, let myself relax again, while I followed the progress of the bubble of gas.

I'd eaten real food that day. The meal had been another engrossing experience. I'd broke my anal compulsion, too—divorced the need for evacuation from the process of eating. It had been so easy it amazed me—it still amazed me. The gas bubble seemed to be backtracking. I felt it against my diaphragm, and then it was working up my throat and I burped, lightly. That too amused me.

I let my mind drift, setting it free to wander through my body as it would. I followed my heartbeat, calm, firm, steady, so very competent and assured, and then the rushing of my blood outward through my arteries. Gradually I entered a state of waking sleep, a state in which I was still conscious, but quiescent, my conscious mind somehow linked with and not contesting my unconscious mind. My breathing had slowed; my heartbeat was coasting; my body was more completely relaxed than it had been since I was a small baby. I was admiring myself. *You've messed yourself up some, but on the whole, you've got yourself a proud piece of goods*. I even felt a little smug.

The door to the room inched cautiously open. I didn't

bother to open my eyes in confirmation. Her step was friendly.

I heard her approach the bed, and then her breath was warm and lightly scented upon my face. I pursed my lips and parted them a little as hers brushed against them in a delicate kiss. It seemed to me then that I was being born again, that I had learned at last a new function for my lips beyond those of grasping at a meal tube, or framing unpleasant words to spew forth. I sensed the thousand nerve-endings in the surface of my lips as one erotic instrument. I returned her kiss.

She was leaning over me and I raised my arms to caress her skin with my fingertips. She wore no clothes. That was fine; neither did I.

Her own fingertip traced a delicated pattern down my chest, embroidered a filigree around my nipples that sent sensuous chills through me. I ran my fingers down her spine so lightly that I touched no skin—only the fine feathery down above her skin. A long shudder undulated through her and then she was sprawling upon me in a full embrace.

We made love that night—a real and genuine love. It lasted a long time, long and slow in the buildup, long in the coupling, and towering in its climax, ascending from plateau to plateau before at last the thunder and lightning struck. And then we lay together, silent, touching and being touched, for a time longer yet.

When the first rays of sunlight peered through the window I kissed her nose and murmured, "Thank you, Dian. I love you." And then fell into exhausted sleep.

Chapter Twenty-Three

Ditmas and Tucker drove down to Bay Complex with me. I felt euphoric; it seemed we'd all been transformed from shallow shells of people into solid substance. The old friction, the old manipulative game-playing was gone.

"You know," I told Tucker after we'd settled into our adjacent seats on the HST, "I really pulled some pretty bad stunts on you, didn't I?"

He nodded. "You did, at that," he chuckled. "How do you feel about them now?"

"How do *you* feel about them?"

"Well," he said, deliberately lapsing into his old corn-pone drawl, "I reckon if you could take me, I could take you. Let's not worry about it anymore. We're two people who were sick for a long time. Now we're on the mend."

"I thought you were stringing on half the girls in the office," I said. "I deliberately chased those girls just to give you a hard time."

"You were right, too," he said. "You *did* give me a hard time. But it was nothing like what I was doing to my wife."

"Oh," I said. "You know, I've never met your wife."

"The problem is," he said, "neither have I."

I knew what he meant.

"Thing is, now I have to start all over," Tucker continued. "Bjonn's been instructing me so that I can create the Sacrament of Life myself. I'm taking a vacation from the Bureau—it doesn't need me that badly now, anyway. We've got *arapads* through all the higher echelons, and the filtering-down process will go right on without me—and I think it's time Fern and I had a second honeymoon. I'm looking forward to it."

"Tucker," I said, "how old are you?"

"Old enough to be your father, son, and that's a fact."

Tears came unbidden to my eyes. *Old enough to be my father*—and he'd lived over half his life in darkness.

I changed the subject. "You know," I said, "only one thing still puzzles me."

"What's that?"

"Why did you devote so much attention to me? I mean, here I was, running around making a paranoiac fool of myself—but why care about a crummy Level Seven agent? What difference did it make? Couldn't you have assumed I'd wake up someday by myself?"

"That's a hard question, Tad," he said. "I'm not sure in

my own mind about that. You were a sore point with me—
before, I mean. I had only daughters, you know—no sons.
In a way I tried to make a son out of you. But you, damn
your soul, you were so ornery with me, it was like you
wanted to stay inside that sick box of yours, no matter how
hard I tried to jolt you out of it. Not, of course, that I knew
what I was doing at the time. But I've thought about it
some, since. I *liked* you; that was the problem. You were
smart, you had a lot going for you, up here"—he tapped
his forehead—"more than you seemed to realize. But stubborn—! You had your horns locked on the Deep Space
thing so badly it threw you every time.

"I wanted to kick you so hard, you wouldn't believe it!
I wanted to rub your nose in the miserable failure you were
making of yourself and say, 'You're making a mess, boy;
clean yourself up.' I tried. But of course I went at it all
wrong."

"You mean, you really wanted me to jump out of that
whole rut I was in?"

"Sure I did. That's why I kept harping on it. I figured
sooner or later you'd get so mad that you'd prove you could
do it, just to spite me."

I smiled, ruefully. "It didn't work quite that way." I
didn't have to state the obvious, now: my sickness had run
a lot deeper than that.

When we disembarked in Megayork, I found myself
looking around me with fresh eyes, my attention divided
between the griminess of the megacity—an unpleasant con-
trast to the countryside above Cloverdale, I discovered—
and the throngs of people surrounding me. As before, when
we'd entered Bay Complex, I found myself searching faces
for the signs . . . for the awareness that signaled the presence
of an *arapad*. I felt like the new inductee in a secret and
exclusive fraternity, looking for the Secret Handclasp, the
telltale tunic-pin. It was a little childish of me, but it was
also a harmless amusement—and while my fellow hosts
were far from ubiquitous in the milling crowds, I sighted
several. Usually we exchanged knowing smiles, then
pressed on about our own business.

"Some of the people who have taken *arapads*," Bjonn had told me, "are not aware of their origin, or of their real meaning. This is inevitable when something like this begins to grow. It quickly outgrows the bonds of easy communication. I'm told that over five billion people in New Africa now have *arapads;* yet, I know none of them myself. That's why we started up the Church of the Brotherhood of Life. Those who have *arapads* will recognize us when they encounter us—and we're establishing many branches now wherever we can find hospitable settings. This is our way of letting them know about us."

"But what do they really need your Church for?" I'd asked.

"The *arapad* confers good health upon its host," Bjonn told me. "But it does so in an ethical, moral vacuum. And it doesn't volunteer any information about its conscious uses. We evolved our knowledge in Farhome over three generations, by trial and error. We haven't filled the tape yet, but we do know a good deal. More than you've learned yet, I might add, although you've done well for yourself, Tad. Our Church exists as a sanctuary for this accumulated knowledge and experience. It offers a moral, an ethical framework, a structure for the symbiosis between *arapad* and human. Not everyone will need us. But most could profit from us. What we offer is not religious dogma. We offer insights, truths, and methods for self-realization. There's mental health—and there's mental health. An *arapad* cleans up an unbalanced brain; it doesn't attack the old memories or the ingrained compulsions. That one must do for himself. And we can help. We exist, as a Church, to help."

"What's your ultimate goal, Bjonn?" I'd asked, finally. "Why did you really bring the *arapads* to Earth?"

"I'm an altruist, I guess," he'd said. "Earth is a vast planetary slum—and so unnecessarily so. Man has always had it within his technological power to change things for the better. But he's lacked the will, the common drive toward that goal. Man has been crippled, all his life on this planet. And he's been poisoning his world with his own sickness.

"It is such a terrible tragedy. And it was almost repeated on Farhome, you know. If we hadn't discovered the *arapads*, well . . . we're only human. We'd have eventually despoiled another planet."

"The *arapads* will turn Earth into a utopia?"

"No. *Man* will have to do that, if he wants it done. But the *arapad* is a handy lever for starting things rolling in that direction. You know it yourself, Tad. Compare yourself, *now*, with the person you were, *then*. You tell me which way the balance has shifted."

"Hello, Mother," I said. "I've brought you a gift."

She looked harried and unhappy and not at all pleased to see me. I wasn't surprised; I hadn't exactly left her with pleasant memories of me.

"What *happened* to you?" she asked, rising from the couch to approach me. "You missed all your appointments for the last, oh, two weeks at *least*. Did you just set them up in order to break them? Is that what you had in mind all along? A way to punish your mother? Every single one of those appointments—do you know how I felt, wondering if you'd show up each time, wondering what you'd say, how you'd explain yourself? I left time open for you, and every appointment you missed was time I could have been seeing someone else, if I hadn't made an appointment for you, time I could have been working—"

"Mother, please," I said. "Calm down, and sit down. I'm sorry I broke those appointments, but it was unavoidable. Anyway, I've—"

"*Unavoidable*." Her lip curled. "Of *course* it was. And you couldn't call your mother—your own *mother*—to tell her about it!"

"Mother, I was in Geneva, and then on the West Coast and then the Moon—"

"I suppose they don't have infomats on any of those places—?"

"Sit down and be quiet!" I said. It was interesting to

discover that I was still capable of anger. "Listen to yourself! Is that any way to talk to a patient?"

"You're not my patient; you're my son," she said.

"That's right," I said. "I am. You might think about that, too."

"I'm—sorry."

"I came to tell you that I wouldn't be needing to see you anymore," I said. "At least, not in your professional capacity. And I brought you a goodbye present."

Her eyes sharpened a little. "I can see you've changed," she said. "And I'm glad to see that. But what's this goodbye business?"

"I'm going on a trip," I said. I didn't elaborate. "Before I go, though, I need the answer to one more question from you."

"What is it?" she asked, a little tremulously.

I eased myself down into the couch opposite hers. It felt good to relax in, and I smiled at her. "Relax," I said. "I'm not going to eat you." Her eyes widened, and I realized that she really was afraid of me. Why? Old guilts? Or did my presence seem somehow threatening to her?

"You said you had a question?"

"Yes. What happened to my father?"

A veil seemed to fall over her face. "He left me. I told you that."

"Yes, but where did he go? What did he do?"

"Is it important, now, at this late date?"

"Yes," I said, firmly, "it is important to me, now. Please tell me."

"He went into space," she said.

The final piece of the jigsaw puzzle fitted itself into place. Suddenly I felt completely whole.

Captain David Dameron took *The Searcher* out when I was eight. It was a hundred-twenty-year round trip. I remembered now the lean face with sandpaper cheeks that bent down to me and told me goodbye, that long, long ago day.

My den mother had called me out to one of the offices

which was off limits for us kids, and there a man with dark eyebrows and a long nose looked down at me and smiled hesitantly.

"Daddy!" I cried. "You're taking me home!"

The smile had gone as if suddenly erased. "No," he said, shaking his head. "I wish I could, Taddy, but I'm going away."

I'd stopped dead and stared at him, feeling hurt and bewildered. I'd lived each day as though it might be my last in the hated den; I'd dreamed each night of returning home the next day. I ached with homesickness. I missed the comfort and security of my parents more than I could comprehend.

"Where are you going?" I'd asked.

"Deep space," he'd said, and his eyes seemed already far away. "I've got command of *The Searcher*, and we're going out a long way, son."

"Take me with you," I begged.

Again, the wistful smile. "Wish I could, son. But I can't. I just can't."

"I'll wait for you. When are you coming back?"

He shook his head. "Too long," he said. "A long, long time from now."

"When I'm grown up?"

"After that."

"After that . . . ?"

"One hundred and twenty years, Taddy; one hundred and twenty years at least. You'd be a hundred and twenty-eight."

He didn't have to say it, and I hadn't wanted to. *After you're dead, son. I'm going away and I won't be coming back until after you're dead.*

It was as if he'd struck me. Tears blinded my eyes and I turned and ran heedlessly out the door of the room. It was the last time I'd ever seen my father.

"I thought you remembered," my mother said. "You were so hipped on space—they used to tell me about you, you know, for a while; I had a friend in Den Administration—wasn't that why?"

"Yes," I said. "And no."

Yes, it explained my frantic drive to follow my father. And perhaps it also explained why, alone of the seven Feinberg Drive ships, *The Searcher* remained completely unrepresented in my collection of childhood trivia.

I remembered now that I had dried my tears and told my fellow denmates that my father was commanding a starship. They'd laughed at me with all the innate cruelty of children who envied me that precious intangible possession. They ridiculed me, and called me a liar, and in their blind fashion they'd stripped my last defense from the face of my tragedy. They took from me even my pride in my father's position.

I killed my father that night. This was the night I knew at last that I'd never go home again. I burned my father's memory and buried it with dry sobs and when at last I fell asleep it was to the lonely knowledge that I had finally been abandoned and lost.

I made my mother a parting gift: an *arapad*. I told her how to contact the local branch of the Church of the Brotherhood of Life—it was in northern Maine, only a few hours away—and wished her luck. She needed it, I felt. I hoped things would improve for her now—and I was reasonably certain they would. She had fallen into her own box, and clutched it closed around her for all these many years. She was of Tucker's generation, and his lesson was hers: *it's never too late*.

I half wished I could stick around, just to be there for her. But of course I couldn't.

I've been taping this on and off over the last few weeks, while on my free time and during those rare moments when Dian has not commanded my attention. I've been busy learning a lot of new skills, for which, fortunately, the shipboard library is well stocked.

I've tried to make this an honest chronicle—not because anyone requires it of me (no one else but Dian knows I've been taping it), but because I demand it of myself. You might say I've been laying the past to rest. I've tried to recreate the self I was during each point of each episode

I've related. The recall hasn't been difficult—I have fine tuning on my memories, thank you!—but there are parts I don't like to tell. It's easy to stand outside my old self and point the finger of judgment at him. He was a shallow, conceited, deeply neurotic fool. That much is obvious. But he is also *me*. For all of my *arapad*-assisted growth, I am still Tad Dameron: different, and yet the same. It is as Bjonn said. I was very sick, but I can't avoid the responsibility for what I did. I must face it, acknowledge it, accept it, and be done with it. My actions of the past are set; they are milestones . . . but not, I hope, millstones.

Now that I am making the great crossing between the stars, I wonder what it was that once so fascinated me about this voyage. My anticipations were so shallow, so meaningless, and yet, so compulsive. They blinded me and they obsessed me. Had I followed them into space then, I should have missed it all.

It's better this way. Dian and I are making the return trip to Farhome aboard the *Longhaul II*. Officially, we are Earth's representatives on the new world. Off the record, we are new colonists. We've been going through the library for holograms and recordings of Farhome, and the more we see of it the more it enchants us. Green and open, rolling hills and abundant nature . . . this is a world where man has a second chance. This time we know enough to avoid the ecological pitfalls. This time we hope to find a niche of coexistence.

Somehow, I have the feeling that's what the *arapads* are all about: they're Farhome's ecological insurance policy, paid in full. The Furies will never come to this new world of ours—and perhaps some day they'll be banished from the old world too.

I hope so. That's what we're dedicating our lives toward.